The Northcote Anthology of Short Stories

Harold Shaw Publishers
Wheaton, Illinois

ISBN 0-87788-589-3

Library of Congress Cataloging-in-Publication Data

The Northcote anthology of short stories.
    p. cm.
   "Northcote books."
   ISBN 0-87788-589-3 (v. 1)
   1. Christian fiction, American.   2. Short stories, American.
PS374.C48N67 1992
813'.0108382—dc20   92-19157
                                                       CIP

---

99 98 97 96 95 94 93 92

10 9 8 7 6 5 4 3 2 1

CONTENTS

INTRODUCTION

*O*nce upon a time, a magnificent story was told. In it, good won over evil, the Creator became known to those created, and people found love and a purpose for their lives. This story's first written form is known to us as the Bible.

Ever since the original story, people have lived those same truths and struggles over and over again. They have retold the Story in their own stories—with new characters in new situations finding love, winning over life's evils, discovering purpose, and meeting the One who made them.

It's not easy to tell an honest story in a way that people will want to listen—honesty is not always lovely. It's not easy revealing old facts so artfully that they feel new again. But sometimes such stories *are* written. And all of us are revived, as well as reminded of what faith can really mean in our world.

In 1992, we sponsored a short fiction contest in the hopes that we would discover some good stories in the process. We were not disappointed. The works that came to us were evaluated in areas of creativity, characterization, theme, and style. We are proud to present to you the best-of-the-best in this volume. They are new and vibrant stories that reflect the original Story and give us all cause to meditate on it again.

We invite you now to take a journey through these pages and meet some memorable people whose life episodes will—if you allow them—bear strangely and wonderfully upon your own. We anticipate that their unique images and phrases will warm your soul as they have ours.

The Editors
Harold Shaw Publishers

FLORRI MCMILLAN

REMEMBERING
IN IKONS

Well sure, I remember David Benson. I could still show you a snakeskin he gave me the year we were eleven. We'd been walking along Swan Creek with our BB guns, and he just grabbed it up without stopping. I never even saw it.

"There was a big old S.O.B. in this one," he told me.

"How do you know? It's just an old snakeskin."

"He's shed of it now," David said, "but I can feel his shape in my hand."

"You can't feel any snake in that old rag-skin! Or see him either."

David walked along silently. Then he answered.

"I can feel lots of things I can't see."

"Like what?"

"Like badness. Evil."

"Oh yah! What does evil smell like then?"

David laughed. "I dunno. Snakes maybe. I can feel it though, half in my head and half out. Kind of close my eyes and touch it. I think I touched God once, when I was saying my beads."

I was shocked by David's blasphemy, but he didn't seem to notice. He held the snakeskin high in the sunlight. His dark red hair glowed as if it were polished, giving off a little shine to his prize.

"Here." He tossed it to me. "You take it; maybe it'll bring you luck."

"Are you kidding?"

"Yah, I am. It's just something to remember me by."

"I'll remember you," I told him and put the skin in my pocket. "The weirdo with lousy BB gun aim."

A couple of days later I found the skin in the pocket of my jeans and pulled it out. It was all brown and crumpled.

That happened in 1957. I remember, because it was the summer David's father was elected Millerton's Young Man of the Year by the Town Council. Everybody agreed that Mr. Benson was a good choice. He was in construction, roadwork mostly, and got a pretty fair number of small state contracts. He owned a medium bulldozer and a Caterpillar tractor with the bank. He kept them parked in a corner of Handkerchief Grove at the edge of town. In the summer he gave the high-school boys jobs.

He had thirteen children (David was the eighth) and a white frame house in town with aluminum siding. His wife, Elita, kept the whole place neat as a pin, the other women said, and all those kids too. They didn't know how she did it.

The award was announced on the first night of Millerton Days. David got to give the signal for the firemen's hose fight and ride in a convertible at the front of the parade the next day. It just seemed natural that he should. In school it was the same way. He raised his hand a lot, but no one called him a teacher's pet. I always wanted to be on his team or to go to the store with him. Everybody liked to share things with David, like Mallomars and drinks from their Thermoses. I could ask him anything, and he'd come through. I wish I could ask him today whether he'd ever looked back on Millerton Days 1957. If he remembered the parade.

We were in eighth grade the day his father died. David showed up at school. All his older brothers and sisters came to school too. He walked in looking straight ahead and sat in his seat in the front row. His freckles were big and smudged against white skin, like the spots of a disease. He hadn't combed his bangs back with hair tonic. They fell over his forehead, a soft, dark red, shining clean so that he looked like a little kid.

Mrs. Halley, the teacher, stood very stiff and tall at the front of the room.

"David Benson's father," she said, "was killed early this morning in a bulldozer accident. The nicest thing we can do for David is to go on together as best we can. We will skip 'The Star Spangled Banner' this morning because I don't think anyone feels much like singing." Her voice was tight with tears.

"Please get out your spellers," she said.

I saw the blue veins standing out on the backs of David's hands, folded quietly on the top of his desk, and knew that he was clenching them.

We understood Mr. Benson's death perfectly. His bulldozer had killed him. Mr. Osten, who farmed near Wheatland, wore Blue Bell workshirts with one sleeve neatly folded up and safety-pinned. He had lost his arm to a corn shucker. Mr. Ardys had one wood shoe with a special steel loop attached to the sole because his tractor kicked into first and pulled a drill over his foot. We had intimate knowledge of the things that held absolute power over our lives: the violent strength of farm machines, the firm, stolid voices of our fathers, the priest's flowing robes at Sunday Mass.

At David's father's funeral his family filled the first two pews. The girls' legs, covered in clean cotton stockings, lined the rows like white pickets in a fence. When the boys went up to the rail for communion, you could see a cowlick on the back of each head, sticking up like a rooster's tail. The priest told them all that now they had two fathers in heaven because they had always been children of God.

The day after the service, I asked David if he had looked on his father one last time before they buried him.

"Nope," he said firmly.

"I thought you might. To kind of hold his face in your mind," I said.

David shook his head definitely. "I didn't have to," he said, and looked hard at me.

"Oh, I know," I answered nervously, "I know your ma didn't make you!"

"I didn't have to," David repeated slowly. "I have him with me."

I can't say what changed David; his dad's death or his God. He grew calmer and surer, and sometimes his hazel eyes widened as if he were seeing everything, all of us, from a distance. The way he acted seemed to make people in town begin to count on him, just the way his family did. Grown men asked his advice about crops and building repairs. The county agent always looked up David when there was a job to be contracted, even though it was his older brother Dennis who worked the Cat and bulldozer. Mr. Solberg, the grocer, told me solemnly that David was "special, a very special young man."

"What makes you so special?" I said when I told David about it. I was kind of mad.

He shrugged. "Don't ask me," he answered. "You, maybe."

Maybe we did give David special powers, just by believing he had them. Anyone could understand the kind of power that came from being in charge of his mother and family, but that other kind—it was strange. Lying in my bed at night I thought about how old women's eyes lit up when they touched a crucifix, how King Midas's touch turned everything to pure gold, and how David's hair made the snakeskin glow in the sunlight.

I admit that I was relieved, three years later, when the priest solved the mystery for all of us. What made David special, he explained to us, was "the power of God's calling." David had a true vocation.

When he left for the seminary at Mankato, there was a farewell party in the church parlor. His sisters piped "Father David" in pink on iced cupcakes, his mother cried, and off he went, a kind-faced boy in a secondhand gray suit that didn't quite fit and crepe-soled boots. We expected to see him back before three years' time and maybe for Christmas in between. It was seven years before we laid eyes on him again.

He only came back the one time, a vicar of Christ now in a rippling black cassock and crisp, short, auburn hair. He arrived on the afternoon Empire Builder. Mac, the stationmaster, stood by the tracks to flag it down. Just about everybody in town was there. The VFW Ladies Auxiliary had taken the big cloth banner that said:

MILLERTON

A GOOD PLACE TO LIVE AND WORK

the one we used on holidays, and sewed a new piece of sheeting along the bottom so it said:

MILLERTON

CLAIMS FATHER DAVID

We waited, crowding together at the station, because David Benson was ours, and he was coming home.

He stood in the doorway of the train coach for a second before he jumped down and dropped his black valise. There were no freckles left on his face. It had a harder, gaunt look to it now. The special vision still beamed from his eyes, but it glittered sharply now, intensified. He gathered his mother in his arms, and we saw the sure, firm line of his jaw as he pressed his face against hers. He opened his eyes after a moment and we saw that they were hot with love, melting, and then cooled by tears. His gaze swept across the station platform, taking the sign, the people, all of us in. His face broke into a grin, and he stretched both his arms above his head, spreading them wide to accept our claim to him.

Father David belonged to the town. It was a sort of burden, as I look back on it, but he was so full of joy and energy on that visit that nobody noticed. He said Mass at 5 a.m. for the farmers, in the afternoon for shut-ins, and just before supper for his nieces whose toy animals he baptized, using the kitchen table as an altar. He took his mother and his two unmarried sisters to the dance in Wheatland on Friday night and whirled them around grandly. The deep lines around Elita's mouth softened as she relaxed under his caring gaze, becoming special with him, as we all did.

He was always ours. What never occurred to us was the idea that in seven years his vision had gone beyond us, so far beyond that we couldn't follow.

I asked him one afternoon if he wanted to go shoot crows over by Swan Creek. The damn crows were eating the seeds out of my sunflower field. We blasted away at a few crows and then went down the bank and sat under the cottonwoods, getting cool.

"You remember how we used to shoot our BB guns out here, right at this curve?" he asked.

I laughed. "Sure," I said. "At bullfrogs, and those big old snakes sunning themselves on the mud bank."

"It must be almost fifteen years," he said and shook his head. He pointed across the water to the barbed wire fence. "One day we got eight big ones, remember?" he asked. "In a half hour. We hung 'em up in a row on that fence."

"You've got a memory," I said.

I could see those snakes, every one four feet long, glistening in the sun.

"All lined up," he repeated and turned to me. " 'For behold, I will send serpents among you, which will not be charmed, and they shall bite you,' " he quoted. "That's Jeremiah, lamenting the woes of Zion."

He was looking at the fence, and I saw the steady light in his eyes recede, growing dim.

"Serpents," he said, with such violence that I felt the town, the past, even me fall away from him.

"Well," I said, embarrassed. "There aren't so many snakes in the creek now. Around Millerton either."

"No," he answered. "Imagine," he said gently, "eight snakes with nothing but a BB gun."

I listened to the creek and his voice, trickling along the edge of sorrow. He stood up and slapped the dirt off his wash pants.

"I'm going to Africa," he said.

I pulled up a reed and split it lengthwise with my thumbnail. I was as stunned as one of those crows.

"I was thinking you might be leaving for the Twin Cities," I said reasonably. "Or going to the Jesuits. But Africa!"

He laughed out loud at the look on my face.

"I'm called there," he told me. "To a country where Christians are in danger, persecuted."

"How many would that be?"

"Thousands. Tens of thousands."

"Negroes," I said.

"Descended from princes and baptized at birth."

"You'd think their own would protect them," I argued, "their own law."

"Their own are the law there," he said. "They're evil men." He fixed his eyes on the barbed wire fence.

"Serpents," I said, following his eyes.

He nodded.

"It's dangerous then." There was no question in my voice.

"Yes. They murder priests."

"Your ma . . ." I began.

"I won't tell her this," he said quietly. "I leave next week. Later I'll write to her. Friends, clergy can smuggle letters out. I don't want her to worry until . . . it's necessary."

The depth in his gaze beckoned to me, and I tried to follow him inward, to make this journey with him, if only in my heart. I asked, excited now, "How long will it take? How long before you come back home? What—"

He stared at me, and my unfinished question hung between us. I was aware, in the buzzing silence, of the stagnant, unmoving coulee water and the heat that rose around us. What had stopped me was David's eyes, empty of the promise to return. After a minute I shrugged.

"You be careful now," I told him and started up the bank.

There was nothing more to say.

———

Luke Akontu came to Millerton in September of 1976, the Bicentennial Year. The harvest was in, except for feed corn.

You couldn't miss him. He was near seven feet tall and skinny as a post, with huge hands. His priest's collar was white and his teeth, that's all. The rest was black: his suit and shirt front, his hands and face, glowing black. Not Negro. Nothing brown, I mean!

He said he was named for the apostle, but he pronounced it Lewk-ah A-Kawn-too so it sounded like strange music. No one expected him except Elita. He had written to her.

How can you understand someone like that? He spoke English. He knew American customs; how to behave at table and in church, but he was still a stranger. His eyes looked straight at us and far away all at the same time. His words were flat and clear as a teacher's, but his voice tipped gently underneath, pitching back and forth. He came to tell us about David.

Father announced at noon Mass that Luke Akontu would talk with us at three in the church parlor.

"He has brought us news of David Benson," Father said.

The parlor was so crowded that most of us had to stand. We had all left our good clothes on, since we knew we'd be coming back at three.

Elita sat on one of the folding chairs in front, holding a rosary that Luke Akontu had given her; that's what Kathleen Benson whispered to me.

Luke Akontu spoke slowly and loudly in English. I could hear the words, but I registered them late, a few seconds after each sentence, like a ricochet. I thought it was like watching a fancy exhibit tractor from the State Fair plow your field. He was telling us about David in our own language, but with a different tongue. His face was still and calm. His eyes burned.

"My country is tropical," he began. "Very hot always, but the heat is dry."

He said that he knew David Benson well. The name was strange on his lips, all the long sounds drawn out softly,

Dayveed. He said that the leaders of his country feared the Christian church as a faith common to all the tribes. They had ordered the archbishop killed.

"In the sickness of this time," he said, "my people first welcomed, then feared these leaders."

He told us that six months ago, after mass murders of the clergy, he Luke Akontu, had swum across the river to safety in the middle of the night. His bishop had arranged his escape through Kenya to this country. He would tell us now about his friend Dayveed Benson, he said. I saw Elita close her fingers over her beads. I wondered how this stranger, who spoke of vague sickness and fear in the tropics, could possibly tell us about David.

"The executions," Luke Akontu explained, "are always held on the airfield outside the city. For this one there were a great many witnesses, perhaps two thousand people, and this was unusual. They stood watching as if paralyzed. I remember thinking that they were fixed by the sun, frozen in its glare."

He shrugged. "Perhaps after all the size of that crowd was not so unusual," he corrected himself. "There were thirty to be shot, a very large number. Often there were only four or five," he said matter-of-factly.

I watched his eyes, which had seen these things happen, and I tried to understand. He said that the victims had been gathered over several weeks' time and detained, which I took to mean in jail. They were from different tribes, he said. They were accused of conspiring against the government. The executions were to be performed by a military detachment.

"The commanding officer sent a messenger, a soldier, to invite my bishop to attend these thirty Christians, you know, to give them succor."

Luke Akontu said he went with David to the executions. I tried to picture it: David, marching into the sun beside this black giant, a soldier with a gun close behind. I couldn't do it. What did the uniforms even look like?

"The prisoners were tied on logs," Luke Akontu went on.

Logs? Lying down on logs? He must have seen our confusion because he stopped for a minute.

"Logs," he said. "Boards. Thick stakes of wood pushed upright into the ground."

There was a communal release of breath in the parlor.

"Dayveed walked along the line of prisoners."

Luke Akontu looked out at us now, his chin lifted. The planes of his cheekbones reflected the light.

"He was given thirty seconds with each man before the squad fired. He spoke quietly to them one by one. He would look into their eyes and touch them—a shoulder or a hand—and then the shots and then the next one."

In the parlor no one moved. We stood packed together, our muscles rigid, witnesses paralyzed in the sun. The silence grew longer. Finally our priest interrupted it.

"Father Akontu," he said, "could you hear . . . perhaps you know . . . what David said to them."

We strained forward, all our eyes on this stranger now, waiting for him to give us David.

Akontu looked puzzled.

"Well," he faltered, "you see . . . thirty victims . . . from so many tribes."

He lifted his shoulders and turned his hands upward in a helpless gesture. I saw that his palms were pink, as if he had been wounded there.

We began to shift our weight and to rustle around. So the stranger could tell us nothing. I felt a hardening in the pit of my stomach and saw it rise in the room, marking the faces around me. Akontu saw it too. He tried again.

"There was no single phrase," he explained. "Each tribe speaks a different dialect. These people were arrested miles from each other. Dayveed, you see, spoke several tongues, all their languages, at least enough to give them comfort . . ."

He looked out at all of us. His features softened, taking on our despair. He stared at our faces as if he were making a desperate effort to understand us.

"Dayveed, he said the only thing there was to say."

The lack of sureness in Luke Akontu's voice seemed suddenly to resolve itself. The pain that burned in his eyes echoed in his words.

"In the brokenness of our life, God is."

Then I heard David and saw him moving among the strange natives, his eyes meeting theirs, taking on their terror. His voice gave them the only answer he had, repeated over and over in thirty tongues. Black hands reached out to grasp him, to pluck at his cassock. Voices rose in crescendos of prayer, a dozen tongues tumbling over words as old as ikons.

Strong arms stretched out in supplication.

Lips cried, Save me! Why won't you save me?

A black face twisted in anger, shouted "Where is your God now? Let him show himself now!"

And David, moving along the line, fought evil with his touchings and wrestled with serpents in all the languages of man: "In the brokenness of our life, God is."

Standing at the back of the church parlor, I remembered David's eyes, looking into mine beside Swan Creek and heard the languages of men.

"Be it unto me according to Thy word," murmured the Virgin Mary in the Christmas pageant.

"Hear O Israel, the Lord your God, the Lord is One," chanted the Rabbi on the Motorola.

"Though I speak with the tongues of angels and have not love . . ." I had repeated, memorizing the chapter of charity.

"In paradisum deducant angeli," Father had intoned at Mr. Benson's funeral. "May the angels lead you into paradise."

Surely David had spoken with the tongues of angels, moving across the airfield in the shimmering sunlight. Surely he had led them, those thirty people, into paradise. I closed my eyes, trying to capture the vision in his eyes, trying to see.

Luke Akontu's voice was flat as a slap.

"I watched him move forward to the next. His voice was gentle, clear. He touched the man. The rifles exploded. The man sagged down and dangled from his bonds. Dayveed was at the next. His voice was gentle . . ."

Akontu's voice repeated the lulling litany, rocking us until we didn't understand his words any longer. It was several seconds before I realized that he had stopped, that the room was silent. I looked up. We all watched him, waiting.

"When Dayveed came to the end of the line, they shot him."

Elita cried out once, sharply, and stuffed her knuckles between her lips. I saw that Akontu had told her before; she had brought the rosary along for comfort. I couldn't recall the look in David's eyes anymore. All I could see was a man made golden as the child of Midas, who touched what he loved and died.

I looked carefully at Luke Akontu. I saw failure in his face. What could this man, black not brown, tell us about our pain, our loss? He was not David Benson, Father David, who went away to strangers and left us, the children of his God, with our unanswered questions.

If he could have come back. If he could have explained to us in our own tongue. If we could have touched him just once more, we would have understood. Now he was gone.

I looked over at Elita and saw the rosary threaded between her folded hands. The rosary that Luke Akontu had brought to her. It trembled gently as she worked her fingers, as if it were alive. Quite suddenly I knew that it had been David's. His rosary, held in his hand as he moved slowly across the airfield. The sight of it in Elita's fingers registered on my brain an image of David, the proof that he *was*.

I closed my eyes, feeling the sting of tears, and saw him clearly.

He held the empty snakeskin high, smiling in triumph.

The sun lingered on his red-gold hair, glowing there.

"Something to remember me by," he called.

When I opened my eyes, everyone, Mrs. Solberg, Ben and Edna Hyler, all the Bensons were surging toward the black priest. They milled around him in a circle, reaching their hands toward him just a few inches, and drawing them back as if they were embarrassed. They were murmuring gentle, half-finished sentences and watching his face. Their hungry eyes never left his pink-tinged, swollen lips, which had delivered David's message to them, a gift from a strange mouth. "In the brokenness of our life, God is"; words strung on a precious thread, an invisible rosary to cherish.

I moved slowly to the front of the room to shake the hand of Luke Akontu, who brought us what we had to have, something to remember.

Florri McMillan writes both fiction and poetry. Her books include a novel, a mystery, and a short story collection. Her fiction has appeared in such periodicals as *Redbook, American Health, Family Circle, Savvy Woman, Quarterly West,* and

Greensboro Review. She has been a Breadloaf Scholar and is currently an Illinois Artist-in-Education. She has taught Creative Writing and Composition at Northwestern University and Loyola University of Chicago.

Of "Remembering in Ikons," Florri relates, "I wanted to show, rather than tell, that the human heart particularizes loss in order to survive it—that we can only bear to remember in ikons." The story was based on an actual execution.

JON MARTYN CARTER

DO NOT THROW TO DOGS WHAT IS HOLY

*T*he dirty dishes lay scattered on the *kotatsu* table, advertising the plain fact that someone would have to wash them when family devotions were over. On Luke's plate, still flooded with soy sauce, a few kernels of corn floated merrily around, driven by the fan behind him. He picked up a fork and poked at them, making little clinking sounds.

My father paused in his reading.

Luke picked one kernel up, held it out for investigation, and then put it in his mouth. My father continued reading. We moved into chapter 8 of 1 Corinthians. He approached verse four, reading more boldly as if doing his best to ignore the clinking sounds that followed.

" 'And as for sacrificing meat to idols,' " he read, but then stopped and did not continue.

My brother held his fork still for a moment, then pushed a kernel of corn into a glob of ketchup that remained at two o'clock on his plate. Earlier, there had been an argument about how much ketchup he took. My mother had said that people didn't support missionaries to go to Japan to spend all their money on Hunt's Tomato Ketchup.

My mother looked up at my father, "Keep reading, dear. Go on about the meat," she said.

"Yeah, what about the meat?" my brother mumbled, putting his fork down.

"There's no sense in reading if no one will listen," my father said.

"We were listening," my mother said.

"No, I think we should pray now," he said, and bowed his head. My mother and I looked at each other and then she followed suit. Luke shrugged and leaned back against the wall with his hands clasped behind his head. He stared at the ceiling for a bit and then closed his eyes.

My father prayed for missionaries on other fields, in Africa and in Papua New Guinea, especially for Florence Marlow in Papua New Guinea who worked with unreached tribes. Florence Marlow's husband, Phil had been eaten by cannibals when his missionary aircraft crashed in the jungle in 1962. My brother once told me that she had devoted her life to finding the very person, whether male or female, who had eaten her husband, so she could share the gospel with him. By this time she must have been extremely old, because she looked about sixty in her prayer card printed back in 1964 that hung on our refrigerator door. Yet my father said she still tramped further into the jungle every day to preach the gospel.

Now my father was praying for our supporters in America. Most of them were old, too.

"We pray for old Mr. Crosier, now that Mildred has passed on," my father said. My mother had recently told me that she worried we would wake up one morning to find that all of our supporters had died and gone to heaven. "Where would we be then?" she had said.

I thought about all of these things and then I realized I wasn't praying, so I thought about the fact that I wasn't praying and I wondered how a person stops thinking about it and starts doing it. I tried to say the words that my father was saying, but there was a voice somewhere else in my brain saying, "You're still thinking about it."

My father mentioned Satoh San, who had had a breakdown the day after his baptism. "Keep his faith strong despite his weak condition," he said.

Then suddenly he was pleading for Luke. *He asked that Luke's rebellion would be quenched and that he would turn back to God.* He prayed for Luke's future wife, too, whoever she might be, and then for mine. There was no way I could pray along at this point. My mother and father regularly prayed for our future wives. All I could picture in my case was some beautiful blond girl who would be about as likely to fall in love with me as I would be to fall in love with Florence Marlow. A few weeks before, I had suggested that he might start by praying that I'd get a girlfriend. Luke acted as though he was asleep, nodding his head up and down and snorting. My father began pleading again for God to take hold of Luke. He asked that the power that had been so persistent with Jacob, and that wrestled with him all night, would wrestle with Luke. He had gone back to Luke's rebellion. Usually he just sneaked it in and went on, embarrassed but persistent. My mother held her face in her hands, rubbing her eyebrows with her fingers. Her lips moved silently, somewhat like Hannah's must have done when Eli thought she was drunk.

My father came to the end of his prayer and my mother echoed his amen. He kept his head bowed, clearly hoping someone else would pray too. My mother put her hands on the table and lifted herself. She started clearing plates. My brother stretched and opened his eyes.

"Paul and I are going out," he said. He stood up and went to the *genkan* at the front door and started putting his shoes on.

"Someone has to do the dishes," my mother said.

My father's head remained bowed. Either he was still hoping that someone else might pray, or he had decided not to lift it until Luke was gone. The front door clattered open on its rails and Luke stepped out. He stood on the porch and mouthed something to me that I couldn't quite get, something about the Shinto shrine and Paul. Paul was my best friend, but he was doing more with Luke just recently. My mother was still looking at me. I felt like a conspirator. I couldn't make any sign to him without her seeing. I faced her, ignoring Luke. "I'll do the dishes."

She turned toward the kitchen and said, "Shut the door, Luke. You're letting mosquitoes in and you know how they eat up your father."

Luke shut it after giving me a final knowing look. After a moment, his image disappeared from the glass pane.

My mother turned the faucet on in the kitchen and arranged the dish pan. I decided to let her set it up for me. If I waited long enough, she would do the dishes herself. She couldn't stand to see dishes sit for even a few minutes. My father rubbed his eyes with the bottoms of his palms like Oedipus did after gouging his eyes out. He looked defeated.

Someone had to say something. "I really wanted to go over to Toshi Yamada's house tonight," I said. "He's showing his slides of his trip to Europe."

"He is?" my mother said.

"Starts at eight," I said, glancing at the clock. It was seven-thirty. I hoped she would take the hint.

"You better get in here right away then," she said.

While I washed the dishes and stacked them, I could hear my parents talking in low tones in the living room, though I could only catch a few words and phrases. Anyway, I was trying not to listen. They would be talking about Luke and his supposedly nonexistent spiritual life.

She raised her voice once. "But right in front of him?" she said.

And he replied, "We can't tiptoe around the subject. We're a family." And their voices died down again.

I felt peaceful with the satisfaction of work. Out the window, the cicadas chanted rhythmically like Buddhist priests. Two children rode by on their bicycles, ringing their bells and chattering. It was getting dark. At seven-forty-five, the neighbor's seven-year-old girl, Akiko, started her thirty minutes of pounding scales on the piano. Once my father interrupted something he was saying to yell out, "Aach, C sharp!"

I soon had a pile of dishes precariously tilted toward the sink on the dish rack. I emptied the water, dried my hands and sat down by the back door to tie my shoes.

"I'm going now," I said. "You know where I'll be."

"Okay, honey," my mother called. "Be sure to tell Mrs. Yamada that we miss her at our Bible class."

Out in the night air, I walked quickly, sometimes breaking into a jog. Really, it had been Luke's turn to do the dishes. My mother had let him slip out. And as for Mrs. Yamada being missed at her class, Mrs. Yamada hadn't come in over a year now. If she did show up, nobody would remember her. Yet, every time I went to Toshi's house, my mother expected me to carry the same message.

Toshi and I had been forced on each other one day when Mrs. Yamada brought him to my mother's class. The class was supposed to be exclusively for women, so my mother had led him to my room and had told me to entertain him for an hour during the class. He wore his high-school uniform buttoned to the chin, and kept turning his cap over in his hands. I didn't know what to say to him, so I put a Beatles record on, and we sang the lyrics together for forty minutes, sitting on the floor and looking at the ceiling. We were more comfortable after that and talked about T.B., eating *sembei* and drinking Coke. He stayed for lunch even though his mother went home.

When I arrived, Toshi opened the door for me even before I had closed the yard gate.

"I didn't want you to ring the doorbell," he said. "My grandfather's already gone to bed. No one else is home." He had already set up the projector, beaming the picture at the far living room wall from the dining room table. He had had to put a white sheet over the Shinto god shelf in order to get as big a picture as he wanted. The shelf was used for offering incense and food to the Yamada's ancestors.

"I don't think the old dead folks will mind," he said, laughing. "Are Paul and Luke coming?"

"I'm not sure," I said. "Let's start. Luke said something about going over to the shrine."

"The shrine?"

"That's what he said."

We lay on our backs on the *tatami* floor, our heads resting on piled *zabutons,* and watched the slides. We saw the coliseum in Rome and the Arc de Triomphe with some crows perched on it. We saw the Eiffel Tower, partially covered by Toshi's finger. There were a number of reddish-orange sunset pictures taken over lakes in Germany and Austria. Toshi had taken one picture of King Olaf getting out of a Volkswagen Beetle in some small town in Norway. The king was facing the other way and holding the top of his hat so the wind wouldn't lift it away. He looked like any old businessman, but I believed Toshi.

After a grueling hour and a half of focusing and refocusing and being blinded by the occasional blank spaces that Toshi had missed when loading the carousel, we heard Paul's motorcycle pull up outside. Over the sound of the engine came Paul and Luke's voices, loud and excited. The engine revved a couple times before cutting off and I knew that my brother had been driving.

"They're going to ring the doorbell," Toshi said, running to the door.

He let them in, saying, "Shh, shh, what's the matter with you? My grandfather's asleep."

They shut up and tiptoed quietly to the kitchen, Paul holding out his blue backpack that was full of something that jingled. They snickered and laughed and wouldn't tell us what it was or show it to us.

"Guess what it is? Guess what it is?" Luke said, as if we cared, slapping Paul on the shoulder and laughing. Their hands and forearms were caked with dried mud, which flicked off onto the table and chairs as they hit each other. Their pant legs were also muddy up to the knees.

Toshi looked down at the little clumps of dirt chipping off onto the floor. "You obviously didn't win at *pachinko*," he said. He had switched back to Japanese, a sign of nervousness.

"Nope," Luke said, taking the backpack authoritatively from Paul and setting it on the table. He put his fingers on the zipper and looked up at us with glowing eyes. He loved to create dramatic moments.

I folded my arms and sighed. "Go on," I said, "We give up."

He paused another moment and then unzipped the bag.

Inside was one of the most beautiful sights I had ever seen. The bag was filled with dirty money of almost every color— purple, green, red, orange, and yellow—representing different stages of rust and decay. Surrounding the money were clumps of green moss, pebbles, and blobs of shiny mud. It reminded me of the picture of Captain Hook's pirate chest in the Peter Pan book.

"We've got to wash it," Luke said, picking the bag up from under our noses and taking it to the kitchen sink.

"Where'd you get it?" Toshi said, following him and trying to stick his hand in the bag.

Luke held the bag away. "Don't touch," he said. "If you help us wash it, we'll split it with you."

Paul turned the faucet on and plugged the sink.

It suddenly hit me. "You took it from the shrine!"

Luke emptied the whole contents of the bag into the sink. It made a huge crashing noise. Toshi threw his arms into the air and cringed. We all froze, listening, but there was no noise from upstairs.

"If he didn't wake up with that, he never will," Paul said.

"You took it from the shrine," I repeated.

"You're right," Luke said. "But not exactly. It's not like we took it from the offering plate."

"The creek," Toshi said.

"The creek, of course!" I said. A shallow creek ran through the grounds of the Shinto shrine during winter and spring and dried up in July after the rainy season ended. People continually threw money into it while it was running, and ignored it when it was dry. When we were small, on the way to school in the autumn, we sometimes found fifty-*yen* pieces on the dry ground and spent them on Cokes or Fanta Grapes, and never told my parents about it. We weren't sure what they'd think.

"Did anyone see you?" Toshi said.

"Of course not," Luke said. "One of the priests came out once, but we hid behind a tree."

"He didn't even look our way," Paul said.

"Still, it was a close one," Luke said. "Come on, let's get it washed. There'll be free drinks for everyone at Winnie the Pooh tonight."

Winnie the Pooh was a coffee shop where we hung out. We were good friends with the cook and waiters and some of the regular clientele. The manager liked us because we drew customers who wanted to practice their English. We usually wound up there at nine-thirty or so to sit around for a half hour before going home to bed. In the summers, we stayed longer.

We soon had a smooth assembly line working. I washed, Paul rinsed, Toshi dried, and Luke separated the money into piles, one for each of us.

"So, why did you bring this money to my house?" Toshi asked.

Luke closed his eyes halfway and shook his head. "If you don't want any, you don't have to take any," he said. "I'll divide your pile up among the rest of ours."

"Oh no, that's okay," Toshi laughed. "It's just that, well, do you realize what you've done? What are your parents going to say?"

"I really don't think we should tell them," Luke said. "They wouldn't understand."

"What's there to understand?" I said. At this point, I had my head down close to the water, studying something that seemed to have moved in the slime between my fingers. I wasn't paying much attention to their talk. It was either a worm or a caterpillar.

"It wasn't stealing," Paul said.

"It doesn't belong to anybody," Luke said. "Who would it belong to?"

"So why not tell them?" Toshi said.

"It was only going to sink further into the ground," Luke said. "Think of it. There are layers upon layers of money, just waiting to be dug up, all going to waste."

It was a worm. It wriggled away below a pile of five-*yen* pieces before I could grab it. I looked over my shoulder at Luke. His pile of money somehow seemed bigger than the rest of ours. How had he gotten me involved in this in the first place? We were talking about my parents, but what if Mrs. Yamada came home, or if Toshi's grandfather actually did come downstairs and find us?

"I don't think you should tell them," I said, shaking my head. "The more I think about it, the more I don't like it."

"It wouldn't be like lying," Paul said. "We're not telling them. I'm sure not going to tell my parents."

"That's a forgone conclusion," Luke said. "Your parents could never handle it."

"You didn't quite steal it, and now you're not quite going to lie," I said.

Toshi laughed.

"What do you mean, 'you'?" Luke said. "You've been washing the stuff."

"That's it," I said. "I quit. I have nothing to do with this any-more." I lifted my hands out of the water and shook them. "Here, give me the towel," I said to Paul.

He looked at Luke.

"Give him the towel," Luke said. He picked up one of the piles of money and started dispersing it among the others slowly, one coin at a time. Each time a coin landed, it made a little jingle.

I wiped my hand on the towel. Paul stood watching the coins fall. Toshi spread some money out in the bottom of the rinse pan and then scooped it up to put on the counter. Luke finished with my pile.

"Here, I'll wash now," he said, coming over to me, taking the towel and throwing it back to Paul. He stuck his hands in the water.

"There's a worm in there," I said.

Luke pulled his hands up quickly and started parting the muck at the top of the water with his fingertips, peering in. He hated slimy crawling things of any kind. When I thought about it, it was surprising that he had been willing to dig down in the dry riverbed to get the money in the first place. Maybe he had made Paul do it. Soon, Paul and Toshi went back to work and I sat at the table, dejected.

I was looking for the broom and dustpan in Toshi's hall closet a few minutes later, feeling like I had been through forty days and forty nights in the desert and had come away unscathed, when the doorbell rang. It rang loud like the gong at the shrine, or church bells in America—loud enough, certainly, to bring old Mr. Yamada down from upstairs.

All clinking sounds from the kitchen ceased.

Then it rang again, deafening in its falsetto.

Toshi hurried from the kitchen, past me, down the hall to the front door. "What idiots would call at this time of night?" he said.

I looked at my watch. It was ten o'clock.

Through the doorway, in the kitchen, I saw Luke and Paul start to sweep money off the table into Paul's backpack, disregarding Luke's neat piles. A group of fifty-*yen* pieces missed the opening in the backpack and bounced in all directions on the floor. A few coins rolled out into the hall and Paul pursued them.

"Never mind those," Luke said, "there's still more in the sink."

Toshi opened the front door and peered out. I couldn't see who was beyond him, but he seemed dumbfounded, gazing out and saying nothing.

Above me, a floorboard stirred.

Then from the front door, I heard a voice that made me cringe. "Toshi, it's so good to see you. Is your mother home? I was thinking, I hadn't seen her in so long, and since Nathan was already over here . . . "

"Come in, come in," Toshi interrupted in his best English. "Come in, Mr. and Mrs. Williams," he said more loudly. "So good to see you." I could tell his mind was racing.

Behind me, all noise stopped again in the kitchen.

My mother and father stepped into the *genkan*. They were dressed up, my father in his seventies' leisure suit and my mother in one of her nicer dresses. My father carried a huge watermelon in his arms. I recognized it as one that Pastor Itoh had given us a couple days before. My parents looked around awkwardly for a minute and then my mother started undoing the clasps on her shoes. My father put a hand on her shoulder, balancing the watermelon in his other arm.

"Oh no, we don't want to come in and bother you," he said. "We wanted to bring this watermelon as a gift." He held out the watermelon.

Toshi took it and held it in his arms like a baby. "Thank you so much. It looks delicious."

"We thought it was just the thing for your family," my father said.

"Is your mother home?" my mother repeated, continuing to unclasp her shoes, despite my father's warning looks.

"She's not here," I said, coming forward. "We were finishing up with the slides."

"She should be home anytime, though," Toshi said. "I'll be sure and give this watermelon to her. Thank you again."

"But I thought I heard the sink running," my mother said.

"Janet," my father said.

At that moment, the sink made that loud gurgling sound a sink makes when the last bit of water goes down the drain. Luke must have pulled the plug a few minutes before and forgotten about it or never thought of its consequence.

My mother looked at my father as if to say, "See?" She called into the kitchen, "Mrs. Yamada, are you in there?" in a high-pitched little girls' voice she used with Japanese women.

"Uh," Luke's voice came back. "No, it's just us."

"What?" my mother said, slipping her shoes all the way off and stepping up into the hallway. "Paul, are you here too?" She proceeded toward the kitchen. Toshi and I followed her. My father remained at the front door, looking helpless.

My mother stopped at the doorway and surveyed the kitchen as if she were still looking for Mrs. Yamada. "Your father and I were dropping by," she said, and broke off. Her eyes had stopped at the clumps of dirt and moss mixed with money that still inhabited the bottom of the sink.

"We have some money here," my brother stammered. "We found it."

"You found it?" my mother said.

My father's voice came from behind us, "Janet, boys, it's getting late. Let's not continue to bother these people."

It was a strange statement, because we seemed to be the only "people" present.

"Where did you find it? Did you dig it up?" my mother asked. She stepped forward, squashing a clump of dirt that had fallen off someone's pant leg earlier. She lifted her foot. "What a mess. I hope you're going to clean all this up?"

"I was looking for the broom," I said.

"Now, where did it come from?" she asked again.

"We found it in the creek," my brother said. "It was in the ground. That's why we had to wash it."

"In the creek? Somebody left it there? Do you know who it belongs to?"

"It wasn't all in one place," Paul said.

I felt like we were in the final stages of a miserable chess game. My mother was moving her pawns in for the kill and didn't even know it. She stepped a few feet further into the kitchen and caught sight of the backpack that lay open and half-filled with clean money on one of the chairs pushed under the table.

"And what's this?" she said, now definitely suspicious.

She grabbed at it, but Luke took hold of it first. He held it up to her.

"See how much we found?" he said. "It's incredible." He seemed to be grasping at a last thin hope that she would simply accept that they had found a few thousand *yen* in a creek and leave it at that. It was ridiculous, but she had accepted worse in the past. He stayed out all night once when he was thirteen and told her that he had gotten locked in the train station bathroom by mistake after the last train came in and the station closed.

She stood looking at the money, her eyes wide. I wondered if she saw the beauty in it the way I did. She was pivoting back and forth on her feet like a teeter-totter, saying nothing. I heard a sound upstairs, maybe the hinge of a door. I wondered why my father didn't call my mother again.

I whispered to Toshi, "Maybe we should clean up the slides and stuff in the living room."

He nodded, shifting the watermelon in his arms, but we stayed where we were.

"Why would there be money at the bottom of a creek?" my mother said slowly.

"People throw it in all the time," Luke said. He smiled, but the corners of his mouth shook. "It sinks down and nobody picks it up. It doesn't belong to anybody. So we went and took some."

"What?" my mother said, sounding confused. I wondered if she really knew what he was talking about, but was making it hard for him to tell her.

"At the shrine, mother!" my brother said, irritatedly.

"You're going to have to be much more clear about this," my mother said. "This is a lot of money."

"The shrine! People throw money in the creek there all the time! It just stays there. Nobody picks it up!"

My mother thrust her hand against her chest, and heaved out a large breath. She rocked forward on her toes, and whispered loudly, "That money was thrown to the Shinto gods!"

"But they don't exist," my brother said.

"You thief!" she spluttered.

"How can you steal something that doesn't belong to anyone?" Luke said. He looked around to the rest of us for support.

My mother heaved big breaths

"It really doesn't, Mrs. Williams," Paul said. "Nobody picks it up."

"So you were in this too?" she said. "I'm ashamed of you." For some reason my mother never expected our friends to be as evil as we were. "You were all in this," she practically yelled, grabbing the backpack from Luke. She held it up above her and took a handful of money out. She turned around and thrust it in my face. "Look," she said. "Can't you see that this is theft?" Her eyes were getting watery. She wiped her mouth. "You're thieves!"

She reminded me of Moses holding up the Serpent in the wilderness. I was caught. Telling her I had nothing to do with it would be a betrayal of my brother. Yet, saying nothing would implicate myself. And what about Toshi?

She whipped around toward my brother again, her whole body trembling. She tightened her lips. "You can go to hell, if that's what you want," she said. "Just go there. Do what you want."

Her eyes strayed from Luke's to Paul's, to mine. And then a blank look came over her face. She was gazing past me, at Toshi. He stood behind me, holding the watermelon in his two hands, trying to look guilty and grateful at the same time. She wiped her nose and lowered the backpack.

"Well," she said softly, "I can see what kind of witness you've been to this boy." She looked around the room again and dropped the backpack on the floor. "I certainly hope you clean this kitchen up before you leave. I hope you do that, at least," she trailed off.

"I need to put this watermelon in the refrigerator," Toshi said. He moved out of the doorway. Behind him, I heard my father talking to someone in polite Japanese.

"Toshi," I said. "Your grandfather."

We all marched out into the hall, my mother wiping her eyes quickly and patting her hair. Toshi's grandfather stood in his t-shirt and pajama bottoms looking at my father's business card, which he held in his hands.

"I was once interested in Christianity . . ." he was saying.

My father gave my mother a severe look.

" . . . but I am Shinto. My ancestors were Shinto. You see, we Japanese are Shinto."

"Look," Toshi said. "They brought us a watermelon."

"Oh, very nice," he said, "very nice, in season too. I was in World War II, you see. But still, I like Americans. Of course we are very different, very different. A beautiful watermelon."

He looked curiously at my mother. She shuffled past him into the *genkan,* her head down.

"I think we should be going," my father said. "It's very late. We're so sorry to trouble you."

"No trouble, no trouble," the old man said.

My mother put on her shoes, not bothering to clasp them. My father opened the front door.

"Very glad to meet you," my father said. My mother and father bowed, backing out the door.

"Very glad to meet you," the old man replied.

"Be home soon," my father said to us, and closed the door.

I went into the living room to work on the slides, while Toshi, Paul, and Luke retreated to the kitchen.

Toshi's grandfather headed back up the stairs, muttering to himself again about how he liked Americans even though he had been in World War II, but he stopped halfway. He had spied the sheet over the god shelf through the doorway in the living room. He came back down and removed it. He held it up to me. "This should never be done," he said, "never. We have very different ways, the Americans and the Japanese."

I shrugged my shoulders and apologized. "I'm sure it won't happen again," I said.

He went back upstairs, and I settled down to emptying the carousels of the slide projector and putting the slides back in their respective boxes. In the kitchen, Luke and Toshi and Paul worked in silence. I wondered if my parents would already be in bed when we arrived home. I pictured them walking home now, my mother explaining about the money, my father grieving over my brother and the terrible witness the horrible ordeal must have been to old Mr. Yamada.

We finished our work in surprisingly little time and I joined the others at the kitchen table. Toshi poured us each a glass of water and we drank slowly. Luke cradled the backpack in his lap, zipped shut.

"What are we going to do with the money?" Paul asked.

"I better keep it for now," Luke said.

Paul frowned. "You're going to take it home with you?"

It was Paul's backpack. He had as much right to it as my brother did. Besides, what was Luke going to do with it? It was like the thirty pieces of silver the Pharisees were left with after Judas hanged himself. You couldn't really enjoy it.

"I still think it's ours to use," my brother said.

"Let's go home," I said. "We don't have to spend it tonight anyway."

"Aren't you coming to Winnie the Pooh?" Toshi said.

"You all go on," I said. "I'm going home."

Luke acted as though he might go with me, and even walked me to the door, but said good-bye to me there. He said he didn't want to show up at home quite yet.

As I was walking down the street, Mrs. Yamada's white Camry passed me, but she didn't recognize me and I didn't wave. I wondered how my mother would act if Mrs. Yamada were to show up at her class the next day.

I cut through the neighborhood park and kicked at the swings. Their chains clashed and tangled and wriggled apart. I climbed the steps to our street. A businessman came out on the veranda of a house in his boxer shorts and smoked. I had put a tract in his mailbox a couple of days earlier about Christ freeing people from a hectic life. My parents and Paul and I had covered the whole neighborhood. He flicked his cigarette and sang to himself.

There was an envelope taped to the front door when I arrived home. The drapes in the living room were partially illumined, lit by the small lamp beside the pump organ. My mother might have been in there reading, or sitting on a chair, listening. Otherwise, the house was still and dark. I took the envelope off the glass pane, trying not to rattle the door, and sat down on the steps. Inside the envelope, I found a ten-thousand-*yen* bill and a note written in my mother's handwriting.

"Dear boys," it read, "if you have to have money, here's a ten-thousand-*yen* bill. Spend it as you like, but please don't come home until you've taken the stolen money back. I won't be able to sleep tonight knowing you are thieves." It was written in a jerky kind of handwriting and unsigned. I wondered if she did it hurriedly without my father knowing.

I thought for a moment and then went around the side of the house. My brother's bicycle was leaning against my father's bicycle under the car port. My own had a flat. I tried to disentangle them without making a noise, but a pedal was caught in the spokes, and finally I shook the two bikes until my brother's came loose. The drapes in the living room changed shades and stirred. I didn't want to say anything to my mother. I jumped on the bike and rode off, leaving the gate partially open. When she called I was far enough away that she may have thought I hadn't heard her.

It was a cool evening, though muggy. I pedaled as fast as I could, down the hill and over the sewage drain, past the junior college and the T.B. hospital, past the *pachinko* parlor, where college students and old men were filling the machines with a hundred times more money than my brother and Paul had found. My brother had once argued with my father that the *pachinko* parlor was the real place to do person-to-person evangelism. "You've got to go where the people are," he had said. My father said we should never be even associated with the appearance of evil. "A *pachinko* parlor is no more than a gambling hall." As I rode, a misty rain began to fall and wet my face and hands. The people on the streets put their umbrellas up one by one and I had to maneuver around them.

When I arrived, Paul and Luke were leaning out the second-story-window. Luke was eating a crepe and Paul had a bottle of Coke in his hand. The bag of money sat limply on the windowsill between them. Toshi's head bobbed up behind them when they pointed at me.

"I've got something urgent," I said. "You haven't spent any money, have you?"

Luke shook his head. "We're discussing Mother's hysterical fit."

"Come on up," Paul said, raising his Coke. "I bought it with my own money. I swear."

I parked my bike and went in. There were still a few couples in the corners of the restaurant downstairs and a businessman reading a newspaper at a table in the middle. I climbed the stairs to the second floor. A group of college students were leaving with their bill, and I had to stand aside to let them by.

"I'll get you a Coke," Toshi said, as I sat down. "Your mother's okay. She was just upset."

"Thanks," I said. I handed him two hundred *yen* and he went downstairs. Paul looked at me guiltily.

"She was completely out of control," Luke said, looking out the window and stuffing the last bit of crepe in his mouth. When he had chewed it down, he started laughing. " 'You can go to hell,' " he mimicked, lifting his arms in the air.

Paul and I laughed.

" 'You're thieves,' " he went on in the same voice. " 'That's all you are. You're just thieves!' " He laughed loudly, but stopped short and looked back out the window. "I can't believe she did that."

"So what is it that's so urgent?" Paul said.

I put the envelope on the table in front of Luke. "Take a look at this," I said. "It's from Mother."

He opened the flap and emptied the ten-thousand-*yen* bill and the note onto the table. While Luke read the note, Paul fingered the money. Toshi came back with my Coke and asked what was going on.

"We've been temporarily kicked out of our house," I said.

Luke finished reading and gave the note to Paul. "We're going to have to take it back," he said. He unzipped the backpack and grabbed a handful of money. "It was fun while it lasted." He tossed the handful up in the air and caught it. A coin slipped through his fingers and bounced off the windowsill and onto the umbrella of a couple of college girls down below. One of them picked it up off the wet street and looked up at our window. "Keep it," Luke called.

Paul passed the note on to Toshi, who glanced at it and put it back in the envelope. He couldn't read cursive.

"It says we have to take the money back before coming home," I said.

"But we can't just leave it out on the ground," Paul said.

"Someone else would take it," Toshi said. "Some kids, probably."

"We could take it to the priests," I said.

"But then they would use it. It would be like an offering," Paul said.

"Better to throw it in the trash," Luke said.

He tossed a coin down on another umbrella, this time an elderly lady's. She hunched over and shuffled on more quickly. The coin rolled into the gutter.

"That one went back where it came from," Luke said.

He took another handful of coins out of the bag.

"Bet you I could hit that green and yellow one over there," he said, pointing at an umbrella with Arnold Palmer's signature that was passing by on the opposite side of the street. He laughed and tossed the coins high into the air. Most of them bounced on the pavement, but a few hit the umbrella. The person underneath ducked with the impact. Three small children ran out of the toy store across the street and chased the rolling coins, their mother close on their heels.

"Look," Luke said, grabbing another handful and laughing even louder, "there's the people the money belongs to!" He threw the handful down. Some high-school students below noticed the money bouncing around them and joined in the chase. "Come on," Luke said, "throw it down!"

Paul started throwing money down along with Luke, and Toshi and I moved the table aside to give ourselves room at the window. Soon we were all four throwing money out the window. A large crowd gathered outside, old and young, looking up at us with cupped hands and talking to each other excitedly.

"Take it, you heathens," Paul yelled, showering it down on them. "It's money from the gods!"

"It's yours, all yours!" Luke was yelling. "We give freely to all!"

Shouts of, "Hey you Americans, throw it here! Over here! How much have they got?" came from all directions.

The street below shone like the scales of a fish, the bright money glittering in the puddles. The red and yellow and green and pink umbrellas moved around and bumped into each other like bumper cars as the people raced here and there for the bouncing coins. Everybody was laughing.

My brother reigned over it all like a king.

When the backpack was nearly empty, he turned it upside down and shook the remainder, showering it in a wide arc over the crowd. All hands went up for a moment, and then again people scrambled for the change that had fallen in the puddles between them.

A few coins had actually rolled so far as the pharmacy, down the slight slope of the street four or five stores away. Two small children hooded in the yellow hat of their kindergarten chased them at full speed. People down the street had come out of their shops to watch the commotion and stood in pairs talking and looking up toward us.

"What are we going to do now?" Paul said. "We're all out of money."

I was turning my head when I saw my mother. She stood far down the street, barely visible through the rain, an umbrella in one hand. She had her other hand to her mouth and she was shaking, her eyes fixed on the little children chasing the coins toward her. She was laughing.

When I turned around, my brother and Paul were sitting at the table, Luke with my mother's ten-thousand-*yen* bill in hand.

"Now, what should we do with this?" he said.

I lowered my head and sipped my Coke. At home, I was sure, my father was on his knees fervently praying for his family: for his sons who were thieves like Achan, and for his wife who had sneaked out angrily in search of them. And surely he would mention the old Japanese man whose ancestors were Shinto and who would stay Shinto himself.

Jon Martyn Carter is a language arts teacher in Athens, Georgia, and he is also the son of missionaries in Japan. "My brother did take some money from a riverbed once and my mother did yell at him." He would like to become a media specialist and eventually go back to the mission field to do church planting. He plans to continue writing, and admits, "most of my stories are about incidents happening the way I wished they had happened."

DAVID BOROFKA

A BLESSING

We are not, as a family, robust breeders. My mother had three miscarriages before I happened along, and then I was a solo act. For years, my wife said that this was the whole problem: I had been so much the object of my parents' attentions as well as affections, and they had lived so long with the fear of losing yet another child that, even after I had grown up, moved away, and married, they still could not let go. And neither could I. For the effect on me has been real. Constantly bathed in the limelight of my parents' expectations, I performed my role of the dutiful, successful son—at school, in athletics, at church, as a child, and now as an adult—with a desperate guilt and obligation, as if some sort of repayment for their overweening affection needed to be made, as if upon my shoulders rested the burden of my parents' other disappointments, as if my life could somehow recover for them what had been lost.

But there was something else. Although an only child, I some-how knew, even before my mother listed for me the durations of her many failed pregnancies, that I was not the *oldest* child. Even at the age of three I distinctly felt as though I were occupying a place that by all rights belonged to others. I came to believe that I had two brothers and one sister, three older siblings who were simply on vacation, a conceit that I shared with my kindergarten teacher one morning and for which I received a spanking that afternoon.

"How could you lie like that?" my mother said when we were home, her voice fraught with concern and grief in equal measures.

I stood mutely before her, consciously aware of having told what was apparently untrue, although the certainty of my siblings' presence was as palpable as toast, their aroma, as it were, overpoweringly strong.

Later, my mother told me about the miscarriages and her grief in language she deemed appropriate for a five-year-old. She said that the other babies had been sick, that she and my father had prayed and prayed, that each time they had been crushed by sorrow until I had come along, and that was why they loved me so much and wanted only the best things for me. Because I was their *only* child.

"God sent you to us," my mother said. "You were a gift we'd nearly stopped hoping for."

It is disturbing to a child to be so complete a monarch over his parents' emotions, and it seemed to me, even then, that I had enormous leverage—I could ruin them if I wished. I could have told them several stories: How I knew that my sister would have loved dancing—she would have loved Chubby Checker and the Twist in its day—and yet I also knew that, had she lived, she would have been fat and sadly disappointed by the cruelties of life. How I whispered with my brothers in the front hall closet, a place comfortable in its darkness and the musty smell of aging wool coats, a boys' club in which I confided my longings and fear; when my parents, concerned by what they perceived to be my loneliness, asked about what I could possibly be doing in a front hall closet, I mutely showed them the comic books and flashlight that I had had the foresight to bring as props. My parents, who could hear my whisperings, chose to believe in my creativity, that I could conjure up imaginary playmates for myself, not realizing that my visions of family life were appallingly literal. Until I turned twelve, I could have told them stories of my brothers' comings and goings and my sister's heartbreaks when one day without warning or fanfare I knew that I would not be seeing my brothers or sister again, that in the growing importance of my own life (and in my need to shine brightly for the sake of my parents) their outlines had dimmed. I could have told my parents everything. But I did not. For pathos has its powers as well, and cognizance of that power doomed me to goodness; to crush them would have crushed me also, and even though at odd moments, I felt the presence of my brothers and sister hovering on an axis just slightly different from my own, I never spoke of it again.

Until I met Janice, who was from a family of seven children. When I said that I envied her childhood, surrounded as it was by chaos and vitality and the literalness of family life, she snorted at my naiveté.

"Don't be stupid. We lived in a two-bedroom house. My parents had babies in their bedroom for eight years while my sisters and I shared the other bedroom and my brothers slept on couches and chairs. We're talking *Tobacco Road,* not *Life with Father.*"

"Still," I said, unwilling to let it go, yet unwilling to speak in anything but the most elliptical terms, "you *have* brothers and sisters. I'll never know what it's like. Not the way you do, anyway."

"I see them three times a year, and we get along. Back then, I would have killed a couple of the others just to get more room."

I trusted Janice and I trusted her familial experience as being broader than my own, and frankly I had begun to doubt my own memories of twenty years before. So, when we decided to get married, we also decided that children could be put on hold. Janice had endured enough family to last several lifetimes; my fascination with family could be classified as less than empirical. We had become part of a trend, one described on the covers of national news magazines: Double incomes, No Kids—DINKs. We didn't like the label or the self-satisfied, self-gratifying consumption its image conjured up. But even less did we like the children of friends, little monsters who turned their parents' conversational abilities into distracted preoccupation, shrill argument, or the saccharine of psycho-pedia-babble. Still, our list of single and/or childless acquaintances was shrinking and the names were getting younger. We both admitted to a certain degree of selfishness, a selfishness that frightened us, but a selfishness we protected with the jealousy of an *amah*. We had a right to our adult privacy. We didn't have to defend ourselves to anyone else.

And then Janice came home one evening after a routine appointment with her gynecologist, who informed her that her biological clock wasn't just ticking—the main spring was playing crack-the-whip. She came home from her appointment and stood in front of the bedroom mirror. "I'm too fat to get pregnant," she said. This was not true. Janice has never been remotely overweight, and yet when I said something to that effect, she turned on me with a look of withering mockery: "You're not the one," she said, "you're not the one who has to become a blimp for a year. Or wear clothes designed by Ahmad the Tentmaker." In the space of a sentence, the world had tipped; we had gone from sterility to fecundity. Tillers of human soil.

And yet time wasn't all that we had to worry about: physiologically, Janice was one of those women who, if she had lived one hundred years ago, would, in all likelihood, never have gotten pregnant in the first place. So we became participants in that divine prank whereby an act that seventeen-year-olds routinely perform as rough as animal horseplay in the humid backseats of Volkswagens (and which, just as routinely, yields unwanted issue) is reduced in thirty-year-olds to something resembling a Mr. Science experiment—with just as much passion and just as much success. It is a phenomenon illustrative of our time, I suppose—so much concern with the avoidance of reproduction, only to result in the frantic application of technology, forcing the body to do what it was primed to do all along.

Others have extolled the absurdities of temperature-taking, ovulation-charting, and the careful choice of one's underwear among a whole host of other indignities; I will not add to it.

Fourteen months later we were pregnant.

"Congratulations," Janice's gynecologist said. He patted her on the knee. He shook my hand. He is the forty-year-old son of a Polish shipworker, and he has seven Catholic children of his own. By his own admission he is not yet finished fulfilling his own personal command of fruitfulness and multiplication. "So happy, so very happy."

Janice did not begin to cry until we were alone in the car. "I'm pregnant," she sniffled. "I'll have to quite my job, I'm going to get as big as a house, have varicose veins, and have sudden strange desires to wear polyester stretch pants and keep soup can curlers in my hair until noon every day. I'll lose my waist, and then my patience when he throws all your underwear into the toilet and tries to flush it."

I had no idea to which problem I should respond. "He won't do anything like that," I said.

"You don't know anything," she said. "You don't know anything about kids and what kids do to parents, especially mothers. The only kid you've ever known was yourself, but you were born old, and you've even forgotten that."

I half expected those ghosts of my childhood to visit in confirmation, but the air behind Janice's head was still, uninterrupted.

"I wanted you to be happy," I said.

"I am," she sobbed. "Don't be dumb."

"No. I won't be dumb."

We drove the rest of the way home in silence, slipping past vineyards dotted green with leaf.

When we went to bed, Janice wore a flannel nightgown and a quilted robe. "You've done enough." She rolled over onto her side, her back to me, and when I put my arms around her, she snored into her pillow.

———

You might, I suppose, think Janice unreasonable. And you might think me more than a little ignorant of the irresistible demands of estrogen. I can honestly say that I conducted more than one secret conversation with myself, that I often dissected the strange logic whereby Janice and I had suffered fourteen months of uncomfortable copulatory arrangement leading to a pregnancy she now said she never wanted. And which was all my fault. I harbored the illusion that I had done no wrong, that Janice had gone off-center. I could take comfort as the aggrieved party. And I would, of course, be wrong.

We endured one week of *detente*. Then one night, in the middle of the night, I became aware that Janice was no longer in bed, that the aggrieved wings of her shoulders no longer pointed in my direction. Light seeped from beneath the bathroom door. I heard sobbing. Convulsed, choking, stifled cries, a wilted bouquet of tears. Janice was sitting on the toilet, her knees pressed together, her arms around her abdomen.

"Sweetheart," I said, not entirely sincere, not then. "Cupcake, tell me about it."

"I'm bleeding." She held for my inspection a wad of red-streaked toilet paper.

"You're bleeding," I repeated.

"Bleeding. That's what I said." She had stopped crying, and her voice was clinical, detached, the bearer of facts, albeit unpleasant. "I'm going to lose the baby."

"You don't know that," I said. "You're not a doctor."

"No. I'm just a hormonally imbalanced woman." She looked at me. "I've heard you talking to yourself. And don't tell me you haven't. Talked to yourself, I mean."

I stood mutely in front of my wife, accused and convicted.

"Go back to bed," Janice said. "You're not doing me any good by staring at me."

———

What can I say of the anguish suffered for those who die before birth? It is as unsatisfying as it is unsettling, as if the burden, although weightless, still buckles the knees, a shadow without object; there are no funerals, no ordered rituals for grief. My brothers and sister had come before me, and I had never known mourning except at that distance. It is not enough, by way of consolation, to say that no name was lost.

We drove to Dr. Wozniak's office at eight the next morning. Recognizing the signs, the nurses quickly ushered Janice into an exam room; they helped her out of her clothes and onto the harsh paper of the exam table with that solicitude reserved only for other women, a connection denied to men. One nurse, a stout woman in a flowered uniform top, smoothed Janice's cheek with the backs of her fingers, saying, "Sh, sh, there, there," cooing and clucking her comfort. For her part, Janice began to cry musically, a lullaby cry of sniffles and restraint. She blew her nose into a proffered tissue. "Post-natal drip," she said, laugh-weeping into her Kleenex.

A second nurse, an older woman wearing glasses with no-nonsense steel frames, shooed me away. "There's nothing more useless," she said, "than husbands. Lucky for you she's strong." I sat in a corduroy-covered armchair and looked at the back issues of *Sunset* and *Parents* and *People* spread out in neat fans on the waiting room coffee tables, unable to pick any of them up, unable to break their happy symmetry.

Half an hour later, Janice tottered from her room. She was holding a piece of paper. "We have to go to the hospital," she said. "I have a prescription."

We did not leave the hospital until the hour before dawn of the next day. An orderly wheeled her out while I brought the car from the parking lot. Stars littered the sky in useless celebration, and I thought of the past twenty-four hours: of pregnancy and miscarriage, and the surgical investigation into my wife's ability to conceive and carry. Dr. Wozniak had spoken to both of us following Janice's recovery from the anesthesia.

"There's nothing wrong, thank God," he said. "Nothing to stop you from getting pregnant again. But not right away, okay? No—" and here he used a phrase that sounded like hanky-panky, a Polish-sounding euphemism for sex, love-making, intercourse— "no *nifky poofky* for three weeks. Use your contraceptives until three periods have gone by, and then we'll get busy, okay?" I did not stop him from using the inclusive pronoun. "It will work itself out, you'll see. Babies will come if you want them. I feel sure of that." Good Catholic optimism, "In the meantime," he cautioned, "no big plans. You'll maybe feel sudden urges to change your life—a new job, a new house, you might even look at each other and think, *Do I know this person?* Very normal, very typical. But don't dwell on these. Live your life as before. Get rested. Eat. Drink. It will get better—trust me."

And so we were in the car, driving away from the hospital, trusting Dr. Wozniak, trying to forget the bloody, blue rope of tissue that had come from between Janice's legs during our drive to the hospital.

"I'm sorry," Janice said. "I wasn't sure, and I lost the baby."

"The fetus wasn't healthy," I said, "and that's not your fault."

Before we left the hospital, Dr. Wozniak had said this, so I felt that I was on safe ground. "This early," he had said, "to lose the baby is a blessing."

"It was sick," I said, aware as I said it of my daughter's presence and my mother's own words, "she was sick and she would have had a horrible life."

"I wished it to be sick."

"You can't blame yourself."

She sat with her hands in her lap, tearing at her cuticles, and I wished that I had bought her something in the gift shop, something for her to hold.

"Don't go home," she said. "I don't want to go home. I don't want to rest right now. Just drive."

We followed the highway that followed the river, tagging along as it rose into the foothills. Ground fog had begun to rise, blotting out the accusations of the stars.

At a bend in the highway, Janice ordered me to stop and pull to the side. To our right was the riverbank strewn with river rock, sand, and empty beer bottles in this the fifth year of drought and hopelessness. To the left two ancient horses stood observing us from the center of dry pasture. A barbed wire fence leaned halfway to the ground.

Our shoes made sounds unnaturally loud in the dawn fog as we crossed the highway. "Here horsey, horsey," Janice called, a whispered shout. "Come on, baby," she said.

Neither animal stirred.

Hiking her dress up to her hips, she put one leg over the sagging wire.

"Janice," I said, "what are you doing?"

"Nothing new," she said. "I used to pet horseys all the time, but lately I haven't had the time."

I held the wire down for her, then followed. The two horses watched us as we approached. Janice touched one, then the other on the neck, and in the spot between the eyes. "Poor horseys," she said, *"you* don't have much time, do you?" They ducked their heads, their eyes well-acquainted with grief. "If I had some sugar, I'd give you some." She stroked their patchy coats.

In my pockets I could find only a stray packet of hospital Sweet-N-Low. "What can I do?" I said.

"You could not ask dumb questions." Her voice broke, as brittle as pressed flowers.

I held her then in the presence of aging creatures, aware of an increased chorus of souls, their lives uninterrupted by birth.

David Borofka is currently an instructor at Kings River Community College in Reedley, California, where he teaches composition, literature, and creative writing. "A Blessing" is somewhat autobiographical in that two women in his family have suffered miscarriages. David was intrigued by the idea that "if we experience life *before* conception, if ' . . . birth is but a sleep and a forgetting,' what does that make of the unborn child who is uninterruptedly connected with the divine and immortal?"

This story is part of a larger collection David hopes to publish as a single volume. Other stories from the collection have appeared in *The Southern Review, Crosscurrents, The South Dakota Review,* and *Modern Short Stories.*

MICHAEL SEBASTIAN GIOBBE

AND SOME ARE MADE SO BY MEN

"And Lot was vexed, down to his righteous soul." *Who wouldn't be,* Teague thought. *That was Sodom, north of Gomorrah. This is Cambridge, north of Boston. Is it really any different—could you find ten righteous men here, if you had to?*

Teague sat at his cigarette-burned desk replete with outworn and various auto parts, no two from the same car. These served as well as anything to chronicle Teague's past year. Only one of these artifacts served a present and useful purpose: a 1972 Buick Electra piston, itself of impressive size, was inverted and made a fine ashtray.

A cast-irony, that was: 1972 was the year that his Excellency Richard Cardinal Cushing, God rest his soul, found Stephen Teague and his fellows worthily prepared to profess their vows, and so, solemnly, with anointing of oil and laying on of hands in

keeping with apostolic succession, received them into the priesthood of Archdiocese of Boston.

Teague grunted at the thought, looking out over his Mass. Ave.
car lot. "The only thing that I've anointed with oil lately is a Chevy
Malibu."

It was a Thursday morning, which meant Friday's auto auction
to prepare for. Two cars, an Olds Wagon and a Volkswagen
Beetle, he was selling at the auction tomorrow. To everything
there is a season, and spring is the season when seniors grad-
uated from Harvard and Tufts, got job offers starting at princely
sums, and finally got rid of the Olds Wagons their parents sent
them off to school in.

The Beetle was different; now that's a grad student's car. The
poor, it is said, we will always have with us. They come to grad
school in Beetles or Pintos or Datsuns, and endure a year or two
of Boston driving and Boston weather. And after moths and rust
corrode and thieves break in and steal, they're perfectly happy to
take the bus. In the suburbs, his VW was a "Special interest car in
restorable condition." Fine with me. Here in the city, it's just
another Beetle.

The morning was consumed in washing and vacuuming the
two cars, changing oil, bleeding brakes, gluing broken door
handles, grinding out and buffing the chalked-out paint on both
cars, making the old seem a reasonable facsimile of the new.

"Ah, pinstripes and a tune-up." Teague laughed to himself.
"Pinstripes and a tune-up." He was being only half cynical, as he
was every time he did these two jobs: together they took less than
an hour, cost him less than fifty dollars, and raised his return by
ten times that.

"As my dad once told me, 'Stephen, you sell one a day, it's a
very comfortable business.' "

Satisfied that he stood to sell two on Friday, Stephen Teague went to lunch, hoping as he had every day for the past year only that he meet nobody he knew from his former line of work. Teague, you see, was not one of those many who had left the priesthood. Before Stephen's father died last winter, he willed the business to his son. After all, Steve wasn't required to take any vows of poverty.

So when the Chancery spoke again of transferring him that spring, Stephen simply went into the used-car business. His desire for anonymity was ill-considered, since he now drove a bright blue tow truck with full flashing light rack and the name "Teague's" on each side in foot-high reflective yellow letters.

Lunch was interrupted by the squawk of his pager.

"Teague, call in. Two-car on Soldier's Field Road." And Teague immediately brightened up and moved out with the ambers on.

The towing end of the business always reminded Stephen of his father: Peter Teague, retired Marine gunnery sergeant, used his G.I. preference and all the connections he had to gain the towing rights to most of Cambridge and some of Boston and the Mass Pike as well. This short, leatherneck veteran of the Pacific war taught his son the towing trade, and later the used-car trade. Peter Teague was one who loved simply having a "mission"—he was never so happy as when racing to an accident, flashing the amber lights. Over a beer at the Black Rose, Peter had introduced Stephen to a generation of Boston, Cambridge, and Mass. State police officers. At Stephen's ordination there had been nearly as many men in blue as men in black. And at Peter's funeral last year—well you'd think Dad spent his twenty with the Metro police instead of with the Corps.

Stephen eased the truck onto Soldier's Field Road and saw the blue and red light a half-mile off. No smoke. A good sign.

He recognized the officer at the scene. Parking the wrecker on the median, he called out, "Pyskevitch! Joe! Hey, Sergeant, what have we got?"

"Hi, Steve. Guy in the Cavalier tried to pull a U-turn across the median. Would have made it too, I guess, if he'd looked first. Pulling into the lane he got broadsided by a Lincoln Town Car."

"That's a rough match-up. How bad?"

"Well, they both went to the hospital. The guy in the Cavalier had at least a couple of fractures and a concussion. The lady in the Lincoln—well, just some scrapes and bruises, and a bad afternoon. Hell, whoever gets hurt in a Lincoln? Wasn't her fault. The guy was being a jackass."

"Car's totalled, Joe."

"Yeah, well, the Lincoln's still good. Just needs a full front-end clip. Anyway, get'em out of here, will you, Steve?"

"Yeah, tell Metro it should take me twenty, twenty-five minutes for both. I'll need the flat-bed for the Chevy, but I can get it off the road now." The Cavalier had been stove in from the right side, the body curled around the passenger door, which was a foot and a half closer to its mate on the driver's side than it had been just before lunch.

"You busy after hours, Steve?"

"No plans. The Rose?"

"The usual. I'll see you there. I'm off at eight."

"Watch the donuts."

Boston Metropolitan District Police Sgt. Joseph Pyskevitch swore cheerfully at his friends and drove off.

It didn't bother Sgt. Psykevitch that Stephen was a priest, or that he walked away from it, or that he drove a tow truck and sold cars. The good sergeant was a devout Catholic but really didn't feel that the priests he knew were up to handling, say,

highway emergencies, accident scenes, working with the state
police or the paramedics. Not that they'd ever need to, of course.
But he'd seen Steve do that for a year. If he got tired of saying
Mass every morning for a bunch of old ladies to do this instead,
Joe didn't blame him.

Fr. David Martino didn't blame him either. Naturally the Chancery sent his seminary roommate out to talk to him last summer;
they were once very close, and still good friends.

"Steve, understand me—it's not that I think you're necessarily
wrong, but why, after nineteen years, this?"

"Look, you know there are things I never agreed with the
Church about—celibate priests for one—but that's since we were
at St. John's together. I can live with that. I have. It's always
everybody's first question. No, the big question I have is—why
be a priest anymore? What are we doing? Dave, are you satisfied
at it?"

"Bud, you sound like one of those theologians that came out
in the seventies. Am I satisfied? I minister the sacraments. I share
in the life of the parish. I teach."

"Those are clichés, David! Do you remember the kind of
vision we had, reading Vatican II when it came out? I wanted to
help the Church change the world, and I wanted to help the
bishops change the Church. Remember?"

"So, you have always—always!—gone after that. Have you
ever been in a parish yet that you haven't taught courses on
Vatican II, the Bible, Discipleship, Life in the Spirit?"

"Weymouth. All Souls, the pastor didn't want the laity involved
in what he thought was 'his' role, so I didn't get permission to
teach at all. Besides, there are always ways to dump on an as-
sociate pastor in the suburbs."

"You mean like parish admin., the parish meetings."

"Yes, and morning Mass, and visiting sick calls on the retired, affluent, and none-too-sick, and hearing the confessions of the terminally pious, God help us."

"It's like getting stoned to death with popcorn. I know."

"And yet every time I tried to teach the teenagers—yeah, they'd respond! They'd understand! They would want to see change. It was always the same damn problem."

"Problem?"

"Yeah, you see their parents on the Knights of Columbus and the parish council would complain to the pastor; they got upset, I got transferred."

"Doesn't make sense."

"Radical vision meets traditional piety. Dave, I've been traded to everyone but the Celtics. Happened ten times now in nineteen years. I've moved more than my dad used to with the Corps."

"I was sorry to hear about him. He was a good man, your father. I was in South America at the time."

"I understand. It's okay. So all I'm saying, Dave, is that I've woken up. The Church doesn't really care about changing the world, the bishops don't know how to change the Church. Just more clichés. And most of all, the Church doesn't want to change. They don't want to have to *become* disciples. They want to hire 'em to deliver sermons and baptize babies. It's a miracle we still have a Church at all."

"You know, the Cardinal has all these same frustrations, and he thinks you're a good priest. You should have heard him at the last conference, when he heard that half his priests didn't know what Renewal was. Fire, brimstone, Pentecost and the Magisterium, for an hour and a half. Shame you missed it. Anyway—so when your father left you the place, then you decided to make the change?"

"No, it came before that. Present company excepted, well . . . it's as if when the Archbishop laid hands on these men's heads, their balls shrivelled up and fell off. I don't mean celibacy. I mean character. I just wanted out. Dad left me the business. It seemed the right thing. It still does. I'm tired of being a professional eunuch."

"You know that only the Vatican is able to release you."

"Right."

"And that John Paul has all but ceased releasing men?"

"Yes, I know."

"The Cardinal thinks you should have a parish. The only one free is Dorchester—St. Columbkille's. But he wants you to have it."

"I'll think about it. At least for an hour or so."

That was last summer. Stephen did think about it. Dorchester is one of the roughest parts of Boston's inner city; he knew that the offer would stand for a while. That parish had a new pastor in the fall; by January the man had gotten himself assigned back to suburbia.

"If I ever return to it," Steve decided, "I'd rather go to the city than to the suburbs. But again, I don't think I'll ever go back." And in last week's mail, the Chancery again offered him St. Columbkille's to pastor. That was sufficient; on Monday he'd go in to make an appointment with the Cardinal Archbishop of Boston. To begin application to Rome. To become a layman, a common Christian again. Or maybe an excommunicated one.

The hour of eight came and went at the Black Rose as Stephen nursed a Michelob; the absence of his friend was quite understandable and not uncommon. At nine he ordered a Harp's draft and paid up; if Joe was too busy to show, he'd be too busy to call, as well. So then, Steve was not expecting it when as he neared the bottom of his glass of the fine Irish lager, his pager went off.

The call was to a section of the Pike that Steve had no contract for; he told the desk dispatcher that over the phone. No, he was told, the call was real, and was for him. Within minutes he was eastbound on the Pike with the amber lights on. Sgt. Pyskevitch had made the initial call.

Teague arrived, with the traffic slowed to a crawl a half-mile on either side. He had to search out a place to pull up the wrecker, for indeed the four-lane highway was blocked across three lanes, by a jack-knifed semi and a red Chrysler convertible which, it seemed, had tried to drive under the tractor-trailer; police, fire, and ambulance already on hand—and two tow trucks. One was on a big rig frame and was clearly for the jack-knifed truck; the other similar enough to his own.

"This makes little sense." He pulled out of the file of crawling traffic and parked beside the closest police car. In it was some corporal he'd never met.

"I'm from Teague's. Got a call from MDC to cover this one." As if the foot-high letters and flashing lights didn't say as much already.

"The towing is covered already," the corporal said, trying to make sense of Teague's presence. "And you can't park there. You don't have . . . wait, now. You—you're not the guy that Sgt. Pyskevitch sent for?"

"I think I am. What's this about?"

"You'd have to talk to the Sergeant. I'm a Baptist myself, I couldn't tell you. He's over by the car."

That was strange. He found the sergeant.

"Hey, Joe, what the hell—"

"Steve. Thank God. It's a rough situation here. Trailer jack-knifed, you can see, damn lucky he only caught one car. But that's pretty bad. This guy's car is in under as far as the windshield; that folded back on the driver, the car folded in around him. He's pinned. Fire department's using the Jaws, cutting him out. Take another hour at least. He's lucid, and awake, but he's losing blood." Sgt. Joe caught his breath. "So I called you."

"Yeah?" Steve noted again the police, fire, and paramedics on the scene, and the two tow vehicles already present. "Why? Seems like you've got everyone here. I don't even cover this section."

"Steve, the guy thinks he's gonna die. He's been screaming for a priest."

"So you called me."

"You're the only priest I know with a Metro Emergency Pager. Look, when I made the call, it was just to calm him down; now the paras think he might need your kind of help."

The man had been cut badly and sat with the air bag fully deployed in front of him. The fire rescue team was working to free him from his car, by carving it into pieces around him. The paramedics had already dressed what injuries they could see, but they could not yet get at the real problem: his legs were pinned under the dash, which was sitting far lower than it should. Flashlights revealed bleeding within and without from the man's knees, swollen to twice normal size. Until he could be moved, he could not be treated. The medic in charge had him on I.V., monitored his vitals, and waited.

"I'm Father Teague," Steve said to the chief medic. "How stable is the guy?"

"We can keep supplying him blood, but I think he's compound-fractured a femur, maybe both. That can kill, you know. He's starting to show signs of shock. I don't know how he's staying conscious, but if you can keep him that way till they cut him free, you might save his life. He's been calling for a priest, I think he's fighting to stay awake until he gets one."

"Then why am I talking to you?" Steve knelt down beside the driver's door. "You wanted a priest. I'm Father Steve. You're going to be okay. What's your name?"

"Paul, Father, I was on my way to a party. I tend bar. The guy just cut me off. I'm late, already, Father . . . "

"Yeah, Paul."

"I can taste a lot of blood—I feel sick. Tired sick. Just don't go, okay?"

The shrieking rasp of the Jaws of Life sawing into the car's body cut any conversation short. Already they had removed the windshield pillars. Now they were cutting the doors off. This was the work of some ten minutes.

"Father—I want the rites. Last rites. I'm scared—I said I'd bring the drinks. I've got to go! My car . . . don't let me die, Father."

"Paul, relax. You're covered. I'm here—look at me—no, don't move your neck. Sergeant?"

"Yeah, Steve, what do you need?"

"I need water, bread, oil, and wine."

"Where the hell am I going to find wine?"

"The guy says he's a bartender. Try his trunk."

The trunk was forced open, showing all manner of liquor and beer. Several liqueur bottles had broken on impact, leaving the trunk sticky and full of broken glass.

"How about it? Any wine there?"

"No—wait. Bottle of champagne—does that count?"

"It's wine enough for the moment."

"Bread . . . hey! My partner gave me a bagel at breakfast. I don't like 'em—it's still there. We've got water. Oil? What kind of oil?"

"Del Monte, Coconut Oil. Quaker State. It's just gotta be oil."

"The medics! Maybe they have baby oil or something." Sergeant Pyskevitch moved out to collect these things, as the Jaws of Life started up again, then stopped.

The fire captain yelled: "There's not a damn thing we can do 'til we move that trailer. We just need it off a few feet, but we need it now."

"Paul—are you still awake? We're going to use the short form. They're winching the trailer now. Paul, are you sorry for your sins, whatever they are, and do you intend never to commit them again?"

"Yes." Paul sounded distant and weak, just as Joe ran up with the four items requested.

Taking up the jug of water, Stephen prayed over it as he had at so many fonts and baptismals for two decades. Now, though, he heard the words he prayed, as if by being earnest in his benedictions he might save Paul's life.

"I cleanse you, Paul, with water for the remission of sins. In the name of Jesus the Christ, I absolve you of all your sins."

As well as he could with the air bag blocking him, Paul made the sign of the cross.

"On the night he was betrayed, Jesus took bread in his sacred hands, and looking up to heaven to His almighty Father he blessed it, broke the bread, gave it to his disciples and said, 'Take this all of you. This is my body which will be given up for you. Do this in memory of me.' "

The car shuddered as the trailer was being winched carefully of its hood.

"Paul, the body of Christ."

"Amen." Stephen tore off a small piece of the bagel, and then wondered—*How is this guy supposed to swallow?*

Stephen took the morsel of bread and soaked it in the now-holy water. *That should make it a little easier,* he thought. This he now placed in Paul's waiting hands, above the air bag, cupped as if to form a throne for the host to sit on. Paul swallowed it without a word. The car shook again. Inch after inch of crushed Chrysler hood was being slowly revealed.

"When they were finished, he took wine, and looking up to heaven to his almighty Father, he said, 'Take this, all of you, and drink. This is my blood, the blood of the new and everlasting covenant, shed for you and for all men for the forgiveness of sins. Do this in memory of me.'"

"Now, Paul," he said, aiming the champagne bottle toward the westbound side of the highway, "just take a sip, a small one. I don't know what shape your insides are in."

Steve popped the cork, drawing all kinds of attention from the rescue team. "It's okay," he said, "I'm a priest." Lord, he felt foolish. The consecrated champagne flowed out of the bottle, spilling the blood of Christ onto the surface of the Mass. Pike. Steve held his tongue from cursing himself for not opening it before the prayer. Now it could not be helped.

"Kyrie eleison, Christe eleison, Kyrie eleison," Teague sighed.

"Huh? What?" Paul croaked, eyes wide, clearly panicked.

"Take it easy now. Paul, the blood of Christ."

"Amen." Paul grasped the bottle by the neck. It was work trying to drink from it without moving his neck, without drinking too much, with a fully opened air bag in front of him.

"You went into that Latin, I thought maybe I already died." Paul was calmer, now, but just barely.

One final squeal of metal on metal, and the Chrysler was free. Steve had stood, praying, barely remembering the blessing for oil, until finally he said, "Look, Lord, I don't remember the words. Just bless the oil. In the name of the Father, the Son, and the Holy Spirit, amen."

The rescue team again fired up the Jaws of Life, leaving no room for words and little place to stand. Steve was only able to anoint Paul wordlessly, making the sign of the cross on his forehead. Paul simply nodded. A fireman moved Steve aside, and the car came apart. Inside of five hurried minutes, Paul—the stranger in the car—was in an ambulance bound for Mass. General.

Joe found Stephen still standing there when they finally towed the tractor trailer away thirty minutes later. The priest wore an odd smile.

"Steve, what on earth are you grinning about?" the sergeant asked.

"Two things. One, I've got a nearly full bottle of good champagne here which, by canon law, must be consumed in its entirety by the faithful. That's us. You are off duty, are you not?"

Both men laughed long, from the heart, shaking off the evening's stresses.

"Okay Steve—Father Steve—what's the other thing?"

"I have to call a guy about a place in Dorchester."

"Dorchester? What the hell you want to do there?"

"Well, you know, feed the poor, clothe the naked, visit the sick and imprisoned. Should be a few of those, I expect. Preach, teach, sanctify—you know the drill."

"I've heard that somewhere before."

"I'm sure you have."

Steve walked toward his tow truck, the amber lights still flashing, carrying a bottle of the very blood of Christ—which looked and tasted very much like champagne.

Michael Sebastian Giobbe is a graduate student of theology and the arts at Regent College. In addition to "any manner of wordsmithing" he enjoys acting and several sports, including soccer and skydiving. "And Some Are Made So by

Men" captures some of the tension in his own life, for he left the Catholic church, took a "long vacation of five years in various evangelical protestant churches," and returned to his Catholic roots. (He considers himself a Roman Catholic, and evangelical.) He has also sold used cars.

Michael hopes to earn a commission in the U.S. Coast Guard and serve as a search-and-rescue aviation officer, but plans to settle down eventually to a professorship in English.

DEBORAH JOY COREY

THE GOLDENROD
FIELD

I ask Mama if I can go to the old folks' home to visit and she says yes, as long as I walk near the ditch and that I am sure not to stay too long and tire Mrs. Harris. I outline my lips with mercurochrome before I leave and sneak out past Mama who is talking to Bucky about knowing Jesus. She tells him that there will come a time when it will be up to him to get saved. "Now?" Bucky says.

"You'll know," Mama says.

Bucky bites his bottom lip and frowns at Mama. He is not big on guessing games.

Mrs. Harris has a big bouquet of goldenrod in a white pitcher on her nightstand. She is propped up on her bed, eating orange Jello cubes and it takes her blurry eyes awhile to know me. She tells me that one eye is clear blind with cataracts, then says, "I haven't seen you all summer. Where have you been?"

I smooth my hands down over my dress, then go close enough to touch Mrs. Harris's wrinkled and black-dotted hand. The silver spoon wavers in it. "My brother Eddie got killed in a car crash," I say, even though that is not the biggest thing on my mind.

"Oh, I heard that, dear. That must have been a terrible thing for you." She pushes a Jello cube on her spoon and feeds it to me. I suck it down whole and sweet. Mrs. Harris eats one and then feeds me one until they are gone.

She looks into my eyes. I think all her living years is what gave her cataracts. I think she is looking through a lot of blurry memories while she watches me. A tractor sounds in the distance and I imagine the brown field dust whirling around it. I picture a boy on the back jumping off to pick up the bales of hay, his smooth tanned arms shining in the sun and his eyes squinted to keep the dust out.

"Mrs. Harris," I say. "Last week I almost killed Bucky. I almost made him drown in the lake."

She touches her lips. "You did?"

"Yes," I say, feeling even worse now that I know his soul was not saved. I remember the time Marilyn told me about knowing Jesus. We were taking turns on the ratty swing in the tree behind her house. Marilyn said all I had to do was close my eyes and ask Him to take away my sins, so I did. There wasn't anything to it. When I got home, I told Mama that Marilyn saved me and she said, "Marilyn can't save you. Jesus has to."

Mrs. Harris gets up and straightens the crochet doily on her dresser. "How did you almost drown Bucky?" Her voice is light and shaky like her hands.

I sit on her bed and study my fingernails. "I threw a wooden apple out so he could dive for it and I threw it too far. I threw it where it was deep." The words pop out fast.

Mrs. Harris picks up the brush and pulls it through her white straggly hair. Her window is up with no screen and the houseflies buzz in and out. "Why did your brother go out that far?" Mrs. Harris asks.

I breathe deep and take in some of the dry day's heat that is floating in the window. "Because that's where the apple was, Mrs. Harris."

"Oh," she says as if she suddenly remembered some important thing. Her hair is getting very flat from her brushing. "I picked bouquets all summer," she says, watching herself dreamy in the mirror. "Whatever flowers were growing in the yard, I'd pick and bring them in. When nothing was in bloom, I even brought in a few weeds. I was the only one to see them, so most would say it didn't matter, but after I looked at them for a while, they began to bother me and I didn't keep them very long."

I look at the goldenrod and there are hundreds of little black bugs crawling over it. Mrs. Harris comes back to the bed and stretches out. She folds her hands over her chest and she is so old and wispy that it is easy to imagine her dead. She looks toward the window. "I didn't have a visitor all summer," she breathes.

I bite the side of my thumbnail and watch her milky eyes until they look at me. She focuses good this time. "Is Bucky okay?" she asks.

I remember Daddy pulling Bucky from the water and running with him to the dock, where he kneaded his back, then turned him over and blew into his mouth. "Yes," I say, "but I think Mama still blames me."

She comforts her head on the white pillow. "Are you mad at your mama?"

"No," I say, "She's mad at me."

Mrs. Harris tilts her head and smiles nice at me. For a time, we let things hang between us without talking. After a while she says proud, "I have a new friend."

I wonder if it is someone real or if it is her imagination talking. Once, Mrs. Harris told me about her husband who lives up in the attic and when I got home, mama said he had been dead for years.

"A boy," Mrs. Harris says, sitting up. "Not a boyfriend, but a friend who is a boy."

"Really?"

"Yes," she says. "Would you like to meet him?"

I shrug my shoulders.

Mrs. Harris sits up and slips on her old fluffy slippers, then reaches for my hand. She scuffs down the shady hallway of the old folks' home, her slippers two dirty clouds beneath her. A bitter smell floats up from the floor and I imagine a river of Javex running underneath us. There are other people moving around, but they are as slow and quiet as Mrs. Harris. No wonder Mama calls this place heaven's waiting room.

Mrs. Harris opens a door of the last room and takes me in. There is a boy sleeping in a wheelchair and his body is twisted. He has a white T-shirt and a big white diaper on. The rest of him is thin and bare. His knobby fingers meet at the center of his chest like wounded bird wings.

"That's my friend, Arnie," Mrs. Harris says. "You must have heard of him. He's one of the Lewis boys from over on the ridge."

I picture the Lewis house with its peeling paint and its cow barn out back. "What's wrong with him?" I ask.

"Nothing," Mrs. Harris says. "He was born like that." She lets go of my hand and scuffs over beside him. I look around the dark room that only has a tight-made bed and a nightstand with a bouquet of goldenrod. She rubs the boy's face. "Hello," she says. "Hello, Arnie."

His eyes open wide and his crooked hands come up and fly around his face. I do not move.

"Arnie," Mrs. Harris coos, happy that she has made him come to life. He opens his mouth and it is a long wide mouth full of sounds. "Yes," she says. "I know, Arnie. I know what you mean."

Mrs. Harris looks back at me. "Come and touch him," she says. There is drool on his chin.

"I don't want to touch him."

"Why not?" Mrs. Harris asks. "He loves to be touched." She brushes his stringy hair back from his forehead and he moves so much that his wheelchair rattles.

"Mrs. Harris," I say, "he's wearing a diaper."

She looks down at him and up and down his spindly legs. "He needs to wear one."

"He's big," I say. "There's something wrong with a big boy wearing a diaper."

Mrs. Harris looks at me with her blurry eyes and says, "There's something wrong with all of us."

I bite my bottom lip, squint my face, and stare back at her.

"Come over here beside him." She waves.

I go, but take my time, stopping here and there to swing my hips.

"Just look into his eyes," she says. "They're perfect. And you know what? He's never done anything wrong. He can't."

I bend closer and he watches me. His body and face jerk, but his eyes are brown and warm. "Why can't he do anything wrong?" I ask.

"He's an angel," Mrs. Harris says.

I touch his chin and he jerks, then makes a noise that I believe to be loud laughter trapped inside of him. I jump back and hide my hand. "He's crazy," I say.

She puts her hand on her hip. "You know, there's a woman who works here who says the same thing. She says she's going to take him down to the church some night and get him healed. Healed from what, I ask her."

"Well," I say, "he isn't right."

Mrs. Harris's eyes water. I look away from her, then go and stand beside the flowers on the nightstand. Behind them is a can of air freshener.

"Can't you see the good in him?" Mrs. Harris asks. She pats the boy like a pet and he coos and grunts at her.

"No," I say.

She squints. "Are your eyes open?"

"Yes," I scold, "they're opened."

Mrs. Harris unlocks the wheelchair and rolls the boy into the hallway. "I'm taking him outside," she sings back. "He loves the sun."

I follow behind and stomp my feet. I came here to talk to Mrs. Harris about almost drowning Bucky and she isn't paying much attention. She has a lot more speed when she is pushing the wheelchair and I hurry to keep up. An old man holds the door for her to wheel her new friend outside. He watches me go by and I wonder why Mrs. Harris couldn't be friends with him instead. "Pretty red lips," he says to me.

Mrs. Harris hurries the boy across the gravel driveway to the lawn. In the sunlight, his veins run blue and look like they could be a map to something. There is a circle of rickety lawn chairs with rickety people in them. Most of them sit very still with their mouths dropped open wide.

Mrs. Harris races through the circle and I follow close behind. I walk fast and even. I hold my hands out to steady myself like I am walking a plank. When we get to the other side, I say, "Mrs. Harris, I came down here to tell you something and you haven't even heard me."

"Oh, yes," Mrs. Harris says. "I heard you. You came here to tell me you were mad at your mama."

"No," I say, disgusted. "I came here to tell you I almost drowned Bucky."

Mrs. Harris bounces the boy over the bumpy lawn. "But you said Bucky was all right."

"He is," I yell. "He is all right. But, but, Mama . . . "

She stops and watches my sputtering lips. "Say it," she coaxes. "Your mama . . . your mama what?"

I take the wheelchair from Mrs. Harris and start to run with the crippled boy. I head down toward the field where the goldenrod is growing. He slaps at himself and hollers deep noises. I look back and Mrs. Harris is scurrying to keep up. Her bent elbows make her hands swish beside her hips. "Run faster," she hollers. "He loves it."

I do not want him to love it. I run down over the hill and rip a path through the goldenrod. The black bugs take flight. Stems and blossoms churn in the wheels while I race him through the lake of flowers. The wheelchair stops short on a rock and the boy flies out. He lands on his side and curls like a baby.

Mrs. Harris catches up and gets down beside him. His body is twisting and turning. She lifts his head and waits for his eyes to look at hers. "Arnie." She smiles. She catches her wind and laughs. She lies down beside him and giggles. "Oh my goodness, that was wonderful. Wasn't it, Arnie?"

I stand stiff and chew my thumbnail down to the skin. I watch Mrs. Harris until she squints up through the sunlight at me. "Don't worry," she says. "He's fine."

I let my held breath go. "How do you know?" I ask.

"I know him." She sits up and rests her hand on her chest. "There's a part of him living right inside me."

I look back at the old folks' home and I can see the shape of a man in the attic window. It looks like the man who held the door for us when we came outside.

"Help me put Arnie back in the chair," Mrs. Harris says while she is getting up.

She lifts his shoulders and I go for his twisted feet and legs. They wiggle in my hands, but I hang onto them tight. He turns his head back and forth, sucking in his wet lips, but his eyes watch me. His body is so light that I wonder if he really is an angel.

We lay him in his chair and Mrs. Harris turns it around and starts up the hill. The hill is steep, but Mrs. Harris's stride is strong and she walks sure of herself when she is pushing Arnie. She pants softly. "That was good," she says and breathes deep.

We walk side by side. The hay tractor still putts in the distance. "Did you remember what you wanted to say about your mama?" Mrs. Harris asks.

I wipe a piece of goldenrod from my dress. "No."

"Did you run so fast that you forgot?"

"No," I say. "I just don't want to say it anymore."

I reach out and steady Arnie's head while he goes over the bumps. It is warm and wet under my hand. I wonder if maybe he *could* be my friend. I pant, worn out from my run through the field. We are getting close to the circle of old people. One woman is slumped over sideways and the sun is lighting up her face. I try to picture her as a little girl, but nothing comes to mind. I can see her as someone's mama, though, and it wouldn't really have to be that long ago.

Deborah Joy Corey is a writer living in Cohasset, Massachusetts. Her first book will be published in 1993, and she is currently working on a novel.

As for "The Goldenrod Field": "I suppose Mrs. Harris is a composite of all the old ladies I've known. Since I was little I've had an affinity for them, and I have watched more than a few slip into confusion and forgetfulness. Despite that, there still always seems to be some order to their chaos, some message for me to hear and take as a lesson. This passing on of messages from one generation to the next, no matter how inconsequential they may seem at the time, interests me."

RUTH ELLEN CANJI

LOTTO

When my sister wet the bed she would pay me a quarter if I would hide the evidence. I did this willingly, out of greed rather than charity. A quarter could buy three penny-suckers. It could buy five pieces of Bazooka bubble gum. I saved the comics that the Bazooka people enclosed with their gum because they offered fantastic prizes. You could buy radios and bicycles if you had enough wrappers. I went ahead and sent off for a sharp new red two-wheeler that never came. I waited for months until I got angry enough to send a letter to the company. You gypped me, I wrote. You can speak to my lawyer. I went ahead and grudgingly bought one last piece of gum—I needed the address, that's why. It was then that I read the fine print. You had to send money! Money plus all of the comics. That really killed me. It's the fine print that gets you every time.

We live in Walker, a town in Illinois that is too small for secrets. I was the first to know when Nora let go because she peed on my legs. We slept in the same bed and we would be a tangle of limbs when I'd feel it. It stank like a cat's. When I felt most kindly toward her my own bladder would ache for release. More than once I considered urinating on the bed for the sheer thrill of it. It was exciting to think of purposefully committing a common act, something that would cause people to look at you in disgust. It's like stripping naked in the middle of church. It's like the feeling you get when the invitation to be saved is called up front, and you know that if you walk up the aisle everyone will be satisfied to know you weren't a Christian all these years. They will be smacking their lips because they caught you after all, and you will be expected to be nicer. You will have to set up chairs and tables at church potlucks.

My mother would string up the sheets in our side yard. She would clip them to the clothesline before school in the morning and they would flap like flags. They reminded me of the white flag of surrender. Nora would cry and beg my mother not to, but she would anyhow. It wasn't to be cruel; she was at her wit's end. She watched Nora's fluid intake. She woke her up at intervals. She threatened to withhold her allowance and accused her of harboring water. The doctor couldn't say anything and so we finally just covered the mattress with a rubber fitted sheet and hoped to shame the wetting out of her. When Nora paid me to hide the sheets all I did was to shove them in a plastic bag under the bed. I worked quietly and put on new ones in the cover of the night while she cried, making snuffling animal noises. Sometimes I pinched her to make her stop, or patted her back. It was all the same to her. It's not most that could let go like Nora. She was like one of those fairybook princesses, abandoned in a high lonely tower. She cried and cried and wiped tears on her hair, and no one could stop her. One time, pretending like I was her Prince Charming, the one come to take her away, I kissed her on the lips. Stop, I said, for I have come to take you away. She didn't get it, and usually I didn't bother. The next day I would run home from school and toss the sheets in the dryer. My mother would be at work and so then I would fold the dry sheets and put them in the drawer. They were crusty, but who would notice? All of them were stained yellow anyway.

We were twins, but we weren't alike. For one thing Nora was stupid. She almost got held back in the fifth grade because she couldn't pass the reading comprehension test. You couldn't prepare for it at all, it was that kind of thing. You had to walk in cold and they gave you a story to read in a certain amount of time and then you answered maybe ten or twenty questions. It was simple. I was already done and I was watching Nora without pity. Her face was balled up in concentration and she was rubbing at her eyes. The story was about how scientists can discover cures for cancer and muscular dystrophy by doing experiments and tests on animals. It was a true story and it had things in it you were supposed to pick up, like: true or false, Dr. Frankenstein believes that removing the stomachs of cats has relevance to the research conducted at Harvard Medical School on acute leukemia. I made this question up, but still they were something like this. And here was Nora with her face screwed up, trying not to cry.

"April," she said to me later, "I just couldn't. I was thinking of Oscar." Oscar was a mangy old stray dog with orangey fur we owned once. We plucked him from the brink of starvation, but he wasn't grateful. If you walked within ten feet of his feeding bowl he would whip his head around and draw his lips over his teeth. It wasn't smart to push him. He had bitten at least two people that we knew of. One day we woke up and he was gone. Nora swore that he'd return and she would sit after dark on the porch. She would click her tongue and call him, "Here, Oscar! Here, boy!" The way she carried on was embarrassing. I know for a fact she wrote poems to him. I used to read her diary when I could find where she hid it; she moved it around every week.

My father works construction in Chicago. They pay you good money up there. It's worth it. The main thing is he can't come back every day because it's a two-hour drive. He has a room there with an old Christian lady; he would come back on Friday nights and bring us Lotto tickets, one for me and one for Nora. He put down fifty cents apiece on our tickets and played our birthday, 6-2-7-7. I like to watch the lady turn the balls in the popcorn machine they have. They mix up the numbered ping-pong balls like candy and she fingers them carefully with her long, red polished nails. It must be hard to touch things with long nails. If I win I plan to go to Chicago and get a manicure. I like the way it looks.

Our father was never very cheerful. It's no secret that he wanted twin boys. He knew it was going to be twins; my mother said she filled up a door when she turned sideways. He would pat her stomach and ask if his boys were okay in there, if my mother was treating them right. She tells me about this some-times. His eyes would light up, she says, and he went to Lamaze classes with her. But of course he changed his mind, she says, when he saw it was us. Two perfect little girls. This is according to her. I think both he and my grandpa blamed her for making two girls. I think they wished we lived in China so they could have drowned us, or let us starve in the hills. They do those things there. They teach us that in school. He might have liked to try again, to get at least one boy. I wouldn't have minded it either, but my mother said no, thank you. You couldn't pay her to go through that again. I asked my father about that once. I asked him if he couldn't just make her have one more. He looked at me for a long time and rubbed his chin. He stared me down; he didn't say a word. I finally gave up and went to my room. That's something I always knew how to do. You could only push him so far. Nora never learned when to stop.

"Daddy," she said to him one Saturday, "Can I have twenty dollars?" He didn't look up from his magazine. He was reading the *Sports Illustrated* swimsuit issue. He was studying Elle Mac-Pherson.

"Come on, kid," he said. He swatted at her like a fly. Her voice is whiny.

"Daddy," she said, "it's for a wolf! It's to save a wolf!" There was this thing they passed out in our junior high. It was a pamphlet put out by the Environmental Protection Agency on ways you could save the earth. If you put down twenty dollars you could save a wolf's life at a wolf haven, or coven, or something like that they have in Canada. You get to name your wolf. You get an 8 x 10 glossy of its picture. For $50 you can visit him or her, but even Nora is not that unreasonable. She whined until he looked up.

"Listen, kid," he said. "Will you shut the hell up about the damn wolves! If your grandpa hears you now he'll have a stroke."

"He did already," she said. This was true, but she knew better than to mention it. Our grandfather was a hunter. He said wolves were mean to the bone and he would as soon skin them as look at them. It was American to kill wolves, and didn't Davy Crockett wear a wolf-skin cap? I thought it was beaver. He said it was wolf, and we never settled the issue before his stroke struck him speechless. He was wavering daily between life and death, this much we knew. It used to be a very solemn fact. At the beginning, we tiptoed past the sewing room where he was laid up, and we spoke respectfully about him. We never mentioned his drinking, but it seemed to me that his stroke had made him drunk forever. It used to take him all morning and a good part of the afternoon to reach that stupid, slack-jawed state. It was better this way. It was easier all around. In between his bouts of drinking he used to have periodic conversions back into the church. He cried and repented; he prayed out loud. Forgive me, O Lord, he would say, forgive this backslider bound for hell. He delivered long and tearful speeches at Sunday dinner while the fat congealed on the pot roast. He taught us songs. My favorite was Father Abraham because you had to march around while you sang: *Father Abraham/Had many sons/Many sons had Faaather Abraham! I am one of them/and so are you/as we go marching on! (Right arm!)* You would shake your right arm, and sing all the verses until you were shaking all over like a crazy person. My father would watch us and frown like he was thinking of saying something. He was probably thinking of the sons he had lost, or of his father's weak heart.

It got too strenuous for Nora and me to be respectful for any length of time. He looked like the mummy from a Saturday afternoon horror movie. He was cold all the time, wrapped in blankets. His eyes were always half open and I told Nora he was growing fangs. I would run my index finger under his lips, feeling his broken teeth, until I scared myself and ran to my room to scream into my pillow. I perfected the Stroke Face, a bleary-eyed look with one half of my jaw dropped slack. I could have a stroke on a dare. Nora would howl before guilt got the better of her. Oh, stop, she'd say, and I would tell her to go to hell. She had a soft heart.

No one could talk about my grandfather in front of my father, never mind that they hardly spoke themselves. My grandfather never forgave my father for dropping out of high school, for having two granddaughters and not going to church. I think my father liked having him laid up, safe and harmless. He got mad if the rest of us reminded him that he was there, alive, possibly emanating silent disapproval. Who could tell what he was thinking? He was gathering the forces of his attention to focus on Nora, so I took it upon myself to save her from a smack.

"Come on, stupid," I said, pulling her by the arm. It was time for the Lotto drawing on T.V., and Sharon Sharp herself was there. She was the director, or the president, something of status. She only showed up when the jackpot reached unmanageable proportions. It made people feel better to know that she was there, I guess. I felt better. I felt like they couldn't fix the numbers with Sharon Sharp there; her name promised that much. The numbers popped up into the slots, 6 . . . 2 . . . 7—and we were screaming, jumping up and down—8. It was a huge disappointment. We'd never come so close. I stared sadly at my nails, bitten to the flesh. Nora ran to our bedroom, and I sat there for a few minutes watching Grandpa. He was stretched out on his cot, his eyes open. "Damn," I said to test the waters. Grandpa was death on ladies swearing. He was drooling, and I thought I heard him moan. He frightened me; he was yellow and withered. I decided to go after Nora.

"Dear Lord, forgive us our sins of commission and omission," said my mother. She was sitting on Nora's bed and holding her hand. She was praying for her and Nora lay back with her eyes half closed, studying the cracks in the ceiling. We used to make up stories from the cracks. If you squinted you could imagine shapes, figures, a mural. Periodic water stains offered new possibilities. I scowled at her while my mother continued. "Take care of my baby," she said, "and steady her bladder." This was too much. Only Nora would let her pray like this; it suffocated me to feel her leaning over with her hot breath and her warmth. She hasn't seen me naked since I was six years old; it's like that, she probes too deep. If I read my sister's diary it's because I deserve it. I want to know things, I want to see her in a clear light. My mother doesn't want to see things clearly, she wants to change them. She wants to squint at sins and bury them deep, after she hears them confessed. I hate to think of her hearing my sins. I hate to think of myself exposed to her, to God, because I feel that they can't help but get a moment's thrill out of the whole affair. Even if you want to eradicate other people's wrongs, bury them ten thousand feet under, don't you get a jolt of satisfaction or recognition when you listen to their sins? Nora let her pray. Nora lets anyone do anything.

It might be her job as a secretary at the church that makes my mother pious. She is surrounded daily by symbols of God. There are pictures of Jesus ascending to Heaven in a glowing ring of clouds. He is holding out his hands, saying, *Why don't you join me?* There are pictures of Jesus with children at his feet, pulling at his robes. In these he is patient, smiling tenderly. There is a blue sparkle cross on a blood-red heart. If you turn out the light it glows in the dark. *Teach us to pray,* it says. There is a picture of Jesus swooping down in judgment. He is a fierce conqueror with a silver sword in his teeth, burning with anger. This is what happens if you ignore the prompting of the other signs. You will be cut down with the sword.

Our mother has told us that we are like flowers, tender, fragile. We are flowers in God's garden and we never know the moment that our stems will be broken. Our lives are no more than thin, delicate stems. Be ready, she says. Death is like going home, it's nothing to fear, but God has to know you. There is a small grace period, until age five, that you get to go to heaven no matter what when you die. You can go automatically because you don't know any better. There comes a time, however, when you are held accountable. You get your sins tallied up and if your name isn't recorded in the Book of Life God will look you in the face and deny you're His child. It seemed cold. Six is not so different than five. I would always ask if God could send a six-year-old to hell and my mother would say yes, indeed, and not so long ago, a six-year-old could be tried for murder. A six-year-old could be put to work in a factory. In biblical times parents could stone disobedient children to death. What's to stop God from sending a six-year-old to hell? God had his own set of values. It was with these things in mind that I became a Christian. I did it secretly, privately, when I was five and a half, and I scratched the date on the bedpost. I didn't know if I'd need proof. Nora prayed to be saved, too, but she didn't write it down. She prayed out loud. I supposed that her faith was stronger than mine. God could look in her face and see that she belonged to Him.

———

Nora wet the bed again. She peed like she would never stop, hot and wet on my legs. She jumped out of bed and tore off her thin cotton nightgown, crying and shaking like a person gone crazy.

"Nora," I said, sitting up in bed, "what the hell is wrong with you?" She stared at me and bolted for the door. It was a very hot night and we had all the fans going. They made a noise like a motor on a large truck and they hid the sound of her running down the hall, slamming the screen door and running down the stairs. I had no choice but to follow her.

She looked like a spirit, like a ghost in the night. Her naked white body was as helpless and soft as the belly of a fish. Her arms and legs churned and her brown ponytail flew out behind her as she ran across the field by our house. She was running to nowhere, there was nothing to see. There might be snakes and spiders in the field, mice and beer bottles. I had slipped on my shoes but Nora had not, and I hoped that she wouldn't cut herself. I hoped that she wouldn't step on a coiled snake, a poisonous spider. The fact that I had never seen them didn't bother me. I sensed they were there. It was too late for people, too late for possibilities to be ruled out. I was thinking these things as I loped behind her, trusting she would stop soon. She was running towards the County Road, a mostly empty two-lane highway. There was nothing beyond it, only the woods that were more like a gathering of tree-like twigs sprouting out of the ground. They were tall and spindly, leafless. I knew she wouldn't go in there. Nora had a fear of wild animals.

I saw the car and didn't see it. It was long and black, like an FBI undercover car. It was going as fast as a flash. It was like the flash on a camera. It was there before my eyes, it blinded me, and then it was gone. I could see it behind my eyelids. It left a glow in my brain, a feeling that veterans get in a missing leg when it rains. It was a dream car, a ghost car, dark and silent as a whale, and I can't remember a driver. When I had time to recollect I still couldn't see any driver. It was like an empty black car, silent as death, came hurtling along the road to deliver Nora to God. It hit her, swerved, skidded, and kept on going. It left her for dead, and she was. I ran to her, looked at her and she was, I knew, even before I ran to wake my parents.

It wasn't long ago that our whole family filled out organ donor cards from the Reader's Digest. We were moved by the stories of people who die for lack of hearts and kidneys, for people born without eyes. Perfectly good bodies are wasted, rotting away underground. They took Nora away in an ambulance. They rushed her to the hospital, dead, empty, a collection of parts. They divided her up, cut her, and sectioned her body to fly to different parts of the country. This is how they do it: her lungs might be rushed off to Arizona. Her brain might be flown to

Ohio. Her eyes, her heart. I spent a long time thinking about this. I didn't feel so bad, you know, about her being dead. If anyone had been there they would have seen that it was inevitable. She heard God calling her and she ran, ran out to meet Him in the road. She left without clothes and shoes. Everyone knows that the body lives without clothes in heaven, it's only spirits. They don't have weight, or mass. It has to be like that in order to accommodate all of the Christians who die, billions of them. The only thing I worry about is, what am I going to do when I find the person who has her eyes? Will it be a girl or a boy, an old woman? I will look into them and see myself, my mirror, my soul in another body. It bothers me to think of her dead eyes staring into my face. But no, they wouldn't be dead. They would be glowing with another person's thoughts. They would be flicking around, seeing things, sucking up more life. Her eyes get to live a second time and see things they've already seen, over and over again.

———

My father, when he's home on the weekends, watches Lotto with me. He buys me my number, the Pick Four, but for himself he buys a ticket for the biggest game they have. There are six balls, numbered zero through fifty-four. He buys just one chance. I can't see any hope for him. He says they either have his number or they don't. It's in code. It means something special to him but he won't say what.

I've been rooting around for weeks in the basement. I can't find Nora's diary. I would like to read her last entry. I have this feeling it's something about me, some revelation that I should know. I found a stack of *Playboy* magazines. They were in an orange icebox under the clothesline, piled under some old flannel work shirts. So many naked women! They were beautiful. They were in incredible poses. They lounged around on top of rough rocks. They stood in the middle of lawns, talking to people. They sunned themselves by swimming pools. I selected one magazine and brought it upstairs. I laid it on my grandfather's lap, opened to the centerfold. I wanted to see what my mother would do! You should be prepared to see things. You should realize that anything could happen.

Ruth Ellen Canji is a graduate student and teaching assistant at the University of Illinois in Chicago. She is hard-put to find an origin to "Lotto." "I bought a piece of Bazooka gum; I bought a Lotto ticket; I saw a bad made-for-TV movie featuring a bedwetter. I can never remember how the different elements cohere to form a story. I keep a notebook of quotes and things that strike me; I usually find some way to use the material." She's considering a Ph.D. in Literature and Creative writing when she finishes at UIC.

JOANNE LEAH GERBER

THE LESSER,
THE LARGER

A green almost black, the pines shivered in congregation. Occasional glimpses of sky as through patterned windows, almost white behind the trees. A girl, a silvering moss with her fingers, velvet against the grain. Beside her, a small cache of pebbles arrayed like constellations.

Although the rock on which she sat chilled her, Jeannine had been here for hours. The trickle of water, run-off no wider than she, was so cold and clear that it glorified the pebbles beneath. Made a quivering mosaic of coral and black, pewter, amber and deep marble green, lit with mica and fragments of quartz. On the moist earth of the path, she had followed the mica like silver confetti to the stream bed. Later, pressing some into brilliant paste in her palms, she had tried to make an imprint of her hand on the granite. The stone surface too calloused, the impression she had left was an indeterminate metallic sheen.

Swaying slightly, she closed her eyes, breathed and listened to the air, all damp earth and pine. Another season, there would be the dry tang and crackle of leaves. Today there was nothing but the small gurgling of water and the vespering of trees.

She knelt up, twisted her hair into a loose auburn hank, pushed it down into the collar of her sweater. Hesitated, then bent until her face was in the stream, just touching, and her palms were flat on the cobbled bottom. The water was stunningly cold. The shock rippled her scalp. She shuddered, fought her eyelids as the stones were magnified, intensified, vivid and close through this window. When they flickered and blurred she withdrew. Temples and cheekbones throbbing, straightened and listened again. Beyond her own gasping, there were no fresh sounds.

She dried the new pebble on the thigh of her jeans. Small rivulets of ice water teased, itched, where the hot mat of her hair trapped them against her neck. She shrugged her hair loose. Finally, held the stone up out of the shadows. It was a white quartz, worn smooth and round by the movement of water over the tiny streambed. Perfect.

She placed it with care beside the others on the cushion of moss. Polaris. Finished now, stretched out on the granite slab, sun dappled, shivering, wondering what time it might be. The afternoon had become unfathomable. At home her father was finally packing his things. Her mother threw words at him still, like great wounding stones. The grove knew nothing of this. Jeannine studied the pebbles. Touching her hands to her face, waited for the pain to recede.

One of these buildings, then. Jeannine parked her car under aged elm trees and decided to try the building on the right first. The leaves underfoot were like Japanese paper.

Up close, the building was massive in a reassuring way, not monumental. A world apart from the rest of the university with its primary bright furnishings, attempt of fuchsia and goldenrod posters to encourage concrete slab walls and nervous new students. Instead, leaded windows in weathered stone, doors of wood set solidly in arched portals. Jeannine rested her hand for a moment on the cool roughness of masonry, then entered, hoping she had guessed right, found the Fine Arts Library.

Not quite. This had to be Theatre. First, just inside, a room animated with costume making. The reek of new fabric. Bristol board sketches, sequin-spangled tulle, conversation. She watched, intrigued. Then a voice began tuning somewhere, splendid soprano snaking up the stairs and down the long corridor. With it, Jeannine noticed now, the alkyd smell of brushes at work. Hoping to see backdrop painting, she continued on through the hall. Halfway along, came to impressive double doors, took a breath, and went in.

She found herself in a maroon and oak sanctum with vaulted acoustics. The Theatre proper. At the front two men like priests in black turtlenecks were reading Shakespeare. Passionately. They ignored her intrusion. The blond one's words and hands arced, conjured—and a set shimmered almost visible on the bare floorboards at his feet. Jeannine started, stepped back soundlessly, conscious of ritual, something numinous behind sleeping footlights and still pencilled scripts. An outsider, she let the doors slip shut before her. She would look for the backdrops another time.

Back in the hall clipping aggressive heels on terrazzo announced a secretary, and in seconds Jeannine had proper directions. She made her way down the steps and out the side door into a field of mud, not bothering with the sidewalk. She was exuberant, infused with theatre. Crossing to the Fine Arts Library became a victory of her red coat over the grey swathe of midafternoon. She left it unbuttoned, relished the subtle battle of the wind for the leaves and her bare throat. Both quivered. She would not be hurried from the half-clothed trees and dishevelled sky. She was the only red movement across the mud, between the stone buildings.

Inside, the heat took over immediately, the red coat surrendered to it. Jeannine was disappointed at the catalogue—fine art on microfiche. She abhorred microfiche, found it too linear, words compressed and contained rationally and alphabetically. To her, they seemed words without language, garbled black patterns on plastic, deceptively frail. An ominous glut of information. Childishly, to foil it, she dropped the fiche on the plate haphazardly. The words marched diagonally askew, affronted, across the glare of the screen. She enjoyed this, glided the lever lazily up, over. Pretended to come upon her subject by chance. Sobered.

She had been studying art at the university for less than a month. Loved it. But the other day in class, a film about the life of Edvard Munch had unsettled her. Like a message half received, was still troubling her. By looking at his works she was hoping to efface pervasive images of his days.

On the worn oak surface of the very last table, where the artificial brightness of the room was tempered by the dull light from the window, she arranged the books. The covers were rough as canvases, she closed her eyes to imprint the texture on her hands. The pages would be glossy, Munch's paintings were not. In the film, he had laboured with oils and acids, thick brushes and knives. Had used paint courageously. Made etchings by gouging and burning—she had almost sensed his sweat rising sharp with the stench of the inks, as he bled life from a stone plate, from scorched wood or metal. She, too, was coming to know the heady drag of roller across a beautifully scarred surface. Cautiously now, as though she were lifting a fresh engraving from the block, she opened the book to the first print.

This girl. Her face was diffused with light, the color of her veins was a map under her fading hair. Her eyes looked past walls and years and the book, her pinched face forgave the world for withholding itself. All this, in lines that almost floated from the paper. It elicited a moment of reverence.

Jeannine turned the page, found a room gentled by the play of sunlight with lace curtains before an open window. But here, too, a young woman was dying. In a chair ribbed strong as a boat, she sat tranquil, her cheek resting on a pillow handworked to give pleasure. Beside her, her grey mother's hands were still busy. Her own, translucent, held a blood-flushed handkerchief in an empty lap. In her face was neither fear nor shame, only regret that there was no child to warm her dark dress, or the empty chair when she was gone. Her shoulders were slight, would travel well, Jeannine found herself thinking, because the years had placed on them nothing more weighty than a crocheted shawl and her own going. She would probably touch once more the embroidered pillow, then slip the room off as lightly as the shawl. At the window, the lace billowed.

Involuntarily, Jeannine reached to brush the luminous folds with her fingertips, met the cool sheen of the page. She felt bruised. These paintings, these girls seen through ancient, tender eyes. The artist himself so young. Scenes from the film came back: Losses. A tall house with many doors quietly closed. Helplessly, in small rooms, people choking up blood. At night, the sound of tuberculosis in Edvard's ears, the color behind his eyes. Just looking on, she had been engulfed by the encroaching intimacy of death. Of northern life in those narrow Lutheran years. Felt his paramount need to paint. To preserve. To evade. But had painting saved him? She turned the page.

Here, promenading on *Franz Johann Strauss,* were homberged men like ghouls, and women with haunted, unlit eyes. All strolling to hell under the benevolent yellow light from the windows, along the dusky familiarity of the street. And in the next work, *the Tempest,* a woman in a sheer dress, almost a wraith, distancing herself from a house solidly illuminated on a hill, a knot of people halfway down. Only a wind-whipped tree sensed that their number was diminished, caught the glimmer of her gown in the darkness.

Overleaf, Munch's signature piece. A man on a boat shrieking. Even with her eyes shut, Jeannine could enter. Feel herself dragged through seas and sky striated in bands of color; orange and scarlet and indigo. The ship surged, enveloped in the hues of an angry sun, of lifeblood poured out, in the colors of a night sky shattered by flares. She shuddered, reoriented herself. Palms flat on the oak table, looked again. The man was carried against his will, trapped against an endless gleaming rail. So he screamed. His hands up by his mouth, he contorted himself. Bent all light and time and sky with his horror. He accused her from the page. Accused everyone. Everyone was the unheeding party at the end of the deck, watching the sun set gaudily on the water, waiting with a wish for the first twinkle in the darkening sky overhead. Everyone refused to bear witness.

Shivering, Jeannine closed the book on him. She was not guilty. It was the closeness in the library that made the room waver momentarily, her heart race. In her own life, nothing had been decided yet. She was only just learning to paint.

Outside she took to the sidewalk, red coat buttoned high against the late September gusts. When she still shivered, she moved her mind deftly from the chill breath of the paintings, the dying girls—from wherever that boat was headed. What had she in common with a dead Norwegian painter? She was nineteen years old. A vigorous girl with many friends. She crossed the parking lot quickly, searching for her car.

———

Out beyond the light cast from the windows, Jeannine could feel the night come solidly down around her. It was too cold, biting into her, but she welcomed it as something real, without artifice. From across the snowy lawn wafted giddy voices and laughter, vivid and overheated as the house and clothing of the guests. She should have been inside—they had all come from the city to see her. Instead, she moved closer to the trees, screened from the party, but not from the sky or the slope to the water. With no wind, the frosted air was delicious to breathe.

Driving out this afternoon with Karl, she had been astonished by the color of the trees, the bare branches showing ginger and burgundy, pewter and taupe against the snow and muffled air. The woods were like a sketch in Conte crayons. In that delicate balance, she had observed through tears, leaf would have been intrusion.

Transformed now by the hour, they were limned charcoal against the midnight sky. The wide crescent moon and the stars hung low, brilliant and perfectly placed as in a child's book of verse. There was an illusion of intimacy in the subtle silvering of everything she could see—as if it were all drawn wonderfully close, and she might walk with no effort in any direction and find herself miles away, beyond the reach of everything familiar. Beyond the reach of the past twelve months and the ruin that she had become.

The illness had robbed her. Aged her. She was weak, her back and shoulders curled defensively against the pain in spite of herself. She had tried to contain it, keep it penned up in her blood, in her hollow bones, where no one could see it. But eventually it had outmaneuvered her. Overwhelmed her. Now, whenever she began to shiver, the fear stalked her that the pain would break out, that she would be shuddering again uncontrollably, her body trying to shake her loose.

A swell of sound from the festive house—someone's favorite song? Jeannine wondered whether any of them realized how lost she was. First, she had been treated to chaotic fancies at night. In her dreams she saw herself functioning, laughing, inextricably bound up in the lives of others, even her studio improbably abuzz. Then abruptly, inexplicably, she would be wearing a backless cotton gown, two ties missing, and the floor under her feet terrazzo-stone cold. The studio invariably fell away and she would find herself on a bed. The bed was an ice-white slab and she on it, almost one too. Very much alone.

She had kept these dreams to herself, even from Karl. They recurred. At some point, ceased to be fancy. She was disrobed, laid out on a table like granite. A shawl of lead lay heavily across her bare shoulders, her breasts. Footsteps receded; suspended a scant inch from her flesh, a machine murmured and clicked. Light flickered somewhere brief as heat lightning; the room seemed colder. The technicians came back. She could feel her sharp hips as they turned her, tried to impress the lines of her body onto the plate. Understanding the difficulty of printmaking, she tried to be helpful. She apologized for the uncouth trembling and they, with their gentle hands, apologized for being so very much alive.

There was no waking up. Her life had been given into the hands of technicians and physicians. Professionals who, in the chambers of nuclear medicine, worked at projecting her days in inky images that said nothing of her own plans. Although they were careful to keep her informed, what they held up to the violet-lit panels remained as opaque and indecipherable to her as microfiche. Waiting for them to finish she tried to conceive paintings, but color and perspective were swept away in the chill tide of loneliness that washed over her in those unlit metallic rooms, in the nausea that came afterwards.

More and more it was taking her unguarded even in the studio, making the weight of a brush beyond bearing. She knew this worried people; it worried her. But the disease was carrying her with it. Like Colville's *Swimmer* she was a woman moving through steel-dark water, caught by some trick of timing or current in a course parallel to the jagged shore. There would be no resisting the swell that gleamed a long way out.

Tonight, she found it impossible to pretend otherwise. Tears of desperation came, she tugged off her gloves and covered her eyes with cold fingers. She could scream, she wanted so to survive. Scream. What was wrong with her life? Had she done something? No, she had to stop, or she would get feverish, have to go in. It had been forever since she last went walking alone. Taking a stiff Kleenex to her face, she worked at calming herself. The tissue smelt of mint—a piece of linty candycane stuck deep in her pocket. The tightness in her chest began to ease.

She concentrated for a moment on the terrain. Should she try for the lake, or simply follow the laneway up through the trees?

The grade was gentler uphill, and the cars had been through. Still, if she could make it down to the waterfront—she turned to look, and was caught again by anguish.

This scene. Austere, unspeakably lovely. Suppose she were to paint it, a study in solitude under the night sky? The shrubs over against the house squatted indistinct as clouds, heavily blanketed with snow, while here, the trees that stood up to the winds were bare or glassy, more line than color. Would catching them on canvas as they were tonight say anything about how they had beguiled her this afternoon, or hint at the green explosion when they came to leaf? Live on herself in her art, as everyone assured her? The truth was, she could not even capture trees.

Not to cry again, she stooped to examine the track of a rabbit in the snow, found finer tracings where birds must have come for berries. Her husband might be able to say which birds, Karl had that kind of knowledge. It had been his idea to come out. AWOL. She had spent a month in the hospital this time, and he wanted to take her beyond the reach of doctors for the weekend. A risk, but at this stage of the battle, three days' peace would be a major beachhead. She had not felt up to it, but Karl had been right about coming.

The day was splendid for getting away from the city. As they backed out to the street, she was suddenly comforted by the sunlight on the softly mottled brick of their home, by the glazed houses huffing in the chill air—her community, all intact. At the hospital it was easy to lose her bearings.

For a time, Karl drove silently, letting her watch the play of light and cold. She noted the crenulated drifts like a frozen wake, marking the passage of traffic close to the limits of the roadway. She traced with her eyes the padded movements of rare pedestrians, the collar of snow that had taken the place of birds along the power lines, transformations of winter. Twenty minutes after the last outposts of the city fell away, they detoured to pick up coffee and fresh pastries at a converted apple farm that was a favorite waystation on trips to the lake.

Watching Karl drive as she savoured the crusty sweet fritter, a wonder after hospital food, she thought how young he looked. His hair was still streaked with blond, not grey, and his body was several years from softening. At the hospital he seemed older. His movements hesitant, almost perplexed. Never speaking of the sentence she had been given, he seemed to approach everything obliquely. He had even developed an amazing resistance to provocation, utterly out of character. Maturity, she wondered, or simply that the visitation of dread disease in their lives had knocked the spontaneity out of him? The first time she had ever seen Karl he was fierily calling up Hamlet in an empty theatre.

She reached over to poke the side of his knee, a trick she used to keep him awake on car trips at night. The gentlest jab made his leg jerk up and smash the underside of the dashboard. He pretended to swerve and they laughed, remembering how she had forgotten and done that just a few weeks after his cartilage surgery—they had nearly crashed, that time. She kissed his ear, tugged her seatbelt loose and moved close, enjoying his warmth and the slight flexing and easing of his shoulder as he handled the steering wheel. The fragrance of cinnamon and coffee, of his light aftershave, was wonderful.

Fields rushed by, deeply snow covered or punctuated with broken cornstalks and rocky hillocks. Farm-clustered buildings set far back from the highway were flushed out of the landscape, ruddy or stonefaced, vanished again.

An hour from the lake, Karl startled her. First, he told her about the crowd he had invited out for the evening; as he put it, their whole rogue's gallery of friends. Then he told her that he had begun to make plans for the summer. He thought they might fly out to Victoria and drive to Pacific Rim Park; they had always meant to go back. Hike, sketch, watch the ocean—they could do whatever Jeannine felt up to. He had already looked into accomodations. What did she think?

She sat up, closed her eyes, gave herself over to memory. Their honeymoon trip came back: Days passed on the wind-swept beach in a kind of reverie. Feeling no need to swim, they had slowly traced the wavering line where the land and their footing dissolved into the Pacific. Retraced it. Wordlessly, watched the luminous swells roll in and in, until their eyes were burnt by the dazzling play of light and dissolution. Jeannine trying to take in that out there somewhere was Asia. Every day, she had filled pockets, and Karl's, with pebbles. The green she called jade.

She remembered how, wrapped in layers of clothes that flapped about their arms and thighs like gulls trying to take flight, they went looking for shelter. On a granular bed, amid a drift-log tangle of massive proportions, they had huddled together to eat sand-encrusted Brie and sticky buns, biscuits and peaches bruised from Karl's rucksack. In those days he carried a blue thermos bottle almost two feet high, which she said should be restricted to workers on high steel. Curled up exactly at sea level, they had sipped scalding tea at wide intervals between caresses, as though they were Afphasn marshalling kafir and warmth at the end of a day's frigid climb.

Afterwards, gritty and stiff, they had sat up into the fierce light and read to each other, one holding the frantic pages as doggedly as a halyard in a squall, one shouting poems into the torrent of air off the ocean. They read until the thermos was spent and the light began to fail. Then watched, silenced, as with splendour and sombreness, poetry was written across the water and sky in a never-to-be-repeated requiem for the day.

Four weeks, almost half a summer. They had imagined then fifty summers to be spent or squandered together; inconceivably, that was not ten years ago. Karl still carried in his pocket a tiny stone, as meticulously curved as a mermaid, and banded like malachite. Her gift to him for remembrance, the exact shade of her eyes. He called it his Jade.

What she had culled from the wind-strafed beach was a resonant truth from their reading of Rilke. Through all these years of painting, it had been both touchstone and calling: that works of art are of an infinite loneliness, to be approached only in the opening of oneself which is love. Now, she was discovering that it was true also of persons. In the unravelling of her life, everyone, even he whom she most loved, who most loved her, was receding. Closing themselves to the hated sickness, shielding themselves from the suffering which increasingly defined her, everyone had begun to take leave of Jeannine. And she, of them. Was this a failure—or a corollary—of love?

Either way, the distance remained. Sadness spreading through her as irresistibly as unwanted sedation, she turned to watch the winter-blitzed fields. Let Karl float plans, try to tie their futures together. Apart from the knee repair, he had never been hospitalized. Had he been the one lying all those nights between stainless steel rails, next summer would seem as elusive to him as had the sun, in its incandescent procession across the Pacific.

Jeannine realized now that her silence the rest of the drive must have been disquieting for Karl. She had further abdicated tonight, leaving his gala gathering of friends. She snapped an iced berry from its branch, held it until the slight heat of her hand had melted it down to the creased waxy surface, reached for another. They were hard as cranberries, sank out of sight when she dropped them into the softer snow under the bush. She looked across to the house. There, where every window was a yellow beacon in the night, the tone was too bright for her, almost surreal. She had felt like an interloper, the only one who had lost faith that there was safety in numbers.

Letting the berries fall, she straightened and gripped her ribs fiercely. Was she dreaming all this? Or was it possible that the doctors were right? She hooked her hands over the blades of her hips. Yes, even through the heavy coat her flesh was defeated. She would pass on, soon. But to where—as what—if she outlived the tenuous hold of the flesh? As spirit? Not good enough.

She spoke this word out loud. "Spirit." It hung, a minute trail of exhaust in the air. From the violet-sheened snow, no answer. Again. "Spirit!" The night was unshaken. She intoned it a third time, quietly, "spirit." Gave up and began to move with the plane of the land towards the lake.

The crust glittered, fragile as a meringue. With each step she had to choose betwen letting herself skitter slightly along the surface, or shattering it with the heel of her boot for footing. Where the ridge on which the house was set dropped away, she slipped more seriously. Slid for a few heartstopped seconds. She did not cry out, even when she came to rest with throbbing hip and scraped cheek in a bramble. She sat very still—the numb face, chafed hands, were remembered sensations. Even the icy trickle where some snow found her neck reminded her of something. Of another time, very remote. As she reached to wipe at the wetness, she suddenly missed her long hair, as though she should be stuffing it back under the collar of her coat. And what was she listening for? Water? She shook her head. Still nothing. Whatever the memory, her senses would not share it with her mind.

She unfolded herself, massaged the hip and got to her feet. Her legs were quivering. Continue down? Suppose she fell again?

She had so wanted to walk alone. Incidents like this became crises, though. The devastation of her whole life was not enough for the disease, it imposed a vigilance in small matters, too. Ironically, she remembered how she used to take it for granted that adversity matured a person, that suffering produced wisdom. That seemed aeons ago. She would have liked to believe it still—to become wise herself, to handle this immensity with grace. But the effort was enveloped in exhaustion, the toll of petty decisions and griefs. If anything, she tended to be more truculent and territorial, more easily intimidated. Tonight she did not want to give in. She tried a few steps. For now, the trembling felt manageable. Her walk was on.

The hill was becoming trickier, Jeannine guessed it must be where the grass moved tentatively, concentrating on her footing and the sound of her progress. Almost to the lake. It was uncharacteristically silent, she had not often come here in winter.

Finally, level ground. Her feet found the track, beaten still under a foot of snow, which led to the landing. It would keep her clear of the rocks and the water. Passing the far end this afternoon, she had been surprised to see the ice already heaved up in places, looking uncannily like the shale flats on Georgian Bay, where she summered as a child.

Georgian Bay. The memory came back now, of making her first primitive prints there, the year she was twelve. She had passed most of that summer on the rocks with a mallet, splitting the monotonous shale plates to expose the blacker fossils within. Dragging her best finds back to the cottage, she would lay onionskin over the washed stone and rub with a soft leaded pencil until the image emerged. When she held the fragile paper up to her lamp at last, there would be a marvellously tiny marine animal, a shell, or a fern. Evidence of life past, preserved. She remembered making dozens. Where were they now? The collection must have been lost, like so much else, when her household dissolved the next spring.

Jeannine looked up. The stars were even lower here, the sky seemed to breathe with them. Involuntarily, her eyes found the Dippers. To her, they had always been Jewelled Chairs—the Lesser, the Larger. It had been her intention, as a girl, to ask whoever ran heaven to let her sit in them as soon as she arrived. She had estimated that a hundred years in each would suffice to give her a good look at the world. From that exalted vantage she would come to understand everything.

She was saddened to know now that she would have to travel almost forever to reach those chairs. And to think that the earth, no more than a chance mirror for its star, much as a puddle burns for a moment with sunlight, would have long since been lost in the heavens. Cassiopeia, Orion, the Pleiades, planet Earth . . . the scale of things had changed, become inconceivable.

Yet, out of childhood, it was easier for her to think of the heavens than of heaven, which had somehow been left off the celestial maps. Her own maps. She regretted that, now.

Back when she was first diagnosed, Karl had taken her to hear an evening lecture on contemporary metaphysics. Desolate, she had been ready to consider anything. But the gist of the message seemed to be that death was a passage from the lesser, physical realm, to the larger, spiritual realm. Her real self was eternal, pure spirit. In breaking out of the confines of the body, she would be elevated from the carnal, into the realm of infinite light.

Her reaction had been volatile, shocking her. On the drive home, she had lashed out unfairly at Karl. He could embrace metaphysics if he wanted to. But she could not see her body as a mere casing to be discarded. Found no consolation in the prospect of an interminable half-life as some kind of conscious shadow, incommunicado. It was utter hypocrisy to pretend that disintegration into two halves, with only one of them surviving, was preferable to her current situation—or to oblivion. Better nothing, she told him, than to sham immortality. Then she had wept, so desperately that Karl had had to pull off the rain-swept road to comfort her. He had held her in the streaming car for an hour. They had never spoken of it again.

But the episode had disclosed to her both disabling rage, and a paradox. Rage, that she had been robbed to her right to another half century of growing into her death. That she had no control over where she was headed. Had given Karl no child. Paradox, that flesh was as the speaker had described it—fragile as grass, momentarily touched with glory, then as quickly withered, wind-borne and gone. Yet the body, even in extremity, resisted death as unnatural. At the hospital, she had seen both the remarkable frailty, and resilience, of physical existence.

She tried now to rub some feeling back into her numb hands. Blew into her gloves before pulling them on, wishing the ornamental rabbit fur went deeper than the wrists.

Barely audible, the lapping of water. She turned. There, a dark tongue where the point arced out around the marsh. She picked her way over, crouched to watch the play of moonlight on the narrow current. The cold rose off the frozen lake as from dry ice. This close, she could hear the tentative swelling and creaking. From the hill this afternoon there had been a few resounding rifleshots as cracks spread like lightning far out across the surface. The overhanging trees were glass-sheathed, but the lake would break out soon at this end. Widening channels and dusky patches testified to the waning of winter and the lengthening days.

She was still preoccupied. In her weakening state, she was finding that she could no longer sustain her anger. Besides, in the end it was not enough. The progress of the illness seemed irresistible, and rage was no antidote to fear—or the questions that visited through the long hospital nights. Lately, she was vacillating. Sometimes it seemed obvious that the only way to serenity was acceptance. Yet, however she tried to reconcile herself to dying, Jeannine found she could not relinquish the hope that she would go on being. She was still hoping, absurdly, for a permanent fusion of body and spirit. A simple reversal of the order of decay—was that so fantastic?

Less so, out here. The light was obsidian on the strip of black water, reminding her of the stream in an underground cavern she and Karl had explored. Tonight the icicles, too, seemed to reach down geologically, from the petrified grass to the water. There was no hint of the ferment that made the bog fetid in summer, so that canoes would negotiate the reedy narrows quickly, pausing for lilies only above or beyond this point.

As so often these past weeks, she found herself wondering about God. A legacy from her parents, she was illiterate in matters of religion. The one provacative story she had picked up, was that even Jesus Christ was not content to dismiss his body and live on as pure spirit. Somewhere she had heard that he insisted friends touch him after his alleged death, to acknowledge that his re-animated flesh was real. Whatever lay behind it, the story gave her an obscure sense of solidarity with him. She had always meant to view Kurelek's Passion paintings, the collection a few hours drive from the city. But could she ask Karl to take her, now?

Enough musing. Since childhood, she had known the value of small distractions from great dilemmas. Still crouched, she cut a star into the waferlike surface of the snow. The edges were a blade against the skin of her glove. Strange how irresolute the snow was underneath. She cut another star, then one more. With a movement of her wrist not unlike skipping stones, she set the sheer fragments afloat on the dark current. Rose when the Chairs were complete at her feet, shadows etched into the shimmering mirror of white sky.

Probably another dead end. But what if, out there—she turned to follow the curved parameters of the impassively beautiful night—beyond her field of vision, someone was watching? Jeannine caught herself scanning for a shooting star. Something.

It was time to head back. She would have been missed by now, and with the overheated tone of the festivities, it might spill out into a general alarm and search party. That had happened at a Christmas get-together, when, disconcerted by the words of a carol, Jeannine had gone out unnoticed to her host's garden swing. She made her way now to the path.

The hill looked treacherous from below. Resined and slick. She would have to tackle it sideways, wedging her boots in to the slope, staying over by the bushes. She turned for a last look across the ice just as something gave way with a great snap south of the narrows. Karl had been right about leaving his skates at home.

Climbing took even more energy than she had expected. She became intent on the placement of her feet, on dragging air into her lungs. She was conscious of leaving a powdered wake up the smooth face of the hill, but could not turn to look, break the rhythm of her ascent. Her boots reached, and passed, the spot where she had slid into the bushes earlier. With tremors now in her legs, and jolts of hot pain from the small of her back, she had a brief image of herself bivouacked there in the softened snow. Felt tempted to turn back, rest. But just as suddenly, the climb was behind her. She stumbled, leaned weakly against a tree, a metronome in her head and chest, her hip.

Music usurped the solitude here, but pleasantly. Voices curled out from the house, pervasive as woodsmoke. Jeannine whispered, "Thank you." She had not ruined Karl's party after all. Alarmed her friends. She had made it down to the water's edge and back. In a moment, would go in and make merry.

Staying out too long, straying too far, she might have given the illness the upper hand again. She hoped not. It seemed a great silvery distance across the lawn to where the snow shone topaz under the windows. Not so far as the constellations overhead, but a very great distance. She felt almost ready now to cross it.

Joanne Leah Gerber of Regina, Canada, is a writer and part-time graduate student at Canadian Theological Seminary. She has studied creative writing, Russian Literature and Aesthetics, and Theology and Christian Thought. Her writing studies have included many fiction workshops with top Canadian writers. In 1990 she won the Saskatchewan Literary Award in Short Fiction.

"The Lesser, The Larger" borrows some material from Joanne's own life: "I am just recovering from four years of serious illness—imagined facing death without faith." She also has "an 'apologetic' goal in many of my stories, which I sell to secular literary journals. This is one of those 'theological' ones." She is working on a first collection of short fiction and collaborating with a composer on an opera from one of her stories. As soon as her health allows, Joanne hopes to resume teaching creative writing and literature to undergraduates part-time.

EDWARD LODI

NUMBER
THIRTEEN

In late August, when Deep Meadow Bog lay draped over the earth like a patch of green embroidery, you could look out across the vines and see the heat shimmering above the unripe berries and hear the insects buzzing and almost—not quite—taste the salt tang of the ocean that lay just beyond the swamp.

One year, when I was thirteen and old enough to swing a scythe, my Uncle Dom put me with a crew of men mowing along the ditches and on the dikes where the tractor couldn't reach. Although it was hard work—on the first day blisters as big as quarters blossomed on my palms and I was stung twice by hornets—I soon toughened; by summer's end the rank smell of stagnant water blended with the fragrance of cut weeds was like perfume to me, and I waded through oil slick patches of poison ivy as if it were clover.

The men who worked for Uncle Dom were a mixed crew, such as you find in those Hollywood movies where there is at least one Jew, one Black, a Southerner, a Swede, a Latino, and a college kid or two. We had Cape Verdeans, Puerto Ricans, Frenchmen, Finns, Poles, and plain old swamp Yankees (as Uncle Dom would say, who was himself like me—Italian). We didn't have them all at once, of course. On the cranberry bogs men came and went. The lure of booze, or jail, or even occasionally the promise of something better, took them away. But usually they came back, or were replaced by someone of an ilk, and the ethnic mix remained more or less the same.

Peter Andrade was Cape Verdean. Summer was almost over when he emerged, like a muskrat, out of the swamp and came plodding along the dike to where we were mowing. The men, spread out over the bog at thirty to fifty-foot intervals, glanced up as he approached but continued to slice through the weeds, swinging their scythes like golfers intent on improving their game. Welcoming the opportunity for a break, I removed the whetstone from my hip pocket and, leaning against the handle of the upright scythe, sharpened the blade with the quick, steady strokes the men had taught me to use without cutting my hand.

Peter Andrade walked slowly, as if on the last leg of a long journey. I had a chance to study him without seeming to. Even for a bog worker he was shabbily dressed. He had on a Red Sox baseball cap (picked up, in all probability, by the side of the highway); a long-sleeved shirt, once red, now faded to a pale pink, frayed at the edges like the last rose of summer; a pair of baggy pants with more patches than an old inner tube; and dilapidated shoes the size of tugboats. A bundle tied up in gray flannel longjohns dangled from his shoulder like a brace of rabbits, but Peter was no hunter home from the hill. He looked more like a sad-faced clown, weary after a long performance.

I was decapitating weeds along a cross ditch between two sections of bog about twenty yards out from the dike that separated Deep Meadow Bog from the reservoir. Peter spotted me, paused at the edge of the dike, then slid down the grassy slope and jumped the shore ditch onto the vines. He narrowly missed a bath, teetering on the far rim of the ditch like the circus clown he resembled, regaining his balance only at the last moment. At that time of year, late August, cranberries—grown to nearly full size—are easily bruised. Peter, obviously versed in the lore of the bogs, walked along the edge of the shore ditch, then turned at a right angle and proceeded toward me along the cross ditch, rather than cutting diagonally across the vines, where he would have damaged the crop. So I knew without his having to mention it that he was looking for work.

"Boss around?"

I shook my head. "He won't be back till quitting time."

He removed the baseball cap, exposing a sparsely forested scalp, and mopped his brow with a rag that looked like it had been torn from a pair of discarded pajamas. I tried to guess his age. Fifty, or seventy, it was hard to tell. A grizzled stubble that discolored his chin offered no clue.

"Got another one of them?" He pointed to the scythe.

"There's a spare one over by the reservoir, near that flume."

Nodding a brief thank you, he retraced his steps to the dike. He jumped the ditch with the bundle like a dead albatross around his neck. I could see Bill Monteiro and a couple of the other men watching, expecting to see him lose his balance and go plunging waist deep into water, but again he made it, though it was only momentum and sheer luck that kept him from sliding back. He sprawled against the steep slope like a parachutist hitting solid ground, clambered to the top, adjusted the bundle, then resumed his slow, plodding gait along the dike to the reservoir, where he found the spare scythe leaning against the flume. He tested the blade with his thumb. Finding it sharp, he joined the line of mowers on the bog.

When Uncle Dom came by at four o'clock to pick us up he didn't question Peter's presence. But the next morning when Peter showed up for work Uncle Dom called him aside. He wrote down his social security number and asked him a question or two. I guess Uncle Dom noticed what I hadn't, that Peter had not eaten for a day or two. He left us off on the dike, but returned at ten with a brown paper bag, which he placed in the grass on top of Peter's bundle so the ants wouldn't get to it. Hungry as he must have been, and weak, Peter kept on working, not stopping to eat until we all did at noon. Although he was down and out he still had pride.

Uncle Dom took on Peter Andrade because harvest time was close and extra hands would soon be needed to bring in the berries. Because Peter didn't have a place to stay—he had been sleeping in the woods, taking his baths in the reservoir—Uncle Dom fixed up the shack at the edge of the swamp where the men stayed on frost nights, when they had to monitor the thermometers and start the pumps if necessary. Peter moved into the shack that first day. Uncle Dom and I stayed after work to help him. Not that Peter required much in the way of moving—all he owned in the world, besides the almost-rags he wore, was wrapped up in those gray flannel longjohns—but the hand pump needed new leathers, the wood stove needed cleaning, and the dry sink hadn't been scrubbed in quite awhile. Mainly, we just wanted him to feel at home.

"The rest you can do in your spare time, in lieu of rent," Uncle Dom said. "The axe is in the lean-to. Cut all the dead wood you need. You'll find plates and utensils in that cupboard. Tomorrow

I'll drop off some detergents and a couple of cans of paint. There's kerosene for the lamp in the lean-to. Just don't burn the place down."

"Ain't touched a drop in three months," Peter assured him. "Can't drink like I used to—gives me pains here." He touched the left side of his chest.

We left him standing in the doorway, like a woodchuck guarding its burrow, tiny plumes of smoke rising from the chimney as proof to the world that Peter Andrade had a home. The next day he showed up for work clean shaven but wearing the same clothes. Pay day wasn't till next week, so Uncle Dom offered him an advance, beyond the money he had already lent him for groceries.

Peter declined the offer. "I'll make do," he said.

"Saving your money for something special?" Bill Monteiro asked (thinking, I suppose, of the muscatel wine he himself was hoarding for).

"That's right," Peter replied.

It was noon. We were sitting in the shade of a tall old pine that stood alone in a clearing between the bog and reservoir. Bill tore the crust from his sandwich and tossed it into the water. "Watch them shiners!" he said, as small fish like silver darts leapt through the surface to thrash over the scraps of bread. Peter seemed relieved by the change of subject. That afternoon he kept to himself, mowing along a steep part of the dike the others had avoided.

The last days of August passed in a lassitude that belied the impending harvest. A week before Labor Day Uncle Dom took me off mowing and put me on the truck to help Charlie Perkins cart empty boxes. We removed the boxes from the screenhouse, where they were stored twelve high, and trucked them to the bog, where we stacked them upside down in clearings along the shore. From a distance, across that embroidered expanse, the neatly shaped mounds looked like miniature pyramids.

"Almost like being in Egypt," I remarked to Charlie, as we sat one day eating our lunch in the cab of the truck. "Those piles of boxes could be the tombs of the pharaohs."

Charlie paused from chewing long enough to gaze out across the bog to the opposite shore, at the stacks of wooden boxes lined against the trees. "Don't much look like desert, though," he said, and bit into his sandwich. Charlie was one of those swamp Yankees Uncle Dom referred to: laconic, always to the point.

Uncle Dom could be blunt, too. That pay day after work he drove Peter Andrade to the A&P for grocery shopping. I went with them. As Peter pushed the shopping cart up and down the aisles, decked out in his baseball cap, faded red shirt, baggy pants, and size fourteen shoes, little children ran after him, as if expecting to be handed a balloon.

Oblivious to the stir he was creating Peter filled the cart with rice and beans.

"They've got pork chops on sale," Uncle Dom suggested.

Peter shook his head. "Saving my money."

"What for?" I asked.

"A stone."

"A stone?" I had visions of rubies and emeralds. Or maybe the Hope diamond. "What kind of stone?"

"A stone for my grave," Peter said. He dropped a box of salt into the cart, then headed for the checkout counter.

"Expecting to die soon?" Uncle Dom asked.

Peter waited until we got back to the shack before answering. "I'm sick. In here," he said, touching his chest.

"Have you seen a doctor, Peter?"

"Don't need no doctor. My time is up. I can't change that."

"A doctor might help."

Peter shook his head. "My father died from heart, and his father, too." He went outside to fetch water, which I helped carry in. "Besides, I'm getting tired," he said, as he built a fire in the stove and filled two pans, one for beans, one for rice. "I was born on the island of Pogo seventy-three years ago and came to this country when I was two years old. I had to quit school when I was twelve to go work on the bogs. I been working on the bogs ever since." He sat on a wooden chair and waited for the water to boil. "I was married once, a long time ago. My wife left me. No children." He remembered the baseball cap and removed it from his head. He twirled it absently on the fingers of his right hand as he talked. "No reason to go on."

Uncle Dom murmured some platitude and we left. As we drove off through the gathering twilight I glanced back. I could see Peter through the shack's lone window, still sitting, twirling the cap—thinking, I suppose of the past. Or of what was to come.

"Your grandmother will be wondering what's keeping us," Uncle Dom said, to break the silence.

"Why do you suppose he's saving up for a gravestone?" I asked.

"Peter?" Uncle Dom shrugged. "A lot of reasons, I guess. Mainly so he won't be completely forgotten."

"Like the pharaohs in Egypt?"

Uncle Dom laughed. "Yeah. Like the pharaohs in Egypt. Only on a smaller scale."

Harvest that year began on Labor Day weekend. The C. R. Barton Cranberry Company owned three picking machines, each capable of harvesting a hundred barrels of cranberries a day, but Uncle Dom still employed scoopers to pick certain parts of the bog by hand. These were places too rough for machines, or where the vines were too thick. To keep the scoopers from moving on to other companies Uncle Dom let them pick some of the better sections where (since they were paid piece rate) they could earn good money—fifty cents for every bushel of cranberries they picked. My grandmother was tally keeper. It was her job to keep track of how many boxes each scooper filled.

"What number do you want?" she asked Peter, when it was his turn to choose.

"Thirteen," Peter said. "That's always been a lucky number for me."

Grandmother smiled. "Just make sure you holler it out loud and clear every time you fill a box."

Bright morning sun, aided by a soft September breeze, had already whisked away the surface dew. But underneath the vines were still too wet. Using an upturned bushel box for a seat Peter waited on shore with the others, his scoop resting across his knees like a folded accordion. He had replaced the red shirt with a blue one, equally faded, and sewn cotton-stuffed knee pads onto his baggy pants. He looked like a counterpart to Harlequin, resting between acts.

Finally, about nine o'clock, Uncle Dom walked down the oak plank that bridged the shore ditch. Stooping, he raked his fingers through the vines, then straightened and said: "Dry enough. Let's get going." The scoopers—men, women, and even some children—lined up along the edge of the ditch and kneeling, began to pick, combing the vines with the wooden teeth of their scoops. As soon as the scoop filled they removed any loose vines and poured the berries into a bushel box.

Bill Monteiro was the first to fill a box. "Number Five," he shouted out proudly.

"Number Five," Grandmother repeated, and duly ticked off a block on her chart next to Bill's name.

The scoopers, spread out in a row, picked swaths toward the center of the bog. My job was to keep them supplied with empty boxes. Charlie and another man used a jalopy converted from a Model A Ford to carry the full boxes onto shore, where they loaded them onto the truck. When the truck was full they carted the berries to Ocean Spray, to be sold as fresh fruit or made into cranberry sauce.

We stopped at noon to rest and eat lunch. Breaking into small groups, the crew sought out shade under trees along the edge of the swamp. I sat with Peter and Bill.

"Me and Peter are keeping you hopping, huh?" Bill said, referring to the number of empties they required. Bill was proud of the fact that he had picked the most berries so far. Peter was a close second.

"These younger folk don't know how to scoop," Peter said. "They try to fight the vines. They work twice as hard as they have to. The secret is in how you slide the teeth so that the vines don't tangle."

"Why don't you give the boy here a break," Bill said. "If you filled up those size fourteen shoes of yours with berries he wouldn't have to carry out so many boxes."

Peter took the teasing with good grace. "You could use that mouth of yours instead of a scoop, and pick twice as many berries."

"I got an idea," Bill countered. "You could use one of those clodhoppers as a grave marker, and spend that money you been saving on something reasonable, like whiskey."

Lunch lasted a half hour. At twelve-thirty we returned to work, not quitting until six that evening.

Tuesday after Labor Day was the first day of school. I wasn't able to return to work until the following Saturday. But on Friday Peter died. He hadn't shown up for work in the morning. Concerned, Uncle Dom drove to the shack and found him in bed. He had died sometime during the night.

"His heart, just as he said it would be," Uncle Dom said, on Saturday morning as we sat waiting for the vines to dry. "I guess he won't get that tombstone after all. The little he saved will barely cover the cost of burial."

"He should've gone on a good toot with that money," Bill mused. "Or bought himself a new pair of shoes. At least he could have gone out in style."

"Each man is different," Uncle Dom said. "Peter—rightly or wrongly—felt that his life hadn't amounted to much. He wanted it to at least end well."

"He was good at what he did, when he didn't drink," I said. "That should count for something." So at nine-thirty when the vines were dry and I had scattered enough wheelbarrow loads of empties to keep the scoopers supplied for a while, I grabbed a scoop and filled a bushel box.

"Number Thirteen," I called out.

"Number Thirteen," Grandmother repeated, then caught herself. "Number Thirteen?"

"Number Thirteen," I said. "Toward that stone he wanted."

Most of the scoopers paused to stare at me. Then the idea seemed to sink in. Bill, filling a box, shouted: "Number Thirteen!"

"Number Thirteen," someone else echoed. And even people who had not known him well filled a box for Peter, so that by the end of the day there were enough check marks next to his name to pay for a modest stone to mark his grave.

Edward Lodi, like the narrator in his story, grew up on Cape Cod in the 1950s and began working summers on the cranberry bogs the year he turned thirteen. "The men and women who worked on the bogs led hard lives. To honor them, and to recapture a piece of lost Americana, I've been writing a series of stories based on those early experiences." Employed in social work in East Freetown, Maryland, he writes fiction, is an avid reader of mysteries and a regular reviewer for *The Armchair Detective*. He would like to collect his "cranberry bog" stories and publish them in book form.

RON MACLEAN

BETHESDA

My wife and I are separated. Recently. Her choice.

These things happen, I tell myself. I read a story about a guy waiting to meet his girlfriend, in the park, after work. It was summer. She was a few minutes late, so he sat down on a bench to read a newspaper. He went up in flames. *Poof.* Spontaneous human combustion. Not a trace of him left. I feel bad for the guy, but the thing I wonder about is what if his girlfriend had been on time?

———

Last week I tried to call Beth. My wife. I was lonely. I figured, it's my birthday, she'll have to talk to me. But she was right. It was a sleazy thing to do. We had a deal. I wouldn't contact her. I'd give her the room to reach some kind of decision. She's more principled than I give her credit for.

———

Blair drained the last ice from her glass and chewed.

"Kevin Reilly," I said.

A smile leaked out from her face. "Banking. House in Randolph. Just had their second kid."

"He was going to move to Vermont and be a carpenter."

She chewed ice. The Friday night crowd was trickling in. Financial services professionals loosening their paisley ties, marketing types for high-tech firms rolling up their sleeves and resting their forearms on the varnished oak bar. The men always arrive first. Most of the bar stools were still free. The room's four couches were occupied, one by Blair and me. Across from us a woman in a tight black mini-skirt stood talking to a muscle-bound blond who was far too earnest to be sincere. She kept tugging her mini-skirt down in back. He spoke so close to her ear that I feared he'd fall in and lose himself in her semicircular canals.

"Here's a good one," Blair said. "Carl Glass."

I nodded. "Absolutely no sense of humor. He drives a Cadillac, belongs to the Country Club, cheats terribly at golf, and hangs out every morning at the deli, arguing politics. He's gotten really fat."

"How do *you* know?"

"He offered me a job."

Blair looked at me suspiciously. "And?"

"In-house design. I suppose it was a nice gesture. I just felt like his charity of the month. I saw the rest of my life stretched out before me, secure and empty. I'd probably end up having a hobby. Popsicle stick art." I shuddered. "Oregami."

The wood floor throbbed gently to the beat of dance music, versions of rap and hip-hop anesthetized for the suburbs. Blair glanced toward the entrance.

"Looking for someone?"

"Patient of mine at the clinic might stop by."

"A friend?"

"Yeah."

"A friend friend?"

"I like him, David. It's not romantic."

Blair motioned to the waitress for another round of drinks. "So what are you going to do with yourself?"

I scowled. I've grown to hate that question. "I don't know that I want to go back to advertising. Maybe I'll go out to Vermont and become a carpenter. I think Kevin upset the balance of nature by not doing it."

"You have absolutely no mechanical ability."

"Thanks a lot." The arrival of a young man in a wheelchair saved me from further humiliation.

"Hi, Blair."

"Hi." She turned to make introductions. "Tony, this is David Mattox. David, Tony de la Pena."

We shook hands. Tony had the largest forearms I'd ever seen. He looked like Popeye after a spinach fix.

"David's an old friend." Blair stirred her drink. "From college."

"You two talking about old times?"

I shook my head. "About getting fat."

Tony looked puzzled. Blair gave me a stern look that said I was becoming obnoxious.

I patted my stomach. "I need to start running again."

Tony smiled. "Come with me sometime. I could use a partner."

I stared at him and then at Blair, waiting for one of them to laugh at what I assumed must be a joke. Finally, Blair bailed me out. "Tony's training for a wheelchair race. He's trying to qualify for a marathon."

I smiled and said the polite thing, that maybe I'd join him sometime. A group of men entered the room, talking and laughing loudly, prepared to begin the hunt for companionship. Tony gave me his phone number. He said I had an open invitation. At the time, I wasn't considering it all that seriously. I have a tight schedule.

———

I watch Donohue. I watch Oprah. I watch Sally. I've listened to one-legged dwarfs talk about their problems. I've seen an Episcopal priest who's using up his 27th wife berated on national television. I've watched every movie Bing Crosby and Danny Kaye ever made, alone or together. I have watched (and enjoyed) Jerry Lewis movies. I have slept for entire 24-hour periods. I have read articles on how to feel better about myself in magazines that, under normal circumstances, I would feel embarrassed to buy. I have wondered if I will ever again find what I consider to be normal circumstances in my life. I have purchased vitamins that were supposed to energize me, creams and salves that were supposed to soothe me, music recorded to relax me, machines designed to titillate me. I have even, in my more dire moments, considered looking for a job. But I cannot keep myself from despair at the thought of Beth.

I torment myself by imagining her on dates. I have begun to realize that, on some level, I must enjoy this kind of pain. I picture her situation in extremes. One night she dates the power forward for the San José Jammers of the Continental Basketball Association; the next night, a beret-clad Persian cab driver who recites revolutionary poetry, collects automatic weapons, and repeatedly tells her to look for him on the evening news. In my worst moments, I begin to believe that she will become accustomed enough to life without me that she may actually begin to enjoy the company of businessmen. But this is as bad as it gets: the low point in my cycle. When this happens, I buy furniture. Awful furniture, that I neither like nor can afford. Last time I bought a horrible white naugahyde chair with arms shaped like wings. And a matching ottoman. I don't know why I do it. Maybe because I like to force salesmen into a postion where they have to gush about this stuff. I suppose I find it perversely satisfying.

———

I am 31 years old. I am living in my parents' old house, left to me last year when they moved to Florida. Antsy and uncomfortable, I take refuge in a corner room that used to belong to my older sister. The house depresses me. It seems dirty and sad. The floors are not swept. The paint on the walls is faded. I keep contact with the neighbors to a minimum. I've enforced a distance: my intensity and lack of activity scare them. They think, I imagine, that I am going crazy. I am encouraging this perception since it gives me the solitude I desire. In my room at night, I shout and punch at a small stuffed dragon. I realize this has to stop.

———

"God, I feel stupid," I managed to say between desperate gasps for breath.

"Because you're being outrun by a guy in a wheelchair?"

Tony pulled himself along with amazing dexterity, his arms working a diligent rhythm, his upper body moving forward and back in the chair with mechanistic precision.

"Not exactly." An attempt at a laugh came out more like a grunt. I was panting, concentrating on a thus-far failed attempt to convince my arms and legs to work in unison. "Ashamed." The words burst out with my exhale. "Way out of shape."

Early morning sky showed streaks of magenta and orange and there was a coolness to the air that signalled fall. Leaves on the trees were just beginning to turn in the yards of the half-million-dollar homes that lined the street. I wondered what these people did for a living.

My third morning running with Tony. I had indulged my curiosity and called him, and found that it felt good to run. I was still at the point of pain. Tony would park his van and we would do a three-mile circle, then he would leave me to walk off my pain and humiliation while he did another seven miles. Ten miles twice a day. Training. Tony was flying out to Tempe in two weeks to compete in a 25k race. His goal was to qualify for the Boston Marathon the following spring.

"How long"—inhale—"you been doing this?"

Tony's arms worked in long smooth strokes on the flat terrain, shorter quicker movements on hills. "Couple of years."

I was straining to match his pace. "You've got incredible arm strength."

"Yeah, but the legs aren't much." He smiled.

"What happened?"

"Accident. I was a kid."

We moved silently through the morning. Tony's chair made a steady rhythm. *Shoop. Shoop. Shoop.* The sound made me want to keep running forever. It was peaceful. Consistent. Predictable.

"Blair tells me you're a painter."

"Used to be."

"What happened?"

"Couldn't make a living. Just wasn't there."

Shoop. Shoop.

"Must be hard letting go."

"Can we talk about something else?"

Shoop. Shoop. Tony propelled himself forward with a rhythm that increased as we climbed a small hill. I felt a tightness in the back of my legs and a hard, empty feeling in my gut.

"How well do you know Blair?" he asked.

I could see Tony's van, about a quarter mile down the road. The light at the end of my tunnel. "We were close in college."

"Think she'll ever make time for a relationship?"

"Whew. Who knows?" I stared down at my feet, which seemed to have developed a grudging rhythm. "She knows you're interested?"

"Don't think so." We pushed on, listening to the sounds of our effort, me looking toward the finish line, Tony gearing up for the middle stretch of his run.

———

What would I say to Beth? I've asked myself that question a lot. Something clever. Something worthy of greatness. Something that would appear on those cocktail napkins that feature inspiring or amusing quotes.

I have schemed. I have plotted. I have not ruled out the devious, or the insane. I have considered sending her a cockateel trained to stay awake all night whispering my name to her while she slept. But I lack the self-discipline such a plan would require and, besides, I hate birds. The problem is that I respect Beth's desire to have space. I'm just afraid that the more familiar distance becomes, the more comfortable she'll grow with it. It takes a lot of energy to overcome the familiar.

———

Tony lay on his back, clad in a red t-shirt and running shorts, and drank from a quart bottle of spring water.

"What do you need to qualify for Boston?"

He wiped a forearm across his face. "One-forty or better." He handed me the bottle. Leaves hissed as a breeze stole through a willow tree behind us. We sat by a small round pond, a place that in the summer was a private swimming club for children from Weston.

"You're pretty close. What, two minutes off?"

He shook his head. "Training times should be faster than what I expect for the race. I'm gonna have to push this last week. I should work alone."

"Can't I help?"

He shook his head. "Don't worry about it."

"I could ride alongside on my bike and give you times at checkpoints."

"You don't need to spend your day doing that."

"My schedule's not exactly full."

Tony laughed. "Okay."

The water was as calm and reassuring as a lullaby. A small dock ran partway out and the pond was encircled like an amphitheatre with birch and willow trees. It was a hard place to find unless you knew what you were looking for. Tony knew a back way in. I felt his eyes on me. "What are you hiding from?"

I plucked a clump of grass and let the wind blow it out of my hand. "What does that mean?"

"Painting. Beth. I can't understand why you give up."

"Beth says she needs time. She doesn't even want to talk to me. Says she'll call me when she's ready. I feel helpless."

"Why don't you go after her?"

"She asked for time. I'm trying to respect that. But I'm afraid she'll start to think I'm not that interested. I don't want to let her forget that I want her back."

Tony shook his head. "You gotta do something. You'll drive yourself crazy."

I thought I saw a fish dart in the water.

"Blair and I went out to dinner the other night."

"Yeah?" I rolled onto my side and propped myself on one elbow. "And?"

"Awkward." Tony laughed. "Always is at first." He sipped from the bottle. "There's a look in women's eyes on dates, like they're not sure if they're supposed to feel sorry for me, or they're afraid I'll put a move on them and they spend the whole night wondering what it would be like making love to a cripple."

The pond was quiet except for the chirping of an occasional sparrow and the soft rustle of the breeze.

"Gonna see her again?"

"Hope so."

I found myself staring at Tony's legs. They were the legs of an elderly, sickly man. They weren't Tony's legs. They didn't fit him. Somehow he'd gotten stuck with the wrong pair. I tossed a rock into the water and watched the ripples fan out and fade.

"I love this place." Tony pushed himself into a sitting position and took a deep, hungry breath, as if he were trying to inhale all the spot's beauty. "There's a story about a pool in the Bible. Bethesda. Every now and then an angel would come down and move the waters and a person could get in and be healed."

"You believe in that stuff?"

"Depends. I'm not counting on anything, but miracles happen."

I grabbed a handful of stones and threw them at the pond. "It's moving. Get in, quick."

Tony laughed and shook his head. "Doesn't work that way."

———

Think about it. Two children are playing in their front yard. The little girl kicks a ball, which goes past the little boy. The boy runs after the errant kick, runs into the street, in front of a car, say it's a man on his way to the store for milk, or cigarettes. The driver has no time to react, no time to stop or swerve or even think. Say the little boy is paralyzed—a spinal injury. If the boy had stopped the ball, if his sister's kick had been more accurate, if the driver of the car had chosen a different route to the store or a different store to go to, none of this would have happened. But it did. Simply because at a certain moment in time, a man was driving on a certain street when a little girl kicked a ball past a little boy and the little boy ran out into the street to get it.

What gets me is the arbitrariness of it all.

———

"They should trade McHale," Tony said, pounding a nail into a plywood board. "They need younger blood up-front."

Blair set down an electric sander. She wore plastic goggles over her eyes and a turtleneck sweater with the sleeves pushed up. "No way. You don't trade a hall-of-famer."

I piled wood up next to Tony and surveyed our progress. We had framed the beginnings of a wheelchair ramp that would eventually go beside the porch. "Trade him."

"You're both morons." A cool breeze stirred sawdust into the air.

"Don't take it personally," I told Tony in a voice of mock consolation. "When it comes to the Celtics, she can't control herself."

"Blow up," she said.

Tony shot her a dopey grin. "And she looks so cute in safety goggles."

"Blow up, both of you." Blair lowered her goggles and reached for the sander.

"Hey," Tony said. "I've got tickets for Friday's game. You want to go?"

The question hung for a moment in the air. I wasn't thinking. I love the Celtics.

"Sure," I said.

Tony rested the hammer in his lap and smiled at me. "Not you."

Blair's cheeks were red. "You guys go."

"I didn't ask him. I asked you."

We were all silent. Leaves fell around us like confetti at a parade. Blair turned her back on us. Tony's face flushed.

"What do you think, David? Maybe she wants me to take her dancing instead."

"Don't be crude," she snapped.

"Don't patronize me. You got a problem, let's talk about it."

I felt like I was intruding on something. "You want me to leave?"

"No," Blair said, setting down her tools. "I'm going. I can't do this right now."

The good news was I got to go to the game.

———

I let the phone ring twice before I hung up. I was up late. Real late. Too late even to be calling California. I hung up because I felt like a fool. What would I do? Beg her to come back? Several times I started to dial the number, but each time I hung up. I didn't know what to say. Somehow it doesn't seem right that what's best for one person would be destroying another. I sat on the window sill and listened to the night.

———

The fifth tee at the country club was an elevated section that looked out into a small valley, across a brook and up to a green four hundred yards away.

"Almost romantic, isn't it?" A host of stars littered the night sky. My neck had begun to hurt from looking up.

"I don't know that I'd call it that." Blair sipped from a bottle of red wine, her eyes earthbound.

I sat down next to her and leaned back with my elbows on the soft grass. "Tell me your troubles."

Blair chuckled and tossed a golf ball in the air. "You're not exactly subtle." She began to juggle two balls. Intense concentration in her eyes. "I don't know what to do about Tony."

"Uh-oh."

"He really likes me, doesn't he?"

I nodded. The stars seemed too bright to be real.

"I've always resented people who say they wouldn't go out with a handicapped guy. I've been pretty self-righteous about it." She lowered her hands and let the golf balls fall to the ground. "When I'm away from him, I can convince myself it doesn't bother me. When I'm with him, I freeze up. I hate myself for it."

A wave of sadness rolled over me and left me cold. I wanted to say something that would solve everything. The stars began to seem harsh in their brightness.

Blair sipped from the bottle and shivered. She pulled a sweater around her shoulders. I grabbed her thumbs and squeezed, pressing hard on the nails. I wanted to hurt her. She tried to pull away, her eyes probing me distrustfully, the way you'd look at a dog you suspected was turning rabid. I let go and leaned my head against hers. The smell of wet grass reminded me of childhood. "Sorry. I have a desperate need to see a romance work out right now."

"We do the best we can, you know?"

A loud hissing behind us startled us both. A sprinkler had kicked into action, showering us with a fine, cold mist.

Blair grabbed the wine and we ran toward the car.

———

The morning that Tony returned from Tempe, it was raining; the kind of driving rainstorm where the drops bounce up off the pavement, where you think it can't possibly rain this hard all day, but it does. It was the first morning in a week that I hadn't run. Four miles a day was easy now.

I was painting the front hallway, Navajo White, when I heard his voice out front. I climbed down from the step ladder, placed the brush on its shelf and went out to the porch.

"Hurry up, man, it's pouring."

Tony wore an army jacket and a rainbow-colored umbrella hat. I couldn't help laughing. "You look ridiculous."

"Just get down here and help me."

We got him out of the chair and sitting down on the wet steps, and I got behind him and pulled him up. Eventually we managed to get inside, soaking wet.

"We've got to finish that ramp." I wiped rain from my eyes. "So?"

Tony smiled slyly. "I did it."

"Yes!" I hugged him and went to get a bottle of champagne I'd been saving for when Beth and I got back together. We toasted his success and Tony told me about the race, how training on the hills had given him the strength he needed to have a strong kick left at the finish.

"How you been?"

I shrugged. "Same."

He grabbed me by the shoulders and shook me. "Do something, man. Anything. Write her a letter."

"And tell her what?"

"Tell her you miss her. Tell her you're hurting. The truth."

Tony looked around the dimly lit, half-painted room. "I like it. It's brighter in here."

———

This is not a joke. It is a moral dilemma, a philosophical question about our level of awareness as human beings, a quest to understand: why are we so often blindsided by things we should have seen coming? Why are we so unable to change our self-destructive ways?

The reality of a person and his notion of himself grow apart. Inertia sets in. You watch the gulf grow between the person you think you are and the person you see yourself becoming, convinced that at any moment you could step in and correct it. Somehow this external person, the one that gets frustrated and angry, the one that works the job and pays the bills but isn't the real you, has taken over and the real you, the inside, the part that still loves, is vapor—it can't break through. Even though somewhere underneath it is the you and the her that still love each other, you can't seem to clear aside all that shit in order to get to it. That's what I want to do. Clear aside all that shit and find Beth again.

On a clear, cool Friday afternoon, a day where the air carried the scent of things dying, I mailed a letter to Beth. The heavens didn't open up. Hosts of cherubim did not begin to sing. Adoring throngs did not line the streets to applaud. But I felt better.

———

Four miles a day with Tony. I could match his pace over that distance and sometimes even push him a little. We were comfortable with one another, felt useful to each other. One weekend we finished the ramp at the house. And we went to the pond as often as we could, knowing that the weather would soon turn and our days there were numbered.

"Blair's avoiding me." Tony and I sat side by side at the water's edge, tossing pebbles at our reflections.

"I'm sorry."

He swatted a fly away from his face. "I'm persistent. It's not like this has never happened before. I know how to accept it. I recognize it in a woman. But with Blair somehow it's different. If she could just let herself get past the guilt and admit that she feels awkward dating me, I think we could laugh about it and get past it. It can happen."

I knew what he meant. I felt new strength in my legs, my lungs, my whole body. Smiling, I tossed a pebble into the pond. "I have this completely irrational feeling that everything's going to work out."

We sat there all morning enjoying the quiet, waiting for the angel to come and stir the waters.

Ron MacLean is completing a doctorate in English in Albany, New York, and is editor of *The Little Magazine,* a national literary magazine published there. He has worked in journalism and advertising, has recently completed a short story collection called *Who We Are,* and is at work on a novel.

" 'Bethesda,' " he says, "grew out of the convergence of two attitudes: the quietly hopeful image of the pool at Bethesda, and the cynical, sarcastic humor of a narrator who is afraid to hope and who, in fact, glories in his cynicism. The tension between those two experiences drove this story."

PHIL MCBURNEY

DAYS OF
DARKNESS

*N*ot the atrocities, though God knows they were bad enough—Japanese soldiers bayonetting wounded men in their hospital beds and raping nurses on the operating tables. Instead, what I choose to carry with me over the decades is the memory of a father and his son.

The politicians knew and they still sent us. What were two divisions of good guys going to do against four times that many, or whatever the odds were? The whole thing was more or less a cakewalk for the yellow hoard—screaming "Bonzai!" as they swept down from Gin Drinkers Line in their little rubber shoes, fresh from killing babies in China. Where was the God of the good guys?

After covering up another dead boy with a sheet, I asked Chaplain Webster that question. He just shrugged and said that countries had been doing this kind of thing forever. When civilizations abandon God, which they always did, he said, no end of foulness rises to the top. His job, he said, was to bring love to the pain. "You want to see God?" he said. "God is love."

We all ended up at North Point Camp, eating rancid rice boiled up in old gasoline barrels. Once you came down with something in that foul hole, nine times out of ten it was dugs up. The Japanese put us in barracks they used for horse stables during the offensive. By the time they'd won the battle, committed all their war crimes, and marched us back to North Point from wherever they found us, we just collapsed and fell asleep right in the horse turds amongst the rats and the roaches. Who wouldn't come down with something?

Beri-beri in this case. After a couple of months, this boy showed up on sick parade one fine morning after his Grenadier buddies—and his father, I learned later—were trundled off to fix the holes in the runway at Kai Tak, holes the Japanese needn't have bothered to blow there anyway, given the pitiful state of Hong Kong's air force. Hong Kong's defenses period were a joke. Their great hope was this gun we kept hearing about all the way over in the boat, this super-cannon that would blast the Imperial Army back into mainland China. The only problem was, it turned out, it was bolted down to face the ocean and they attacked from the Kowloon, so it proved about as useful as brass testicles on a female monkey. Not to mention the transport vehicles, which never arrived, and the mortars, which had no rounds.

So this young John Ellis showed up at the infirmary, fresh from the farm so to speak, boots in hand, like some two-legged elephant, his feet swollen to the size of loaves of bread. I knew a man marked for death when I saw one. I didn't need a crystal ball either—we didn't have adequate supplies of drugs or medicines and barely enough clean water or decent food. We're talking about men re-using tea leaves until all flavor and color were gone, then sprinkling them on their meager plates of rice and fish spines.

I only ever saw one miracle, if you want to call it that, though I doubt that God had much to do with it. A fellow came down with cholera, and we had to make a choice as to who gets the medicine and who gets "let go," so to speak. So I gave this guy pure water, boiled, that's it, and told him it was medicine. Well, if he doesn't rise off his sick bed in three days, like Christ himself.

But this young John was going to rise nowhere, though on the first day I saw him, he looked like a perfectly healthy specimen from the knees up. When I told him he was confined to the infirmary, he shouted, "The hell I am," and struggled to get his boots on. He must've known what it meant. But there was no way on God's green earth he could ever get those boots on. Snowshoes maybe. His father, Archie Ellis, and some friends came to visit at the end of the day.

It took a week for the beri-beri symptoms to show up on the rest of his body, bloating him up so much you could hardly recognize him. Doc told Archie they would try and get him to Bowen Road—that's a hospital—but that line of thinking was strictly wishful. This John, like I said, had the shadow of death cast over his bones from the moment I laid my peepers on him. To his credit—whatever that's worth fifty years later—he lasted several weeks.

The evening John died, his father and friends came to the infirmary at the end of the work day. John was bloated up like a cow's carcass left in the hot sun, his face shrunk to a tiny facet of his huge head, his scrotum the size of a soccer ball. Ask someone who's seen it first-hand; they'll tell you that's what happens with beri-beri. You can poke your finger into the flesh and the indentation remains for hours.

He hadn't urinated in four days, a week. His lungs rattled like crumpling paper bags. The way I saw it, he was two men: one a fat sack of putrifying flesh, the other, the real man, wanting to rise out of him like a spirit. He lay there, sleeping mostly, the five of them huddled around the bed as if expecting something monumental to happen. After an hour or so, John opened his eyes and said, as casually as if he'd been chatting all night, "I think I can pee now, boys. Can you turn me?"

"Atta boy," someone said. They clapped, and a few cheers and whistles lightened things for the moment. Think about it: grown men cheering at such a thing. It took all five of them, plus me, to roll John's soggy carcass. He was able to trickle some urine into a tin can beside the bed. When he was done, we rolled him back and Archie wiped the sweat from his face. The exertion of voiding his bladder had exhausted him and he could only smile briefly as he closed his eyes. The boys stole glances at one another in silence until Archie spoke softly, "You guys go on back to the hut. I'll send word if anything happens." They filed out uneasily, leaving Archie alone on the bed to cradle John's pumpkin-sized head in his lap and hold his swollen hand.

Chaplain Webster—Jim is what he insisted we call him—walked in then, his red face and shock of white hair almost luminous in the dingy light of the infirmary. He had a way of hugging the men—boys to him, since he was about forty-five himself—or a way of getting hugs out of us, whether we were "believers" or not; that was quite disarming. After he would talk with us one-on-one—those of us who sought him out or went beyond his cheery hellos. Like a huge gray-haired bear, he would engulf us, lifting shorter men almost off their feet. He did this so naturally that we grew used to it, accepted it; some of us even welcomed it.

Chaplain Webster said a prayer for John, then sat with Archie all night and talked, both men reminiscing the way we do about the dying and the dead. I'd seen men die, but this got my attention, being so much a reversal of the natural order of things. Sons bury their fathers in a sane world.

Late in the night, John came to and spoke through the phlegm that clotted his windpipe. "You've been a good father to me," he said, then a pause. "You see to Elizabeth. Tell her to get married again and get on with her life. That's what I want. We were just kids anyway." He was still a kid as far as I could see, a fine strapping young man saying good-bye to his father because of a politician's decision to put up a token defense of a defenseless colony. For the sake of the "empire." To appease the British. Stupid. Stupid and unforgivable. And we poor buggers who lived were sent off to Japan to do slave labor—pulling tapeworms out of our noses, dying in coal-mine collapses, or just wasting away. I read the stats later, though the government kept them secret for a good long time. Almost as many men died after combat as in it. And now I'm supposed to buy their Toyotas and like it. If life makes any sense, you give me a clue.

Toward midnight, John's breathing labored as the fluid began to choke him. It makes the heart give out in the end. But there's a lot of life in us that scrabbles and scratches and digs to hang on. First, he became delirious, talking all kinds of dreams and nonsense. Then he kicked and thrashed for several hours, clinging to that ember still in him. Finally, though, he calmed like a lake and toward the end we heard him speak.

"John?" Archie asked.

"I love you, Dad," he said. The words were steady, purified, stated as a matter-of-fact. That simple phrase still resonates in my head.

Finally John said, "It's over now. Don't let go." Had I been religous, I would have said his spirit lifted from the sack of soggy flesh and bones that confined it, was free of it, became something more or better, some fresh new life, in the blinking of an eye, so to speak. If it wasn't that way, it should have been.

Archie and the chaplain stirred at first light, stood up and tended to the corpse, trying without success to place the hands over the bloated chest. "I'll tend to him, Archie," Chaplain Webster said, and finally Archie just left, entered the morning light, which showed his face wet beneath the stubble of his beard. Would the bastards make him work the Kai Tak strip on the morning of his son's death? Of course they would.

I pulled a sheet over John's head when Archie left. Then we spent the day digging the grave for the burial of John Franklin Ellis—1920-1942.

That night at the funeral, Chaplain Webster read to us in a low voice from a tattered black Bible: "As thou knowest not what is the way of the spirit, nor how the bones do grow in the womb of her that is with child: even so thou knowest not the works of God who maketh all." We stared like boys agape at an auto accident. The flimsy coffin seemed too small to contain an adult human being. "But if a man live many years, and rejoice in them all; yet let him remember the days of darkness; for they shall be many."

Yes, the many days of darkness we were headed for: destined to be slaves in shipyards and factories and mines; sent home finally, if lucky enough to live, to spend our days mumbling into beer glasses in Legions and the smokey beverage rooms of cheap hotels.

As we began to spade the earth over the top of the coffin, a huge orange ball of a moon rose in the sky. The men came to Archie, one by one or in small groups, to sympathize with him. There were very few words, for what was there to say? Finally he stood alone, except for the chaplain. With the last few tender pats of the soil with our shovels, Archie's eyes were drawn to the moon and he appeared to study it for some minutes, surprised perhaps, as I was, by its beauty in these odd circumstances. Then Chaplain Webster walked to him and wrapped him in his bear-like arms.

As I too looked at the moon—an inexplicable ball spinning mindlessly around the earth, the earth a ball spinning mindlessly around the sun, held in orbit by God knew what forces—I wondered if there was any sense to things.

John Franklin Ellis' dying taught me a lesson, left a trace of hope, maybe a hint of God. It was that pure drop of love he left behind when he said, "I love you, Dad," as if his life had been distilled and love was the only thing of value left, the only hope for him or his father, or any of us.

I looked at the moon that night and imagined my parents standing in its light halfway round the planet, wondering if their son, hardly more than a boy himself, was alive or dead. My own father had wept at my leaving, the first time I had seen his tears. Chin quivering, ashamed of his emotion in true Anglo-Saxon fashion, he had grabbed me and pulled me into him roughly. My arms came up reluctantly, tentatively, around him. How I wished I had embraced him with all my fierce young strength.

Oh, these fragile connections of love and flesh, these human beings who embrace in the darkness, these gifts, these glints of light.

Phil McBurney teaches English in Winnipeg, Canada and has published fiction in the *Winnipeg Sun, Green's Magazine,* and *Dreams & Visions.* "Days of Darkness" is based on the experiences of a World War II veteran. "The story of what happened in Hong Kong to Canadian troops, their brutal treatment and starvation in Japanese prison camps, is not well known, even in Canada. My research into this bit of history has provided a rich source of story ideas."

He is currently developing a radio script for the Canadian Broadcasting Corporation and hopes to work more with scriptwriting and become involved in the theatrical community in Winnipeg.

ROBERT GALIK

TO WALK
IN GILEAD

7
May 2130 hrs

Lieutenant Tandee burst in on Herrington during surgery this morning, demanding he sew up Badolato, who had chased a stick into the barbed wire surrounding their compound.

Herrington, naturally, was outraged. More so, when Lieutenant Tandee drew his revolver and threatened to shoot the patient on the table if Herrington didn't immediately comply. The good doctor is still so livid he could hardly eat at dinner. If he could put his hands on a firearm, I have no doubt he would go after the lieutenant—a mistake Lieutenant Tandee would relish. I'm sure the lieutenant deliberately upsets my man at every opportunity. Why else would he go directly to Herrington this morning, without even checking with me? At the time, I was wading through the reams of paperwork required to keep this place running, and would have seized any excuse to do something else, even if it meant attending that wretched mongrel who eats until he vomits, when the rest of us barely survive on our self-imposed rations.

I might add that Herrington is not above intrigues of his own, petty though they may be. For the past month he has taunted Lieutenant Tandee each time they pass, nodding and saying, "Good day, Major-General Stanley." Then to whomever is near-by, he remarks, "Don't you agree that Major-General Stanley is the very model of a modern major-general?"

The dark glasses and blank expression he perpetually wears cannot hide Lieutenant Tandee's bewilderment. He understands well enough that this confusion with his name and rank is no mistake, yet he cannot imagine what it means. He has never heard of Gilbert and Sullivan, much less *The Pirates of Penzance*. The only music Lieutenant Tandee knows is rock music. That, and rap music. Oh, and I mustn't forget country-and-western. We're treated to some such musical entertainment all day long, since there seems to be a radio in every window of every build-ing Lieutenant Tandee has appropriated for his troops. The music continues at night as well, even when the lights in their mess are dimmed and they are watching movies. (Their preference is for American westerns.) We hear their radios as we lie on our beds in the dark, doing what we can to conserve electricity. At night the government station broadcasts the president's speech-of-the-day. It is replayed every hour, like a top-twenty hit, and frequently followed with a speech by the vice-president, exhorting those rebels still holding-out to surrender and turn in their weapons. Judging from the radio reports, which pronounce government victories following every skirmish, I don't understand how there can be any rebels left. Maybe this explains why there appears to be a different vice-president speaking every week.

Mercifully, at midnight the station goes off the air for six hours. Just before the national anthem is played, a news person reads the weather forecast for the next day. It is this minute of electricity that I most resent giving over to our occupying force, since the weather here is exactly the same, day-after-day, nine months of the year, fluctuating only between unbearably hot and sweltering.

Frequently at the forecast's conclusion, I hear Herrington's voice call out from the darkness of his room, "Wonderful! That means I can work on my tan again tomorrow."

Although he has never said anything, I know Herrington faults me for not hating Lieutenant Tandee as he does. Yet there he errs. For I hate the lieutenant even more.

Yes, here I am—too old and tired and dissillusioned to hate. And still I do. I hate Lieutenant Tandee for being better at his job than I am at mine. The consummate soldier, he can kill (indeed, *does* kill) and apparently without remorse, while I amputate an arm to save the man, then escape to my office to wait for the nausea to pass, like a first-year student. Lieutenant Tandee looks out at the starving thousands gathered around our encampment, people who wait there because they believe we will give them food, because we once had food to give. And rather than tossing them the core of an apple he is eating, and which is more than some of them are accustomed to consuming in a day, Lieutenant Tandee orders one of his men to drop it down the hole of an outhouse. "Why give it to someone starving," he reasons, "when doing so only prolongs their suffering?" I am certain that behind those dark glasses he is cursing me, the outsider who came here to do exactly that, to prolong their suffering, the intruder who arrived with promises and hope, but now has little enough of either.

Because of the time it took to quiet Herrington today, several reports require attention before I turn in. Following which, of course, there promises to be another full night of radio, courtesy of Lieutenant Tandee's men. Today is Friday—I think. It's hard to be sure, even with a calendar. Friday is Oldies Night, an oldie being a song that hasn't been aired for a week. What I dread most is Tuesdays, which is Rap Night. What little English the soldiers know they learned from music, largely rap music. So quite often they sing along, although with little comprehension of what they're saying—until they come to the swear words, which they all shout exuberantly. Vulgarity is clearly the international language.

PS. We're told to expect the supply trucks tomorrow for sure. Of course, like the weather forecast, that's something we've heard before.

PPS. Both Badolato and Herrington's other patient are recuperating nicely.

———

8 May 2145 hrs

The supplies did not come today.

One truck did arrive with emergency provisions which headquarters managed to purchase and beg. But what little it brought will barely see us through another few days. Births and deaths aside, the number of people who have taken up residence outside our camp has stabilized. They came here, some of them from hundreds of miles away. Now they suspect they will starve anyway. They seem to accept such a fate, even the children who spend their days watching our puppet shows. Mr. Rabbit is doing what he can to teach them their alphabet, and hygiene, and how to help a person choking on food. That last is not the irony it would seem, since chewing is the luxury of someone eating for enjoyment. Lately, however, an eerie quiet has overtaken even the puppet shows. The children are too hungry to laugh.

———

9 May 2115 hrs

The trucks did not come today.

Each time I manage to get through to headquarters they tell me the supplies will turn up. After all, they cleared customs weeks ago. I tell them, "Perhaps so. But they haven't arrived here yet."

Headquarters responds, "But they cleared customs weeks ago."

I don't understand what is happening. The radio has not reported any rebel activity between here and the border. So? Has the government stolen our supplies? Have the drivers sold them on the black market? "Yes, but they cleared customs," headquarters will tell me again tomorrow.

———

10 May 2200 hrs

The trucks did not come today.

Late in the afternoon, someone spotted a dot advancing on the horizon. Herrington drove out to investigate, and found an old man carrying a boy. The man didn't understand what a jeep is, or that Herrington wanted him to get inside and be driven the rest of the way. At first the boy seemed to be dead, although he turned out to be merely asleep in the man's arms. There are unfamiliar tribal scarrings on the man's face, which means he must have come a great distance. His dialect is equally strange and, except for a word here and there, no one can communicate with him. He allowed Herrington to give the boy nourishment, but accepted none for himself. Then he set up a campsite apart from everybody else, staking out a few animal skins to shield the boy from the sun.

Late in the day I drove food and water out to them. Once again the old man refused any for himself. Lieutenant Tandee, who had been informed of their arrival, was standing a short distance away at the time, having gone out to interrogate the man for sightings of rebel activity which might have been observed during the journey.

Irritated by my failure to communicate with the man, I snapped at the lieutenant, "Haven't you realized by now that there are no rebels? Quite possibly there never were. Rebels are an invention of your government to justify their continuance of martial law."

He shot back, "Do you mean to say, rebels are the same as your supply trucks, which also do not exist?"

It would be impossible to win any confrontation with Lieutenant Tandee, his impenetrable expression being an armor which deflects all challenges. I, therefore, returned my attentions to the old man, and pantomimed eating the food in my hands. The man laughed.

"Can you not see that he does not want your soup," Lieutenant Tandee called. "He does not even realize it is food you offer. It does not look or smell like any he has known. He assumes that it must be medicine, that you mistake him for a sick man. That is the only reason he is not insulted by your offer. He came here because he heard you have powerful magic, magic which can save his son."

"You understand his language?"

The lieutenant did not respond, and his expression remained typically blank. I pleaded, "For his own sake, explain to him that this is food. Tell him he needs to eat it."

"Food to him means game. That which he kills himself is food."

"Tell him that there is no game here. Game will come with the rains. Game follows the greening of the grasses, and that follows the rains. Until then, this is all we have. He needs to eat this if he is to survive."

Lieutenant Tandee's glasses gave back a darkly distorted reflection of the earth and sky. "You are ignorant of it. However, I recognize the markings on his face, so I will tell you. This man is a warrior. In years past he would have slit your neck and drunk your blood to survive. For anything less, he does not now need you. Go away. Leave him to die with a warrior's dignity. Stop pretending to be Jesus Christ feeding the mobs with a few fishes and loaves. You are not equal to the role."

Unaware that we were arguing about his very life, the old man squatted, looking out at the empty horizon.

———

11 May 2030 hrs

Everyone is surly with frustration. The unrelenting heat only makes it worse. My hand grows leaden, and each day it becomes more of an effort to force myself though that simple declaration, *the trucks did not come.*

This afternoon I drove out to check on the old man and the boy. The boy is recovering nicely, and was animated, almost playful. Once again the old man refused what food I tried to leave for him. He gestured to let me know that he intends to hunt for game. Unfortunately, he will find none. I give him another few days, a week at most.

———

12 May 0430 hrs

During the night a soldier tried to rape one of the women living outside of camp, first luring her into one of the empty warehouses with promises of food. However, the soldier was very drunk, so the woman was able to call out for help. Her cries brought more soldiers, including Lieutenant Tandee. The would-be rapist attempted escaping into the darkness, but was shot by the lieutenant and, at the very least, will walk with a limp for the rest of his life. To Herrington's thinking this is one more reason to despise Lieutenant Tandee. Consequently, he was furious to have the man standing behind us in the O/R.

"I heard he didn't call for the man to stop, didn't fire a warning. Just shot him—as calculated as that. There's not an ounce of humanity in him."

Herrington glanced around to observe Lieutenant Tandee, who was meant to overhear this. But the lieutenant's face remained typically indifferent, further enraging Herrington. "It's two-thirty in the morning, and there's precious little light in here as it is. Yet he still wears those damn dark glasses? Does the man have eyes at all? I've never seen them. Perhaps someone once told him that the eyes are a window to the soul, and he's afraid we'll discover he hasn't one—a soul, I mean."

Even as Herrington ranted on, however, I wondered (and not for the first time) if Lieutenant Tandee's presence isn't a mixed blessing. Officially the government's troops are making sure that food and medical supplies don't fall into rebel hands. Yet, since our own security measures are as lacking as everything else,

Lieutenant Tandee's troops are also safeguarding us from potential violence by the starving thousands, people who have nothing to lose. Even more to the point, by his presence Lieutenant Tandee is guaranteeing we survive his troops.

I have not tried to go back to sleep since the incident with the soldier. The bit of sky I can see from my desk is beginning to color, which means that soon it will be time to officially begin the day.

——

12 May 2345 hrs

"My god, the bloody earth is on bloody fire," exclaimed Herrington, glancing out the window. It was an unsettling way to conclude breakfast, although an accurate description of the sight which met our eyes. Backed by the rising sun, a triangular plume of dust climbed hundreds of feet into the air, catching the dawn, then refracting it into a huge, scarlet eruption. A bloody fire it seemed, indeed.

What it was—really—seen through the glasses, was a convoy of trucks and jeeps and vans, possibly a hundred or more. Increasingly, staffers took up the cry, "It's our supplies," making it into a chant. Yet obviously that was not the case, not unless we were about to receive five year's worth of food and medical aid. There were far too many vehicles, even allowing that some carried military personnel as a security measure.

"Then that leaves only one possiblity," offered Herrington dryly. "They're hopelessly lost. Everyone in that line is lost. That's the line Matthew referred to when he spoke about the blind leading the blind."

In fact, he was not far wrong. They were reporters. I learned so from Lieutenant Tandee, who was having his men clear the road into camp. "What's the matter," he asked, "is your head-quarters completely ignorant? Or do they simply fail to inform you? The president is coming today—*our* president. But don't look for him among this caravan of idiots. These are reporters, in addition to the handful of your people and of mine. The president is coming later, to greet the supply trucks and to head the distribution of food. You see, in the whole of the republic, this camp is the very last to receive food. Who could imagine it? That they would have overlooked this pisshole of a camp? Almost as unthinkable as that they now should remember it. These fools are coming because such a moment needs to be recorded for history. The headlines of the world will read, 'President Ends Hunger In His Country.' Our government will earn new respect."

"You knew about this last night, didn't you? You knew as you watched us operate to save the leg of your soldier, isn't that right? Why didn't you say something? Why didn't you spare us even these few hours of agonizing whether supplies would ever get here?"

"Doctor," he responded, "why would a man with no soul tell you anything?"

Within an hour, the convoy began arriving, and with it a small army of people: staff workers from headquarters, doctors, nurses, government ministers, security troops and laborers. Mostly, though, it brought us reporters. Reporters pressing for interviews. Reporters taking photographs and video footage. Reporters peering around buildings. Reporters pointing at the sky. At the ground. At the people. Reporters aiming transmitters at invisible satellites. Reporters using cigarettes to bribe soldiers because they assumed permission was necessary to move among the starving thousands—people who, in turn, were quietly observing all this madness.

Retreating from the onslaught of questions, I found Elliott from headquarters waiting in my office. "But where is the food?" I demanded, suspecting it had been left behind in all the confusion.

She nodded towards the dust-cloud still settling in the distance. "Behind us. We started out together, but then several trucks experienced mechanical problems. I rather guess those problems will be corrected about the time the president arrives. This whole day is being orchestrated, and the arrival of the trucks will add one more photo opportunity."

"So where is the president?"

"Flying in. That way he manages a few extra hours sleep. The poor fellow is still exhausted from leading the fight to reclaim your supplies."

"You mean the rebels actually broke their agreement? I don't believe it. Why would they do such a thing?"

"You shouldn't believe it. But that's the official explanation, and we're allowing it to stand unchallenged. It's better than informing the world that the trucks were being held in a government compound a half-mile from the presidential palace. Now don't start yelling—"

"Yelling? I'd be insane if I didn't yell. Elliott, what's going on?"

"I wanted you to hear the rumor from me first, because you can't possibly dodge these media-types for long. The president is hosting a dinner for you and your staff tonight, so even if you avoid the press all day, they're bound to corner you then. They've all heard the gossip. Now listen to me; you must tell them it isn't true. It can't be true. The president has always been behind our efforts. You must tell them that. No, don't say anything yet; just hear me out. It's done. You'll soon have your supplies. Who knows? Maybe it works out for the best this way. The world will see what happens here today, and be touched.

However, if you even suggest to these bloodhounds that the rumor may be fact, they're bound to let it overshadow the real story, which is that starving people are being fed."

"But Elliott, he's a monster. To manipulate suffering like that—?"

"People like him have always been the problem. As have economic systems. And prejudices. And indifference. Yes, and the idea that it's God's will for people to starve. Yet we've fought them all, and we'll continue to fight. The president got away with it this time. We can make it impossible for him to do it again. Oh, dear, can it be? Are you still the idealist you were when you showed up at our office twenty years ago, announcing that you were going to feed the world? I told you then and I remind you now: that's not how we do it. We feed one person at a time. One-by-one-by-one, that's how we're dealing with this problem."

"Fine. In public, I'm willing to say such wonderful things about the president that his wife won't recognize him. I have no problem with that. But there's no way I'll attend any dinner he's hosting. I'm not that much of a hypocrite. What's happening here is a publicity stunt, and it's going to lull people into thinking the problem is solved."

"It won't, because we won't allow it. Because we can't allow it. And you will attend the dinner, if only as a favor to me. Oh, don't you see? Part of any struggle—for some the hardest part—is letting go. Most of the time that means passing the battle standard along to somebody else. But you're one of the fortunate few. You get to set it down because you've won."

"Won? No. Or at most, temporarily," I snapped.

"But at least, temporarily," she insisted, smiling.

The sound of a helicopter passing overhead forced us to pause. "That must be the president," Elliott said. "I understand the old boy is furious. He'd intended for his staff to select a camp closer to the capital." She gave a short, ironic, laugh. "Let's go enjoy the show."

"You go on. I'll catch up after I help with the supplies."

"Today you'll do no such thing," Elliott insisted, wrapping her arm around mine. "I've brought laborers, and have already seen to the arrangements. This once you're going to relax and enjoy yourself. Period!"

We stepped outside. A quarter of a mile away, the presidential helicopter hovered above an area cleared of people. I assumed the thing would land any second, yet it remained airborne, giving us time to select a good location for viewing. This also gave the photographers plenty of time to focus their equipment. Lieutenant Tandee, meanwhile, assembled his troops close to the landing spot, and brought them to attention. Finally the helicopter began to descend, slowly and dramatically. The instant its legs touched ground, Lieutenant Tandee and his men delivered a crisp salute.

Suddenly, however, for a reason which none of us could fathom, the helicopter flew straight up again—shot up, as though it had been dynamited from its perch, higher and higher, spinning as it rose.

On the ground, all was chaos. Lieutenant Tandee drew his gun and scanned the area for signs of a rebel attack. His men, unable to hear his shouted commands, chased their berets, which had been sucked off by the updraft and which now ballooned through the air like dry leaves in a whirlwind. Badolato, too, joined the melee, racing onto the field, bandages trailing, snatching up berets and tripping as many soldiers as he could reach.

As abruptly as it rose, the helicopter began to sink again. Gradually it settled to the ground once more, this time several hundred yards from the former site. Lieutenant Tandee worked furiously to reassemble his troops and move them towards this newest location. Although he succeeded, their line was not so straight this time, nor their salute so sharply executed. The helicopter's door opened and the president's arm appeared, waving at the astonished crowd for several minutes, possibly testing the air for bullets.

At last he began to move out from the helicopter's shadowy interior. As he did so, a squad of his freshly arrived security guards rushed onto the field, separating Lieutenant Tandee's troops from the president's view. Passing Lieutenant Tandee, one of the president's generals deliberately knocked him aside. Even from a distance we could see that this general was hardly more than a boy, possibly all of sixteen, his uniform already heavy with metals and ribbons. "You stupid shit," he shouted at Lieutenant Tandee. "Don't you realize you're blocking the president from his photographers?" (Indeed, we surmised later that the helicopter's strange behavior was a last-second decision to move the landing site closer to the cameras.)

The unexpected blow had taken Lieutenant Tandee by surprise, nearly dropping him to his knees. But he rebounded immediately, his dark glasses shattering the reflected sunlight. And although the boy-general remained unaware, since he continued hurrying to greet the president, I witnessed what happened next. I saw Lieutenant Tandee grope for his revolver, watched several of his men drop their rifles to a ready position, prepared to follow his lead. In that moment, I believed Lieutenant Tandee meant to shoot his assailant—for that matter, that he was going to assassinate the president, too, for promoting such a fool.

But prudence (a trait I'd never suspected Lieutenant Tandee of possessing) stayed his hand. He regained his composure, regrouped and realigned his troops off to the side, out of the way of any cameras.

I'll omit here the details of the day, since Elliott has promised to assemble and send along copies of all the articles. They will be enough of a document of the occasion. I expect to see photographs of the president welcoming the supply trucks into camp, the president opening the doors of those trucks and helping to unload the provisions inside. There will most surely be photographs of the president handing over the first plate of food. In fact, merely by chance, the closest person to him at that moment was a man. But as the president was about to pass over the plate, one of his advisors yelled for him to stop, that the president should hand that all-important first portion to a woman or a child. I objected, saying that it makes no difference. Further, I pointed out that the man is crippled; he has only one foot. Yes, shot back the presidential assistant, but a missing foot will not show up in the photographs.

In the evening the president hosted a banquet to honor the staff of our camp. When called upon to speak, I lauded the president's efforts, using such florid language that I expected to see my audience laughing. But apparently only Elliott recognized the joke, and she squeezed my hand under the table when I sat again.

Actually, the dinner had one ironic twist. The supply truck carrying the food for it must have hit a bump, unlatching one of the two cages holding live chickens. The hens, which came from the presidential coops, all escaped somewhere between here and the capital. We have canned meat which might have taken its place, of course. But the president's personal chef, being accustomed to working with only the best ingredients, chose to make do with smaller portions from the poultry which remained. Thus, the president departed his festivities a hungry man.

"We're amazed at what you're doing here," many reporters commented. "We want to do an in-depth story. Would it be all right to return and spend a day? Then we can really get to know the problems you face." (A day? and they will know what we're up against?)

I had to shout my response, that they were most certainly welcome to come back, since they were all racing to claim a seat on the jeeps which would take them out of here. As the dust increases with every vehicle, it's advantageous to sit as close to the front of the convoy as possible.

I invited several staffers back to my room for some cognac, compliments of the president. When they left, I went outside to clear my head. As I walked, I realized that something was different about the night—although it took me awhile to recognize the change.

The silence had ended. The camp was perfectly still, yes, yet the night was not quiet. The government radio station had gone off the air, but the air held a hundred indistinct noises. Somewhere a man laughed, prodded on by another man's voice, as if the two were sharing a joke. People talked. A baby cried, to be silenced by the first notes of a mother's song. Lovers whispered the same vows which lovers have repeated for as long as there has been language, making the words fresh again.

I paused to look up at the sky, which was moonless, and brilliant with stars. The spectacle was dizzying. I began to feel infinitely peaceful, though infinitely sad, and I seemed to be melting, body and soul, into the sight, rising up into the night, floating away—

—until I became aware again of those sounds, those human noises, and gradually they settled me back onto the ground. My thoughts turned to the boy, and to the man on guard beside him. One of the flickers of light came not from a star, but from their campfire. Was the old man also looking up at this very sky? How strange—that men from different cultures and opposite sides of the world could be sharing such a moment. I wondered if the old man, unable to feed himself, considered himself a failure. I certainly felt myself to be one. For even with plenty of food now, I knew I still could not feed him.

———

14 May 1600 hrs

I was not there, so I did not witness it. But several soldiers did, and they are amused to recount the story as often as anyone will listen. That is why, with my eyes closed, this is how I picture it.

Lieutenant Tandee is driven out to where the old man and the boy are camped. "Old man," he calls out. "Now that you have had time to reflect, I wonder if you recall seeing armed rebels on your journey?"

"I already told you I saw no such men," responds the old man.

"You continue to look hungry. Have you caught enough game?"

"I have caught nothing, because there is nothing."

"You say that because you do not know where to hunt. I have frequently caught food by those distant trees there." The old man is skeptical, but the lieutenant insists, "Come, I'll show you."

Lieutenant Tandee and the man trek to the trees, while behind, the jeep and its soldiers follow. "Here I have come across game," Lieutenant Tandee remarks as they approach several scrawny thorn trees.

"There are no signs of animals here now," says the old man. "No droppings. No grass is crushed." He circles the area.

Lieutenant Tandee calls to him, "You doubted me. But look there."

The old man's mouth opens at the sight of so much game, this small flock of strange, fat birds pecking at the ground, black-and-white, their feathers gathered around their faces like a ceremonial headdress. Cautiously he approaches, and lofts his spear at the closest bird—which does not fly away, does not even seem to recognize the danger. Impaled, it dies instantly. Strangely, a disturbance which should have sent the rest of the flock soaring, disturbs them only a little. Or possibly they are too fat to take to the air, for none go far before standing transfixed, pretending to be invisible, watching the old man's approach. Some struggle a bit longer than others when pierced by the spear, but all eventually die. All six.

———

14 May 2230 hrs

"I must protest the noise coming from your men's barracks," I said to Lieutenant Tandee. "Ordinarily it's bad enough. Yet lately they do not even properly tune-in the government station. The static is so bad that a person would almost think there are chickens cackling behind the music."

"I will talk to my men," the lieutenant responded dryly.

I hesitated, awkward in my gratitude, then told him, "Rumor is, you helped the old man to find food. Thank you."

Lieutenant Tandee said nothing.

"I'm curious. Why did you do it?"

"Possibly because I could, where you could not. Or possibly because he reminds me of someone. Before you ask: of my father."

"Your father was a warrior?"

"My father was a fool."

"Whatever the reasons, you ought to feel very pleased. You helped feed the last hungry man in this pisshole of a camp."

"Does it matter? He is a child to be tricked so easily. So he does not starve today or tomorow. It does not mean he will not starve next week."

"Perhaps next week you'll show him where to find more food."

"Even supposing I do, what will happen the week after? Or the week after that?"

"By then, perhaps the rains will have come. And perhaps game will have followed, and be abundant. Perhaps the old man and the boy will be able to find their way back to their own land and people."

"And if the rains do not come?"

"They will."

"And if the game does not come with the rains?"

"It will."

"Supposing it does. What will happen when another dry season comes and there is no food for a long, long time?"

"I don't know, Lieutenant Tandee. But I'm sure you'll think of something by then."

It would round things off so nicely to be able to say that the lieutenant, behind those infernal glasses, smiled. But he did not, just kept watching me blankly, as if he supposed I'd gone as batty as Herrington. Oddly, it's also the way Herrington studies me when he's waiting for my response to one of his more bizarre pawn openings.

If it's true that adversaries eventually become like one another, I assume that before long I shall have trouble telling the two men apart.

———

My dear Elliott:

Thank you for the news clippings and video footage. I have not yet been able to sit through the latter, however, for I squirm uncomfortably each time my face comes on the screen. Initially, I didn't even recognize myself, and asked, "Who's that?" Herrington assures me it's an accurate likeness, but then he always did lack tact. I notice that on video the president looks quite tall, which is some satisfaction, since apparently the camera lens can distort anything.

Please know that I'm in a much better frame of mind than when you left here. I suppose I've been regarding my job as an uphill struggle for so long that it's difficult to let go of the idea. Moses, you recall, wandered forty years without entering the Promised Land. My dear Elliott, now I know how he would have felt if he had been permitted to walk in Gilead.

Our camp has been here for so so long now. Oh, not exactly here, on this exact spot. If you remember, it was a few thousand yards away, closer to the riverbed, where a bit of soil covers the bedrock. There we arranged our dozen tents spaciously, like dinnerplates around a Sunday table. We anticipated staying a few weeks, two months at most, long enough to assist the people here through to the rainy season.

But the rains failed to come. What came, instead, were more hungry people. And the following year the rains were not what was hoped for, not what was needed. By that time, word had spread for hundreds of miles about the doctors here, and so who could think of leaving?

The third year the rainy season did arrive and, like a bad guest, came early and behaved rudely. The river, which until then had existed largely in name only, overnight became a flowing reality, and as the days passed, not all the new-grown grasses, nor the flowers which suddenly covered the earth from horizon to horizon could draw in enough water to keep that rushing, angry serpent within its banks. Quickly it threatened to include our tents among the debris of uprooted plants and animal carcasses. We were compelled to move the entire camp in one rain-soaked afternoon.

This spot is where we replanted it—a hodgepodge of tents, more than three dozen of them by that time. Although we always intended to restore the place to better order, somehow the time could never be spared. What happened, instead, was that our small generator had to be replaced by a larger one, and one-after-another of our tents made way for more permanent structures, sometimes of wood, sometimes of mud and brick. Our footpaths, alternately of dry dust or wet sludge, multiplied, and became a maze. Quite without our realizing it, they evolved into streets, streets with names—names ironically given at first, but which in-turn sprouted signposts. And these somehow added respectablity to such byways as Doctor Street, School Street, Crapper Avenue, or Hungry Person Boulevard. So, quite to our astonishment, this camp became, first a town, then, a city. Those of us who were here when those initial weeks stretched into months used to joke and say, "Who knows, perhaps one day this place will even be on the map."

Now it seems we are.

Robert Galik resides in Middletown Springs, Vermont. He has been a reporter, customs inspector, and college English teacher. About the origin of "To Walk in Gilead" he says, "Years ago, when I lived in N.J., I was active in an organization called The Hunger Project, which is dedicated to ending world hunger. Recently, I was wondering how close to the goal we've come. (Probably not very.) And it occurred to me when that day does come that the last hungry person is fed, the world press will probably—at most—give it 15 minutes 'air' time." Currently he is writing a political thriller, *The Fantasy Man*.

JOSEPH SOLLISH

MIND'S EYE

*T*he last time Walter started out to take the bus into town the few blocks to the bus stop proved exhausting and his daughter-in-law Moira had to come get him in her car. She scolded him gently, saying, "All you have to do is ask, Dad, you know that. Ben and I will always be only too happy to drive you anywhere you want to go." That's what she said, but Walter knew he was as much a burden to them as he was to himself.

It was different when their children, his grandkids, Paulie and Billy, were younger and he would earn his keep by babysitting so Moira and Ben could go out in the evening. But that all ended one night when Paulie got sick and Walter became so stressed he couldn't find the telephone number where Moira and Ben were, and little Billy ran across the yard to a neighbor for help. Walter was humiliated when they began paying a teenage girl to sit with his grandchildren.

He was sure Ben and Moira were worried he was developing Alzheimer's, but there was nothing to be concerned about. Walter could still beat Ben at chess, on the rare occasion when his son had the patience to complete a game with him, and he could debate the current world situaton with the best of his peers at the Senior Center in town when he felt like it, which wasn't very often since he had to ask Moira to drive him there and pick him up when he wanted to leave. His mind was fine; it sometimes just took him a little longer to say what was on it, that's all. Anyway, he didn't have anything earth-shaking to tell the world, so what was the hurry?

"What's wrong, Dad?" Moira asked.

She had been watching him brush something away from his face several times as she stood in the doorway of his room, ready to go out. No, he had told her earlier, he didn't feel like going into town, he would read in the garden, out in the sunshine, after a while. His loneliness seemed to feed on itself, driving him more deeply into isolation.

"What is it?" she asked, that concerned expression always on her face when she looked at him.

"I don't know," he finally answered, batting a hand up towards the right side of his head again. "It's like something's flying around or I got something in my eye."

"Could I look?" she asked.

He turned his face up to her, opening both eyes wider.

"The right one," he said. "Could be a hair or a piece of dust, but I don't feel anything."

"Now hold still," she said, in the same tone she used with the children, peering into his eye. "Look up. Now look down. Side to side. Gosh, I don't see anything, Dad. Maybe you just rubbed it, irritated something."

He blinked his right eye rapidly, then shut it tightly, screwing up the entire right side of his face, then cautiously opened the eye.

"Still there," he said, rolling his eye. "Something black, but on the outside, floating around. Strange-looking."

"Does it hurt or anything?"

He shook his head. Then he sighed and shrugged, resigned to the mysterious ailments of old age. "It's nothing. You go, go on, I'll be fine."

In the doorway she turned, saying, "If it continues, we should call Dr. Huff and have your eyes examined. Maybe you've been reading too much, you strained them."

He snorted.

"All he'll do is give me a stronger prescription and sell me a new pair of glasses. As it is, I can already see into the fibers of the paper, as if I'm reading with a microscope." He shrugged again. "I'll be all right, don't worry."

At dinner that evening, Ben asked him, "How are your eyes? You having some kind of trouble?"

Walter looked over at Moira, always amazed at how she managed to communicate to her husband everything that happened during the course of the day so that by the time Ben came home, he had been fully briefed on Paulie and Billy, Grandpa, phone calls received, mail, bills, the status of current house repair projects, where she went, who she saw and what she bought, so Ben could simply select any item he chose for follow-up at dinner. It was a good system, except that Walter could see that Ben never had a chance to talk about what had happened to him during his day at the office, which was just as well since he was a corporation lawyer and what could be duller, except maybe accountants.

"He had something in it," Moira said. "I told you."

"Is it still there?" Ben asked.

"My friend Marty got hit in the eye in baseball practice," Billy said. "It got all red and swollen, and then black and blue. They had to take him to the hospital."

"Billy, Grandpa didn't get hit in the eye," Paulie told his younger brother.

"How do you know?" Billy demanded.

"Is it still there?" Ben repeated.

The old man nodded and shrank into his plate, to escape being examined like a witness in the box.

"Does it hurt or anything?" Ben asked.

Walter shook his head. "It's nothing, don't worry about it."

"But if it bothers you," Ben said, "interferes with your vision." He looked over at Moira. "Maybe you could make an appointment with Dr. Huff and drive him in."

"I already offered, but he didn't want to," Moira responded.

"But you know how he is," Ben insisted. "Go ahead, make the appointment for him."

The old man hated when they talked about him in the third person. Sooner or later, in every conversation, he became "him," like a child, without any rights or say in the matter, or as though he wasn't there at all, just an unseen ghost, observing the scene. He could imagine the conversations they had about him when he really wasn't there.

Moira nodded. The old man opened his mouth, ready to protest, but shut it again and looked down in his plate, where the strange black thing seemed to be floating around between his face and the soup. He flicked at it with his spoon, but it floated off to the side, and Walter looked around self-consciously, aware of being watched.

———

Walter trailed Dr. Huff and Moira into the examination room. Dr. Huff's pink face rose out of his white coat at them as he turned to Moira, who was smiling the patient smile of an adult with a reluctant child.

"Mrs. Sheffield, you told my nurse he had something in his eye?"

"Yes, Doctor, he said he—"

He? Now these two were doing it, Walter thought.

"I don't *have* something in my eye," he interrupted sharply. "I *see* something in my eye."

The smile left Moira's face. "Well, look," she said softly, turning away, "you don't need me here. I'll wait out in the reception room."

Saying, "Yes, sure, we'll be fine in here, don't you worry," Dr. Huff closed the door behind her and settled Walter into the examining chair with a "Well, let's have a look, shall we?" as he turned off the lights. Pushing aside the apparatus with two huge eyes used for eyeglass examinations, the doctor swung a frame in front of Walter and asked him to rest his chin on the crosspiece. He then shone a rectangular light into Walter's eyes while peering closely into them from all angles. Walter could smell Dr. Huff's minty breath-freshener.

"Any flashes of light?" the doctor asked, pushing the apparatus aside. "Do you ever see any bright flashes of light?"

"Yes," Walter answered, "off to the back somewhere, on the side, I think."

Dr. Huff nodded and said Uh-hmmm. He turned the examination room light on again.

"Well, now I'm going to dilate your eyes, Mr. Sheffield, so I can see back to your retina. You know what that is, dilating the eyes?"

Walter murmured that he'd had it done before, and the doctor placed the drops in his eyes, saying, "Now this will take effect in about twenty minutes, so you can go out and sit with your daughter-in-law, if you like."

"All right if I stay here?" Walter asked.

"Oh, sure, sure, that's fine, make yourself comfortable. I'll just turn the lights down so you can rest easy."

Walter closed his eyes, felt the slight stickiness of the eye drops. He settled his head back against the headrest and immediately started thinking of Alice, his wife, as he did whenever the world stopped intruding on the life in his mind, conjuring up images of them having dinner in a restaurant, driving with Alice at his side, in bed holding her close to him, feeling her warmth, but as always, he couldn't see her face. All his life, Walter had played a kind of game in which he called up the images of people he knew. By just closing his eyes and saying the name to himself, he could clearly see Alonzo Graybar, the chairman of the accounting firm where Walter had worked for thirty years, Pete Hamish and Don Tarvini and anybody else he'd ever worked with, his oldest son Josh, his daughter Melissa, Ben, Ben's wife Moira and their two boys. Even neighbors and people he hardly even knew or cared about. But the one person whose face he was never able to call up at all was Alice, not once during the forty years they lived together and the ten years since she was gone. Her face always eluded him, even now, in the darkness of the examining room, no matter how hard he tried. The sadness of failure settled over him.

The doctor's voice startled him.

"Well, taking forty winks? That's good. Resting is good."

He checked the dilation by flashing a tin penlight into Walter's eyes, saying Uh-hmmm. Then he had Walter rest his chin on the frame again, while he meticulously examined the right eye, telling Walter to look up, up right, side right, down right, straight down, down left, side left, up left, and straight up, after which he said a few more Uh-hmmms and repeated the same routine, using a smaller, hand-held light and colored lenses, bringing his face so close to Walter's that Walter felt the stubble on his cheek and could tell Dr. Huff had taken a fresh squirt of his minty breath-freshener.

"One more test now," the doctor said with a practiced laugh, "only promise me you won't go to sleep," pressing a button on the side of the chair to lower Walter into a horizontal position. Slipping his head into an attachment with a light, the doctor went through the whole procedure again, peering through an eyepiece while the light penetrated Walter's eye, interspersing Uh-hmmms now and then.

Sitting Walter up again, Dr. Huff turned on the softer examining room light. Walter's eyes felt stiff.

"Well," the doctor smiled, "the good news is you don't have any cataracts, and we tested you for glaucoma the last time, so we can rule that out, too." He paused. "I suppose I should call Mrs. Sheffield in."

"Never mind her, Doctor, you can tell me. What's your diagnosis?"

The doctor hesitated, then shrugged inwardly.

"Of course, we'll need additional tests. I'd like to have you go over to St. John's for an ultrasonograph to get a precise picture of your eye."

"But?" Walter urged. These doctors, they were like actors, always puffing up their parts.

"I think we may have a retinal problem of some kind. Let me explain."

He pulled down a wall chart displaying a colorful picture of the inside of an eyeball that made Walter want to gag.

"Here's the retina," Doctor Huff pointed, "back here, a thin, transparent membrane. It contains the rods and cones that are sensitive to light, also the nerves that carry impulses to the optic nerve here, which leads to the brain. You might say that the retina is the film that processes the images projected by the cornea and lens up front here."

Walter nodded, but the doctor had paused only for a breath.

"Behind the retina is this layer of tiny blood vessels," he went on, "which supplies oxygen and nutrients to the eye. Sometimes the retina separates from this layer of blood vessels. What causes it? Well, barring accidents, age, mostly. With the years, the vitreous, which is this jelly-like matter over here, liquefies, and a small portion of it may detach from the retina. This is what causes the appearance of a floater, that thing you see in your eye. Or flashes of light when your eyes are closed or you're in a dark room. This could mean a tear in your retina, or a detachment, which is more serious, but either one could lead to impaired vision, or even loss of sight. Nothing to fool around with."

His voice had assumed a sober tone, and now he brightened, saying, "If it's just a tear, we can use lasers to seal it up, no problem. But it looks to me that your retina may be detached, Mr. Sheffield, in which case we'll have to go in the hospital for surgery."

Walter considered this while the doctor asked, "Shouldn't I call in your daughter-in-law?"

"What? No, no, I'll explain it to her."

"Oh. In that case, I'll have my nurse set up an appointment for the ultrasonograph."

"Fine, fine," Walter said, slipping off the examining chair.

———

At dinner, Ben said, "Moira told me about your eye, Dad. Sounds awful."

"Sounds worse than it is, actually," Walter said. He was aware that the two boys were studying him with renewed interest. "They fix up thousands of them every year with lasers."

"My friend Larry's father had a vasectomy using lasers," Paulie said.

"Carl Trench had a vasectomy?" Ben said. "I didn't know that."

Walter was glad they were off his retina and onto somebody else's vasectomy. Being the subject of their concern made him feel still more helplessly dependent.

———

Now that Walter knew what it was, the floater in his eye no longer upset him, and he actually began to get used to it, learning which movements of his eye would cause it to come floating into full view before slipping down and off to the right out of his vision after one or two seconds. He practiced doing that and was pleased at achieving some degree of control over the floater. By the end of the second day, he could keep it in full view longer, so he could examine it and study its shape. That's when he noticed something strange.

He saw that the floater had the shape of an elongated profile, like a cameo on a brooch, and there was something vaguely familiar about it. After hours of patiently moving his eye from right to left and then holding his breath so the eye remained perfectly still, he finally succeeded in keeping the floater in full view, but then his eyes smarted and tears welled up, completely interfering with his observation of the floater.

. Encouraged and excited by his progress, he waited until the smarting stopped, then tried moving the floater into full view again. After a dozen attempts, while holding his breath made him slightly dizzy and his mouth and lips became parched, he succeeded. There it was. No doubt about it. The floater looked just like Alice. He could see her prominent nose, her deep-set eyes, her hair piled up on her tilted head, and her mouth slightly open, as if to say, "Walter, what shall we do today?"

Desperate to bring her closer and to make her image clearer, Walter experimented with various backgrounds, staring into the bathroom mirror, studying the garage wall in bright daylight, focusing on the dark living-room draperies. Paulie and Billy reported his strange behavior to their mother, who then shared her growing concerns with Ben, but Walter continued his experiments throughout the house until he discovered that if he faced a solid, off-white area, he could hold Alice's image for a longer, clearer, close-up view.

Removing the two Bermuda prints Moira had hung on the wall in his room, he sat on the bed, his head pressed firmly against the wooden headboard, eyes focused straight ahead on the wall. His heart leaped with joy. *Hello, dear Alice,* he said inside his mind. She smiled, turning up the corners of her lovely mouth. There she was, finally, her picture in his eye.

When Paulie came into his room to say that dinner was ready, the old man didn't respond. He just sat on his bed and stared straight ahead at the wall, his mouth slightly open.

"Grandpa, dinner's ready," Paulie repeated, moving closer. "Grandpa?"

Paulie went downstairs and reported that Grandpa was sitting on his bed staring at the wall and didn't want to come down. Ben and Moira exchanged glances, and Ben went upstairs.

"Dad," he said, "is anything wrong? Dad?" He touched his father's shoulder.

The old man seemed startled as he turned his eyes toward his son.

"What?" he asked, a distracted expression on his face, something pulling his eyes back where they had been fixed on the vacant wall.

"Is it the eye operation?" Ben asked. "Are you worried about having the operation?"

Walter looked straight ahead again, a sly smile touching the corners of his mouth as he maneuvered to keep Alice in view.

"Operation?" he murmured, with a shrug. "What operation?"

Joseph Sollish, retired, has been a creative director for advertising firms in Los Angeles and New York. He has recently published some of his short stories in various literary magazines. He also paints and carves stone sculpture. "Concerned with my own eyesight, I went to a doctor for an examination. He explained all the different problems related to aging of eyes, and while waiting for him, in the dark, to continue his examination, the whole story spun out for me." He hopes to continue writing, with an emphasis on short fiction.

DANIEL TAYLOR

CHICKEN
MAN

Introduction to Exegesis: 4 credits.
The first task of exegesis is to understand what the writer
actually said in the language and setting of his day. This means
that the student needs to become acquainted with the gram-
matical, lexical, textual, literary and historical aspects of the
biblical text, and he/she needs to know and use the various
exegetical aids that are at his/her disposal.

The ring of the phone was an annunciation. He welcomed it
as a relief from the blank screen and the maddening blinking
cursor of the desktop computer, a graduation gift. He let the
phone ring a second time. It still gave him pleasure to have his

phone ringing in his own office. That the office was tiny as a monk's cell made it all the better. He lifted the receiver with the reverence due a holy relic. He put it to his ear and listened briefly before speaking. "Pastor Greg."

"Hello, Reverend. This is Sam Rivers. I got a problem, Reverend, and I thought you could give me a hand."

Pastor Greg tried not to sound delighted. The Lord works in mysterious ways, His wonders to perform. Only one person had voted against his coming to "Witness in the Valley Baptist Church." Eloise, his part-time secretary, had as much as told him it was Sam Rivers.

She said it round about. "Everybody was just thrilled to have you coming, Pastor Greg. We haven't had a full-time man of God for better than five years, and he was so old we suspected God had called him home two or three times already and he just wasn't paying attention."

Then she had puffed herself up a bit and added, " 'Course, one man spends so much time with chickens that he hasn't much more brains than one." That was all she said, but with a congregation of fifty-five, counting the two newborns, it didn't take much to figure out that Sam Rivers had been his lone critic.

NT010 Introduction to Greek: 4 credits.
Presentation of fundamentals pertaining to the Greek verb, noun, and clause with respect to forms and simple relationships (syntax). Reading and understanding of materials with elementary vocabulary. Equivalent of a year of Greek. Offered as an intensive course each summer (July, August, and September). See page 56.

"Yes, Sam. Of course. I would be very happy to help you in any way I can. In fact, looking at my schedule book here I see that I am free all day. When would be a good time for you to come in?"

"No, Reverend. It ain't no office help I need. You'll have to come out here."

"Well that will be fine, Sam. What do you say I swing by there after lunch today?"

"I don't eat lunch myself. You be here after you're done. I'll be waitin'."

"Yes. Right. I often skip lunch myself. Actually, I try to jog a lit—"

"And don't wear no preacher's clothes."

BT212 The Church: 3 credits.
New Testament picture of the church (exact term and parallel terms, phrases) in the light of the historical situations where the people of God of the New Testament period are described.

He turned down the long dirt driveway at the crossroad, just beyond the undulating wooden bridge. He had stopped by the parsonage to trade his vest and coat for a sweater. To be safe, he'd also thrown his running shoes in the back seat.

Sam's house seemed less a manmade thing than a random outcropping of the ground. It gave a general impression of whiteness. Its clapboards met only grudgingly at the corners. Green and black asphalt shingles spread over the roof like a disease.

To the left and behind the house was a long, low metal shed, offering a dull reflection of the sun. Sam Rivers stood at its door. He began walking toward the car.

"Thanks for coming, Reverend." He looked the pastor up and down and gave a slight shake of his head.

"More than happy to, Sam. I haven't had a chance to get to many people's homes yet. I like getting out of the office to where people live." The pastor half-turned to move toward the house. "How can I be of help to you?"

"It's o'er here." Sam turned and started walking toward the metal shed. The young man followed carefully behind.

Sam pushed the door open and they stepped inside to a world of wire and artificial light and vibrating life. It didn't seem possible that so many living things—brown, white, yellow, red, and mottled—could be in one place. Rows of wire cages, four layers high, ran into the darkness at the other end. A high-pitched babel and slightly acrid smell swept around the young man. Wrinkling his nose, he registered the scene through squinting eyes.

"It's the chickens, Reverend. I need help with 'em. Some's still laying and some ain't. With four in a cage, ain't no easy way of telling which ones is and which ones ain't. I wouldn't a asked you, Reverend, except you maybe know Ethel died last year and I ain't got no one now to share this place with. After last Sunday's sermon, I figured this here was the kind of thing you were talking about."

PR214 Persuasion in Preaching: 3 credits.
An analysis of the techniques of persuasion as applied in preaching. Emphasis on contemporary persuasion theory in regard to gaining attention of the audience, motivation, persuasibility, audience analysis, ethos, and ethical implications.

"You start this side of the aisle and I'll start the other. Put the layers back in the cage you get 'em from and just toss the others out here in the aisle. I'll take care of them after."

Sam turned to the cages, then stopped and walked toward the door. "You get started, Reverend. I got to feed Jesse."

"Jesse?"

"Our goat. Be right back."

The pastor felt like Moses sent back to Egypt to free his people. Surely there must be an alternate plan.

He knelt on the dirty floor of the shed, peering in at the chickens as though they held the key to the mysteries of the world. He unlatched the door to the cage. He waited briefly, hoping one of the hens would offer itself for examination. None volunteered.

He reached tentatively for a sleepy-looking mottled chicken in the far corner of the cage. At the first touch of his fingers, it became a small cyclone, leaping and squawking and thrashing about. Pastor Greg's hand was out of the cage and back at his side before his brain could form an opinion.

He found himself trembling and wanting to curse. He closed his eyes for a moment, hopeful that when re-opened he would see anything but chickens.

But chickens he did see, hundreds of them. Above his head as he knelt on the floor, there seemed a heavenly host of chickens, clucking to him strange tidings he could not understand.

BT204 Christology: 4 credits.

A study of the origin, meaning, and usage of Christological titles in the primitive church. Special emphasis will be placed on the pertinent Christological passages. Includes a study of quests for the historical Jesus.

Pain and confusion competed on his face. He stared again into the cage, the four hens returning his questioning look with cocked heads.

There seemed no escape. He tensed his stomach muscles and reached again into the cage, this time with both hands. Catching a red and white chicken, he pulled it out, keeping its wings pressed to its body.

It occurred to him that he didn't know what he was looking for. How was he to know if this was a layer or a freeloader? He held the hen up close to his face, hoping to read in its eyes the answer to this and all questions.

The door of the shed slapped open and Rivers returned. The pastor stood up quickly, holding the red and white hen. "Well, I got one here."

"I see that. I'll start on this side."

The young man shuffled a little.

"Yes, I've got this one here. Let me see. I'm having just a bit of a problem knowing whether this particular hen is still laying or not."

Rivers was reaching into the cage on the opposite side. "Two fingers she's laying, one finger she ain't."

Two fingers she's laying, one finger she ain't. What did that mean? He raised the chicken up and glanced at its feet, but quickly lowered it again. *Chickens don't have fingers. Chickens DON'T have fingers,* he repeated to himself.

He decided to watch Rivers out of the corner of his eye to see what he did. But he saw only the brown workshirt of Rivers' hunched back, constellated with patches of sweat.

"Two fingers in the vent shows it's stretched. She's laying. Only one finger—she ain't." With that, Rivers put back the hen he had in his hands and reached for another. Pulling it out, he turned to the young man. "Got it, Reverend?"

"Got it."

It was a revelation. This was the life of a chicken. Chicken eschatology. Two fingers, you lived. One finger, you died. Productivity is reality. Lay and let live. Feed for those who feed; death for the rest. It made him want to laugh, to cry.

All afternoon and into the evening he checked chicken vents. Two fingers—back into the cage. One finger—thrown out into the aisle. Two fingers—another year of grain in the dish and water in the bottle feeder. One finger—a twisted neck and a quick trip to chicken eternity. One finger, two fingers. One finger, two fingers. One finger, two fingers. It was the great chicken judgment.

And what about those in between? What about those that were more than one finger, but not really two? Who was he to judge? What if he were wrong? The responsibility was too much.

No, he concluded. The undecideds went back into the cage. He would take a stand at that point. Somewhere in the great scheme of things there had to be room for grace.

All afternoon and into the evening.

By nightfall he was exhausted and clouded. His hands and forearms were a crosshatch of scratches. His clothes gave off an unprecedented smell. His back had abandoned sharp pain messages and settled into a steady knotted ache. Rivers had been deaf to his attempts at conversation, moving silently and efficiently away from him down the rows, casting out the undeserving, making his decisions quickly without apparent struggle or regret.

The young man, however, moved slower and slower. In his weariness he became rebellious, saving every third one-finger slacker, then every other. He started judging by the color of beak or the cock of the head rather than vent size. By the end he lost all criteria, even picking some of the stringier looking chickens off the floor and sticking them back in cages when Rivers wasn't looking.

BT219 The Lord's Supper: 3 credits.
This seminar on the Lord's Supper will deal with its historical origin, textual variations, theological meaning, and practical significance. Different church traditions will be examined and time will be spent discussing the Eucharist in ecumenical dialogue.

The pastor spent the entire next day in the parsonage, the phone off the hook. He wandered around room to room. He tried reading short bits of Scripture. He wept. He laughed nervously. In mid-afternoon he packed his car. An hour later he put everything back.

He did not eat all day. As darkness came he went to the kitchen and pulled the silver spike handle of the ancient refrigerator. The only thing in it were a few jars and a bunch of purple grapes.

He reached without enthusiasm for the grapes, then closed the door and leaned against the counter. He surrendered to the great weakness in his legs and slid slowly to the linoleum floor, the back of his head coming to rest on the bread drawer.

Not long after he heard a single knock at the front. It took him a few moments to want enough to stand. When he opened the door a cool wind blew over him. He watched a pickup truck pulling away, its headlights carving a narrow path through the darkness.

On the porch was a metal bucket. In it were three headless chickens, plucked. A scratched note lay on top of one of them. "For your help. Eat them all before too long."

The young man lifted them into his house, greeting them as he would a friend.

Daniel Taylor is a teacher and writer in St. Paul, Minnesota. "The gem of the story came from a story told to me many years ago by my father about his first church as a young pastor in the 1940s." He is currently engaged in a long-term project as the stylist for a new translation of the Bible. He has had other short fiction published by *Cream City Review* of the University of Wisconsin.

EDWARD ANDERSON

BENEDICTUS
QUI VENIT

Benedictus qui venit in nomine Domini
Blessed is he who comes in the name of the Lord

*I*n South East London, down past Touley Street, the presses at Brecken and Sons pound their steel forms, day after day, hour after hour. They begin at five in the morning and run continuously until eight at night, from Monday to Saturday, week after week. Only on Sunday is it quiet, when the half-light from the windows shows them angular and grey. The presses are what drive Brecken and Sons forward. It is their brute strength that everyone serves, and their production that everyone guards.

There are about thirty presses to a room, lined up in three rows with each press surrounded by stacks of "blank" metal sheets, cuttings, tools, and an operator. The operators put the blank sheets over the bottom negative form of the press. A safety guard swings into place and the "hammer" holding the positive form falls, pounding the blank sheets into plaques, covers, or hubcaps. After a moment's pause the safety guard swings back, the hammer raises, and the pressed metal sheet is removed. The operators do this repeatedly and nothing else, keeping pace with the presses. To save time because they are paid by piece work, some operators remove the safety guard and place the blank just ahead of the falling hammer. Some have lost their fingers this way. They say one man lost his forearm, when he reached across to straighten a crooked blank as the hammer fell. He jumped back and ran between the rows incoherently screaming and waving his arms, until he could be grabbed and taken to the hospital. People stood around shocked, redescribing the event, until they were hustled back to work by the foremen so the presses could start again.

When he was twenty-eight Morris went to work at Brecken and Sons. His father, who had worked from when he was eighteen until he retired, put him onto an opening at the factory when Morris could not find work. Morris had finally decided to apply. He walked from the bus through the old brick entrance, and into the personnel office. He registered at the desk and sat down, waiting to be seen. After a while the manager called him in. He looked over Morris's application, commented that he had known his father, and told him to be at work the next day at eight. Morris then walked out to see the secretary for routine instructions.

He sat in her office, leaning forward, his hands on the arm rest, his foot doing irregular taps. At some points he would look agitated and apprehensive, and at other times he would look unawares or deep in thought. His brow would furrow as if he was ready to speak, but nothing was said. He looked around the room. There was an electric clock hung two-thirds up the off-white wall to the right of the desk. Behind the desk there was an impressionist print of a Norwegian mountain landscape, with crude impasto paint and slightly jarring colors. A table with a lamp and some magazines stood in the corner, and another chair sat next to his.

"Welcome to Brecken and Sons, Mr. Tailor," she began. "I'm Mrs. Whitney, Mr. Foultey's secretary. There are just some routine matters we need to deal with, and then you will be free to go." She was young, had nice reddish hair cut short, was slim, but she was also in some senses plain. When she talked it was very carefully with little theatrical and slightly exaggerated movements.

There was a pause as she looked at his application. "Oh, it says you've had some education. I hope you're not going to up and leave us right away if you get something better?"

Morris shifted in his chair. "Well I need the work," he said. "And Mr. Foultey seemed to think it was all right."

"Yes, yes," she said, "I didn't mean to say you were. I meant I hope you won't be bored. Anyway, first, I want to make sure the information we have here is correct. Your full name is Morris Clifford Tailor?" Morris answered yes.

"And, your National Insurance number is . . . let me see . . . NA-10-19-88-C?"

"Yes that's correct," he said.

"And you live at Flat number three, 527 Walbutton Street in Clapham?"

"Yes. That's correct."

"Good. And you don't have a telephone now, but you will be getting one shortly. Is that right?" Morris acknowledged again, and she began another subject, moving on to boots and overalls, company policies and holidays. Her hand gestured grandly, and she lifted and turned her head with a touch of self-importance. Even the desk seemed to mean something of importance as she carefully and formally arranged the papers, and then, even readjusted them with a slight emphasis.

"We at Brecken and Sons," she said, "feel that we have a good team spirit in the work place." Morris's hands tightened and he looked down, focusing on the floor. She paused a moment and looked at him, then continued speaking. A couple more topics followed, until she came to the end of her list. She had been half looking at him and half looking down, arranging the papers on her desk, but when she was finished she glanced up.

"Do you have any questions?"

Morris looked back and seemed to say something, then stopped, and then started over. "Who is the 'we'?" he asked. He moved as if trying to summon some strength, then sat back with an odd almost cynical expression.

"You what?" she said, startled and perplexed, and slightly off guard. "The we?"

Morris shifted in his chair and looked past her at the picture on the wall and pursed his lips. "Earlier, you said that 'We at Brecken and Sons,' and so on, and I wondered who the 'we' was that you were talking about. Was it the owners or managers, or who?" It seemed he sat up a little bit more with each word he spoke, with each word pronounced a little more boldly.

"Why us," she said, becoming slightly unsure. "Whoever works at Brecken and Sons."

"Us?" said Morris. "Do they ask you your opinion on anything?"

She paused a moment, then said, "I think you should be thankful you have a job. And yes, Mr. Foultey does ask for my opinion on some things."

Morris leaned forward in his chair, looking directly at her. "What does he ask your opinion on? How to make coffee? You think bein' a secretary they care about what you got to say? And Mr. Foutley's not an owner anyway." Morris could hear muffled voices in the office next door, and his lips went dry in the silence, as she looked down at her desk, and lifted the corner of a piece of paper. She looked back up, her face flushed, her eyes watery.

"If you're upset because o' what I said about you leavin', I said I didn't mean it. But if you're makin' fun of me," she said, her voice thick, "it's not funny. An' I don't see where you come on puttin' on airs. You workin' here same as me." He felt another silence, but cold, and gripped his hands on the chair and tried to find a word. He tried to straighten and resist, but didn't move.

"I'm sorry," he finally said. He glanced at her, then looked down, avoiding her eyes. He stood up and took a few steps towards the door. "I'm sorry, I didn't mean . . . " He paused, and then started to say something but stopped. After a moment he walked out.

Morris crossed the street to the bus stop, and leaned against the pole as he waited. He half expected to see Mr. Foultey come from the building, running and shouting after him. He thought he might lose his job for the incident, and he realized that he had no other options. He had never felt as vulnerable before. A bus pulled away from a traffic light several blocks down. It was going to Greenwich Observatory, and instead of returning to his bedsit, he decided to take it.

When he got to Greenwich he walked up the hill toward the observatory through the common, stopping about three-quarters of the way up. He sat down on the grass and looked out over the green part, and the city below. He watched the Thames flattened across the view, solid and heavy, and immovable. He thought again of the secretary and tried to understand what had happened. He had never intended to say those things, even though he had wanted to, and he had been shocked at himself when he did. Not shocked that he felt resentment, for when she had said "We at Brecken and Sons," he had seen it as one more presumption put upon him. On the one hand he was being offered inclusion, that he could join the "we"; yet the "we" was somehow always one step further, in somebody else's hands. And the "we" was firmly established, and the "we" was not to be discussed. Yet he was surprised he had said it. He had not realized how close to the surface his frustrations had been.

He was also surprised at her response. He had seen her as a wall that would not give; an inanimate portion of an inanimate "them"; a piece of office furniture that was as untouched by him as the metal desk she sat at. Yet, when he had struck at it, the image had collapsed, and in the end he had only struck another person: and in the end a person not unlike himself. The abuse gnawed at him.

He looked down the hill as the sun set. A smartly dressed woman of about forty was walking her dog. *How far away she seems,* he thought. He looked at the bushes around him. The tips of the branches and even the thin pale leaves seemed outlined, hard, and penetrating almost to the point of pain.

He remembered when he was about twelve he had read the story about the life of American Indians on the Great Plains. He read how they lived in response to the "Great Spirit," and how their life revolved around it, and of the rituals they kept to commune with it. The afternoon he finished the story he went out and found Clyde and Greg, and talked them into going to the park to make their own contact with the Great Spirit. They stood in the rain, staring upward toward what they could see of the sun, their hands outstretched, their faces chilled. Clyde and Greg ran off but Morris stayed, and waited, and thought for sure he felt something: almost a sense of quiet conversation or explanation, or a touch on his face. As if to prove it, some light broke through and lit the edge of a cloud, and he saw the wonder of it before the grey mist closed in again. He was still standing there when Clyde and Greg with some other kids came running and taunting him. One large boy from the estate jumped on Morris's back and drove his face into the ground, then got up and kicked him repeatedly before running off. Morris lay there crying. After a while he walked home but he never mentioned anything to his parents, neither of the attack nor his moment with the Great Spirit. After that day he began to keep such things to himself.

He pulled his legs up, rested his chin, and watched the lights across the river. He thought of that moment looking at the clouds and light, and wondered what it was he had felt. He looked at the sky as if to find it again. Almost lost in the evening sky, a seagull flew overhead, and the clouds shifted slowly back and forth, but there was nothing else. *Only imagination,* he thought. *Only a boy lost in imagination can think like that.* Here above the town he could see only things and more things, and empty spaces and pain. He could remember only things, and perhaps that was all there had ever been.

He looked at the black stretch where the river was, with the scattered spots of reflection the only clue there was something there. Obscure and muted voices came almost not heard. He looked at the city below. *We are the imprisoned,* he thought. *A little comfort and a little power and we're satisfied.* Images came: a giant, two or three thousand feet tall, barefoot with no shirt, with tattered plain trousers held up by a rope, and a blindfold tied over his eyes. He was bald with stooping shoulders, huge feet and hands, his arms hung at his side, and he lumbered across in dumb ignorance, treading on the ignorant world below. His mouth gaped open, and he turned this way and that, calling on somone's name with deep slurred words: or the river, like a huge solid black mass, moving through the city ripping up all the things; the things that were houses and tables and chairs and people. *What does it matter,* he thought, *you can't kill a dead person.*

His thoughts went silent as he became ashamed of what he was thinking. Instinctively he looked around in case anyone saw him. But no one was there, and it was quiet around him. A sense of his own insignificance clung to him. He stretched out on his side, and his hands rubbed through the grass, feeling each blade. Below on the river a tugboat went by, floating in the darkness, lit up by its own floodlights, with its engines heard faintly throbbing across the distance. Slowly and purposefully it passed out of sight. The wake piled up behind it and billowed out in decreasing waves, until those too piled against the embankment, then pushed back to meet those coming after: one after another until everything was calm again.

At eight the following day Morris arrived at the employee's entrance. It was located in a recent building fabricated with metal and cinder block. He walked through with the arriving shift, caught in the jam as everyone lined up to punch their time clocks. Some were half asleep, some called greetings. Most were quiet, shuffling forward into each other until inside the factory. Morris asked someone where Mr. Stewart the foreman was. He was directed through the first two rooms into the heat-treatment department. There, one of the employees pointed to a medium-sized man of about sixty, standing over by one of the vats talking to a maintenance man. He was grey-haired with glasses, but strong looking. Morris walked over to him and Mr. Stewart turned around. He had thick eyebrows, a wide neck, and looked very directly, even intently it seemed, toward him.

"Yes, young man," he said. Morris was surprised at hearing a foreign accent with an English name.

He answered, loud enough to be heard over the machines but not shouting, "I'm Morris Tailor. I was told to report to you. The bloke over there said you were Mr. Stewart."

"Ah, yes," Mr. Stewart answered. "They tolt me you were to come. You come vith me and I vill show you vwhat to do." He turned back to the other man. "Tom, I vill show dis man his place and 'ten I come back to you." Tom acknowledged, and Mr. Stewart turned back and started walking with Morris.

"Vwe do not like it vwhen you are late here." Mr. Stewart continued, "So you must be on time. You can holt up the line maybe ifv you are late." Morris answered yes.

"And if vyou talk too much, maybe you do not 'tink, and make a mistake so you vaste time, or hurt yourself. So 'tink about vwhat you do."

Morris answered yes again, and continued to listen as Mr. Stewart led him between the rows of machines. Instructions on breaks, restrooms, personal calls, and other items passed by his ears, until they stopped at a small press that was on the end of a line of similar presses. Like the other machines it was grey green, square, and solid, with a ribbon of clean steel coming off of a large roll feeding into the back. Other rolls were stacked beside the press, along with the standard compliment of tools and scraps. A metal work table stood a few feet nearby. Morris examined the machine as Mr. Stewart described how to operate it. All around them the other presses in the room continued stamping and producing. There was something both impressive and oppressive, with the sheer volume of their concentrated force. Morris touched his hand on the slightly oily side of the press.

"Mitser Tailor," said Mr. Stewart, "Do you understand?"

Morris looked up and answered, "Yes." Mr. Stewart peered at him a moment, and then had him run the machine. A couple minutes of silence followed as Mr. Stewart watched Morris.

Finally Mr. Stewart said, "I vill come back later. If vyou havf a question, you ask around, or later I vwill tell you. 'Tere are some here say I am a hardt man. But you find, if vyou do a goodt job you find me not so bad. You do O.K."

Mr. Stewart walked away and Morris turned back to the machine. The ribbon moved with a steady thump on each press, faster than he expected, without variety. When that roll was finished, he replaced it with another from the stack by the press, which in turn was kept filled by a man who came by with a hand cart. The man would drop the rolls then give a short nod for a greeting, pick up the baskets full of clips, and go away again without a word. This continued until twelve when Morris had his lunch break.

Morris walked outside in front of the employee's entrance where several other people, also having lunch, were sitting on the wall or on the grass. He found a space where the wall butted the side of the building and he could lean back and sit down. He sat a moment and breathed deeply, then shifted so one leg was hanging down, tapping against the wall. Everything around him except himself, or anything not connected with the job, seemed so free. Even the trash blown by the wind seemed to have some dignity of life. If it was blown without a will, at least the wind was spontaneous, and the world changed around it. A slight smile came to him with the thought that perhaps he could write a romantic song with lines like, "I wish I was a little rubbish bag, and you were a dustman's glove." Or, "We'll stick together, like wrappers in the wind."

How badly he needed to talk! And how few there were he could do that with! He thought about trying to find Tom, a classmate up in Birmingham and taking a trip up there: or, perhaps Sarah could be found, or a couple of others. Perhaps they could rebuild their friendship again despite the years.

A group to his left had become much louder, shouting and laughing, and caught his attention. A red-haired man they were calling Mick, and Jill, a woman whose voice carried strong and clearly, were leading the group. At first, Morris could not understand what they were excited about. Mick stood up and said he was sure it was 12:43, another said 12:47, and someone else said

12:45. Jill called them a bunch of "bleedin' morons," and said
12:46. Eventually, Morris figured out they were waiting for someone called "Stomper" to come past; who apparently was a she,
and would come into view from behind a building on the left as
she walked along the street.

Morris's watch read 12:42. He shifted a little for a better view
down the street, and looked over at the group that was getting
more and more excited. He looked back at the corner of the
building, and only half noticed that the group went suddenly
silent, with Jill holding her arms out, and saying "hush" to anyone
making noise. And they waited.

A couple minutes later at 12:45, a nun, dressed in a black habit
but without a hood, stepped into view. The nun was too far away
to notice the noise from the group, or perhaps was oblivious to it,
and continued in a steady gait undisturbed. Morris watched her,
intrigued at the sight. She was about fifty-five and carried a black
bag with her, not unlike a doctor's bag. Her hair was tied up in a
bun and still brown but mixed in with large amounts of grey and
some white. She held her head straight forward, not hung down
but not haughty either. He noticed her habit draped like a tent
over her overweight figure, with her hands and face plump and
white, her cheeks ruddy and her nose a little red. She had a
distinct way of walking, where her feet seemed to reach further
forward than normal, hitting the ground flat on each beat, yet
with her body maintaining a consistent posture. It was the way
that her feet struck the ground, that Morris assumed was cause
for her nickname, "Stomper." He watched her cross in front of
the factory along the street, obscured for a moment as a bus
went by, then step out of sight behind a grey brick building to
his right.

"Oi," Morris called over to the group, and·a couple of them
looked over. "That nun, the one you were callin' Stomper, does

she come by often then?" One of them got a puzzled expression as if trying to understand what Morris said.

"F——n' right she does mate, every f——n' day," he said. Morris nodded and lifted his hand to acknowledge, but the man had already turned back to the group. The shadows, slowly moving around the building had taken the sunlight, and the corner of the entrance grew chilly. Morris got up and stretched his legs, waiting for the bell to ring.

The next day at work, the image of the nun returned to his mind. She intrigued him. She had passed by so complacently and normally, yet she was so out of context with the world around her. The street she walked through had long ceased to care for anything she represented. The language of her dress was too archaic for people to understand, much less respond to. She was neither despised nor respected, but was simply a curiosity. How could someone not see? And if Stomper did see, what was she seeking to prove?

She reminded him of an article he had read, of young birds, that at the right time in their life can be shown, for example, a watering can, and from then on believe that they are one; chirping and courting the tin "companion," to the exclusion of their own kind. Perhaps at the right time she had seen a picture of a "saint" in a black robe, and without thought that vision had become her reality. If she had not been so ordinary looking, if she had looked more like a "saint," then her "costume" might have made more sense. But what was incongruous was that she herself seemed so conventional. Her expression was satisfied and methodical, like a matron in a comfortable job; so unlike the holy painting.

Morris rested his hand on the guard near the hammer on the press. He watched the hammer as it stamped clip after clip, again and again. Each stamp was rapid and percussive, with secondary sounds coming from the belts, rods, gears, and hissing from the hydraulics. The noise was almost tangible, and in a sense not really a sound at all, with any identity, but rather an effect. *How odd,* thought Morris. That day at the press, in many ways he felt most peaceful. Here the machine and the noise could almost drive sense from him. And it was sense that had crowded him with questions and expectations and fantasies. If you can grow in education, he thought, perhaps you can grow in ignorance, and then everything could simply fall where it would, and he would not care. He thought again of Stomper dressed in her habit. She really was most conventional. She looked different, but actually she was conventional. Her dress, her belief, her rituals, simply conventions of another sort. Perhaps that convention did to her what this noise did to him.

"Mitser Tailor, you need your mind on your vwerk." Mr. Stewart walked up behind Morris. Morris straightened and looked around, flushed.

"I vatch you, and you look off and do not be carefvul. You must vatch te ribbon, it can jam maybe, and you must vatch te basket vwhen it is full," Mr. Stewart continued. "Andt you shouldt not put your hand 'tere, it is not safe. Now vwerk, and tink about it." Morris apologized and moved his hand, and Mr. Stewart continued on his rounds.

That lunch, Morris went to the pub for a game of darts, but the following day he again sat outside at the employee's entrance. He had glanced up from reading a newspaper when he saw Stomper halfway along the street. She looked as absurd as she had the two days before: still steadfastly treading the ground with her flat footsteps. He looked at his watch, it was 12:46. In another minute she reached the edge of Morris's view and stepped out of sight.

Perhaps she was returning to work after lunch? She passed by at the right time, but why would she have been so punctual? Was she that eccentric? Wasn't it more likely that she was getting off work? But if so, why every day around 12:45? Morris tried to regather any little facts that might give clue as to who she was. He remembered her little black bag. Perhaps she was a nurse coming off of a shift. Or perhaps she was actually a matron at some school, only working part-time. He could imagine her at a parochial school, pottering around a couple of plain little back rooms, one of which had little single beds in it, leaning over little boys and girls saying yes to this, and no to that. Or, he could see her getting a pair of glasses out of her bag so she could read the label on an aspirin bottle, and getting several out before she could find the right one. Every day she would go to these little rooms at exactly the same time, and every day leave at exactly the same time, keeping everything exactly the same: protected and warm, and unquestioning.

He noticed a man sitting on the grass fairly close who had his back against the wall watching the street. He looked about 35, fairly slim, and had long hair over his shoulders. Every now and then he pulled on a cigarette held loosely between his fingers. He had a hangdog look about him, but his features still looked approachable.

Morris called over to him, "Did you see that nun that went by?" The man turned, but looked as though he had missed the question, so Morris repeated it.

He answered with an impulsive but also off-hand voice. "Yeah, she comes by every day," he said. "I think a few times she hasn't shown up, but most days she does."

"Well, what do you make of her then?" Morris asked.

The other man let out a muffled laugh, and gestured with his hand. "Bloody 'ell," he said, "I don't know. She's alright I guess. A bit off maybe. She reminds me o'some o'them types you see over in India. Those blokes what wander on the street and people give them food an things an' get prayers or somethin' for it."

"Why? Because of what she's wearing?" said Morris. The other man took a pull on his cigarette. He glanced at Morris who was facing the street at that moment. There were light fluctuations of expression on Morris's face, not in response to anything around him, but to some private thought rising to the surface, and he found it odd.

"Sort of. But not that she looks the same, but she does the same sort o'thing."

"Which is?" Morris asked.

The other man breathed deeply, and shrugged his shoulders. "You know. Going roun' the street sellin' religion an' all. It's not like she 'ides it. She's doin' it for somethin' and wants you t'know, it seems. But why you askin'? Are you religious or somethin'?"

"No. I just wondered that's all. I saw her walk by and was just trying to figure 'er out. I saw that get-up she's wearing, an it caught my eye."

"Well, it's 'er game that's all," the other man replied. "We all got one. You don't get nothin' free, an' she's on the take somewhere, you can be sure o' that. I 'ave an aunt what says she's religious, but she's got a game too. An' she wants you t'know it."

"And you wouldn't buy a prayer from her then?" asked Morris. The man started to answer but the bell rang, and they stood up.

"You ask some f—n' questions," he said, and they walked inside.

Morris went back and started the press. The small metal clips came out, one at a time by the thousands. One roll finished, and he stopped the machine, fed in another roll, changed the basket at the other end, and then started the press again. He made sure it was running well, then relaxed and watched it stamp thousands more. The man with the cart came by and dropped off some more rolls, briefly nodded at Morris, then took the full baskets away. Morris almost said something, but decided otherwise.

Later Mr. Stewart walked up to the press. He looked around Morris's work space. "It is O.K. for you Mitser Tailor?" he said. Morris acknowledged. "Goodt. I 'tink you are doing O.K. now. But still you must be carefvul. Ve need 'tese pieces on 'te line. It is a big order 'tat has come." Morris acknowledged and Mr. Stewart started to leave.

"Mr. Stewart," Morris called. Mr. Stewart stopped and looked back. "If you don't mind me asking, was Mr. Stewart always your name?" A look, almost like fear or guilt, colored Mr. Stewart's face and then passed again.

"Vwhy 'to you vant to know?" he said, his expression flat. Morris's face reddened.

"I'm sorry. I didn't mean anything by it. I was only curious. I thought Stewart was an English name, that was all." Mr. Stewart looked at him as if weighing the tone of Morris's voice, and then seemed to relax a little.

"It vwas first Striewski. Vwhen I come to England I change it," he said.

"When did you come to England?" Morris asked.

"That is enough for questions now . . . You must get busy," Mr. Stewart said, then walked to another press with his clipboard in hand. Morris watched the figure of Mr. Stewart moving down the aisle. He was not unlike the machines, square and solid, always working.

On Thursday, Morris was again outside as Stomper marched by. A mother with a little child passed her on the street. The child looked up and stopped, fixedly staring at Stomper, his mouth gaping open. His mother began to pull him, looking embarrassed. The child was standing on the other side of Stomper, and they were too far, so Morris could not see fully, but it seemed she first deliberately ignored the boy, then looked down and smiled. But the child stared without response, until his mother finally dragged him away.

What would a child see in Stomper with such fascination? Perhaps her habit caught his attention, or some manner she had? She was similar to a child, thought Morris: the way she lived protected from the world in her conventions. Her incongruous and oblivious appearance belonged to a child. Even the flat-footed way she walked seemed like the steps of a child. A smile passed Morris's face. *Perhaps she is the biggest child that child has seen,* he thought.

That evening as he was going home on the bus, he saw a bookstore still open. He imagined Stomper reading her Bible, and in response the thought struck him to look at one himself. He got off the bus and went into the store, searched through the rows, and picked out an inexpensive one. He felt strangely awkward and noticeable carrying it to the till, and kept it in the bag until he got home. After dinner, he sat back in an old secondhand couch in his bedsit, and idly turned the pages, reading what first came to mind.

It did not make full sense to him, random images and snippets of verses being what he first noticed. At one point he looked down and read, "Once, when John's disciples and the Pharisees were keeping a fast, some people came and asked him, 'Why is it that John's disciples and the disciples of the Pharisees are fasting but yours are not?' " He looked further down the page. "But the time will come when the bridegroom will be taken away from them; that will be the time for them to fast." The image of Stomper filling her habit like a tent came to mind.

He turned some pages and read, "And if your eye causes your downfall, tear it out; it is better to enter into the kingdom of God with one eye than to keep both eyes and be thrown into hell, where the devouring worm never dies and the fire is never quenched." The barbarity of it shocked and yet compelled him. He thought of the gentle images of sheep and Jesus on a hillside and of family churches, things he saw on posters outside churches; they mixed in with images of fire and worms and eyes being torn out, and they followed each other around in his mind's eye, like a strange and confusing circus. He sat back a moment and looked around the room: at the gas heater and table and lamp. He thought he heard rain falling against the window. *Where does this fit in?* he thought. *How does she believe this? Or does she really?*

He read on, "Everyone will be salted with fire. Salt is good, but if the salt loses its saltiness, how will you season it? You must have salt within yourselves, and be at peace with one another." He could not follow the connection between the verses, and the references to salt were confusing. He looked at the last line again. "Be at peace with one another" he read, the word "peace" going around in his head several times, and settling deeper into his mind. He stood up and walked to the window, peering out. The street lamps were on, their image distorted by the rain now falling heavily on the pane, and running in rivulets down the sides. *Peace with an answer,* he thought. *Not peace at any price.* He could not live like Stomper, secure in her conventions, as long as her world stayed comfortable and the same. He went and sat down on the couch again. He read for another hour, occasionally pausing, until he grew tired and went to bed.

The next morning repeated the day before, clip following clip, until at lunch time Morris was anxious to be outside. He sat by the entrance. Stomper came. He wondered how she would interpret the verses he had read the night before, and what she would say about the fasting?

She was about three-quarters of the way along the street, when a car driving close to where she was ran through a large puddle in the road. To avoid the spray Stomper stepped back and turned around, holding her bag out in front of her. For the first time he saw the left side of her face. He went cold. Large purple areas of skin covered her, wrinkled and drawn, melted from a burn. Her hairline did not start until nearer the top of her head, and even though she tried to cover it with hair, a nub could still be seen where her left ear had been. Morris's mouth was dry, and he stared intently. He watched as she leaned over and wiped off some of the spray that had reached her, her burn marks still visible. She seemed so human, and so little.

How long has she been like this? he thought. Was she a young woman when it happened? Was she beautiful? Was she conscious? How painful was it? Instinctively, he imagined having fire burn on the side of his face, but he pushed the thought away. He looked at the other people around him, but no one else seemed to have noticed. One man leaned on his side with a paper, and three others together could be heard having a muffled conversation. He turned toward Stomper, but she was gone. For a moment he questioned if he had actually seen anything.

The bell rang, and Morris stood up, finding himself shaking, and he went inside, trying to avoid people's attention. The noise of the presses surrounded him as he went back to his machine, and he stood away from the aisle, facing in, watching the hammer as it pounded over and over. He thought of the child he had watched, who had stared at her as she went by. How often that must have happened as she stood in a queue at a shop, or rode a bus, or as then, as she walked down a street: people's eyes always focused or averted, never casually resting and moving past. A twinge of pain caught him. An image came of her falling down as fire stuck to the side of her face, and he rubbed his eyes to distract himself. Before, she had seemed so protected, so untouched and comfortable. Like this, she seemed unbearably delicate and vulnerable.

And he heard his own voice running on in his mind. *She's absurd; she's complacent; she's conventional; she's ignorant.* The voice seemed dull, and his criticism piled into a mound of irrelevant sounds. What had he accused her of? Existence? Which particular fold in her dress had committed the crime? Was it her foot? Perhaps her nose? What high idea had he accused her of failing? In the back of his mind a thought began to form, pushing itself to the surface. It had been his failures he was judging, not hers. She was simply herself, attempting some measure of meaning; and perhaps in some measure succeeding. And who was he?

The basket filled and he replaced it with another. His thoughts went quiet. He stood there as the machine ran on, not thinking nor feeling anything in particular: lightheaded, quiet. The afternoon continued on and finished. He was replaced by the next shift and clocked out, and still he felt nothing.

The next morning he slept in since he was not going to work. Early the previous night he had gone to bed exhausted, but had still awakened around 2:00, feeling both alert and tired before finally going back to sleep. He drank his coffee slowly, and decided to walk down to the shops to buy some warmer clothes, and for something to do.

He left the house and walked along the street but not in any hurry, stopping to look at whatever caught his attention. A fine rain was falling almost like a mist, but he found it pleasant and did not avoid it. He looked in the window of an antique shop, noticing an assortment of toys displayed, particularly an open music box with a small ballerina in the middle. She was poised on her toes in a pirouette, with her arm gracefully outstretched, and her head raised. She was well made, refined, and lifelike. A shopkeeper inside leaned over, and following Morris's eyes, picked up the music box, holding it up and offering it to him. Morris waved his hand, no, and stepped back onto the street.

Down the street he stopped at a crossing and waited for the light to change. A man in a fashionable leather sports jacket came up and stood next to him, shuffling and moving from foot to foot, looking at the cars, then the light, and the cars again. Morris glanced at him, feeling his agitation. As Morris turned away the phrase came into his head, "to do good." It was as if the words came of their own, just a breath, but distinct and immovable. The light changed and he began to cross the street, the man next to him walking quickly ahead. *To do good.* The phrase came again, feeding into his thoughts. "Where is goodness?" countered Morris, turning the word goodness over as if struggling to debate it. He thought of the years of frustration and humiliation and wasted effort. They demanded an explanation. *Goodness has nothing to do with this place,* they said. *Goodness has no power. It has nothing to do with this life.* He came to a small grassy enclosure with shrubbery and a wrought iron fence. He stopped and let his mind slowly clear. He saw the man in the leather jacket now further up the street, walking with quick but jerky and awkward movements, like a parody of life. Morris rested his hand against the railing, and felt the wet from the rain cool to his touch. He looked again at the man now almost out of sight. *So human,* thought Morris.

To do good. It quietly came again. His eyes followed the line of a tree as the trunk lifted itself from the ground, and split upward into branches, splitting again into the ends of twigs, still with some leaves, hanging over the street. *The tree "does good,"* he thought: piece upon piece, delicate and created. Even the concrete on the pavement "does good"; each slab laid with effort, an act of creation, however crude. He remembered the acts of generosity and even mercy that he had known: some as small as a clerk running to give him change he had forgotten; some as important as Sarah listening to his plans. Before, he had seen them as individual acts, which, though pleasant, possessed little power to change a life. But as he stood there, it seemed that together they had been the grace that enabled him to live.

"Maybe in this sense there is goodness," he whispered: not as a high ideal, nor even as a nicety, but as a force or strength, hidden and eternal. It was in this way that goodness lived: slowly gathering up the petty acts of cruelty, reclaiming what was lost. He had tried to use it as a payment for evil, but it could never be. If it was to be found, it would only be as loved for itself. It was justified in its own intent. It lived in its own creation. Morris looked around. It seemed as if behind everything, holding every stick in place was this surge of goodness; holding even him in the grip of life. His chest tightened as his hand gripped the railing and his expression disfigured. His breathing came in heavy convulsions and sobs, as large warm tears found their way down his face.

He raised his head, not knowing how long he had stood there. He tried to find something to blow his nose with, and looked around, feeling embarrassed in case anyone had seen him. His head felt sluggish. He looked up at a break in the clouds, the edges glowing in the bright light of the sun, and diffused by the rain still falling. Slate-blue shapes intermixed with blushes of lavender and gold. Rain swept into places of sunlight and hung briefly in the air as windows of stained glass. "Blessings," said Morris. He breathed deeply, then took a step onto the pavement.

Monday, by the press, he watched a plant he had placed on the work table there. He had bought several on Saturday, and was intending to take one at a time to work and rotate them every day or so. The stem was slender and darker green, with wide leaves that looked lush but also delicate against the grey-green metal table. He had bought it as a symbol of all that he felt was happening in his life: as a statement of his discovery of goodness and the hope that had brought him. Over the weekend he had been busy writing down ideas he started to have on spirituality and prayer. He had read the Bible he had bought again, and had even called around to see his parents on Sunday. Morris felt that he had a future again. There seemed so much to learn, that he did not know where to begin. He leaned and rearranged the plant just a little. It moved ever so slightly with some draft.

Mr. Stewart walked up next to the press. He stepped around Morris and stood still in front of the plant; his eyes squinted, looking through the lower part of his glasses. Morris shifted uneasily.

"Is 'tis your plant Mitser Tailor?" he asked.

Morris answered, "Yes."

" 'Tat is good," Mr. Stewart said, "My vife, she keeps a gardten and now I do also. 'Tat is good . . . You do O.K." He mumbled something to himself. He checked his clipboard and walked over to another machine. Morris watched him as he talked to another operator. He thought that perhaps later he could talk with Mr. Stewart about this garden that he kept. That would be good. Morris felt full.

———

Margaret Bowinger watched the rain outside the door form into streams. In a minute she would walk outside and she prepared herself for the ordeal. She had always been nervous of exposed and wide open spaces, but she had not considered it a problem. It was simply that she had preferred the security and peace of quiet rooms and smaller places. About five years ago she had found herself becoming quite anxious about going outside, but once outside had managed well enough.

Recently however, an acute fear had been settling on her as she would step outside, and hold her gripped until she was inside again. She could find no actual cause for it. She had a large burned area on the left side of her face, but she considered that she had long ago learned to deal with that. She had understood it as God's will for her, as part of sharing in the sufferings of Christ, and had reconciled herself to the cross that had been placed upon her. She did not know why she feared the open spaces, and strange people. When she had mentioned it to Father McKinley, he had prayed with her and heard her confession, yet still she was afraid. With her mind she knew it was foolish, but still the fear would settle. She criticized herself for her lack of faith, and had never said anything to the other sisters. She survived by walking the street concentrating on her destination, looking neither to the right nor left, keeping a steady, firm, but quick, pace. Sometimes it seemed as if the street became a grey tunnel with only her own path visible. She would have to talk with Sister Louise. Sister Louise was a very wise person. She had been very helpful to her before.

Edward Anderson has lived in numerous places, including four years in S.E. London where his story is set. He has also worked a variety of jobs, some in factories similar to the one in "Benedictus Qui Venit." His interests lie primarily in the arts (both parents are artists) but include "music, some sports and movies, and good conversations with friends." Currently he is in the fourth year of an M. Div. program and hopes to combine some aspect of ministry with literature, theology, and possibly art.

PATRICIA C. HANLON

SO SEND
I YOU

*J*ulie paused at the back entrance to the mall, standing half in shadow, half in white morning sunlight. Another Julie squinted back at her in the brown glass door, the face sliced diagonally by the tall shadow, the dark hair scraped back into a hasty and severe ponytail. She looked awful, but that didn't matter much, not anymore. She looked away from her reflection, down at the callused hand pressed against the glass.

—Go in. Now. Just go ahead and push it open.

The thick door shut with a sucking noise behind her, and she felt the chill and whoosh of conditioned air, and heard—just barely, the way you could just barely see pinprick stars on a clear night—the hum of tube lighting. She hadn't expected to feel it so sharply, this sense of having landed in enemy territory.

"Mommy, look at that girl." The child strained against his mother's hand, pointing toward her.

There it was, in the child's gesture—a little bit of the fire already, the fire of the Lord's hard love. She would come out of that fire eventually all pure and shining, like gold purged of its dross. But that wouldn't happen until the end of all time, when the new heaven and the new earth had begun. All the brothers and sisters at Glory Farm would be there, if they persevered in their walk with the Lord, and it would be like a mild spring morning forever. The oat grass, soft like goose down, would cover the hills and valleys, and there would always be flowers— lupine, honeysuckle, poppies, bougainvillea. She imagined a mountain, too, obscured by bright mist at its summit. They would all climb up the mountain together, into that great, unimaginable light.

The child scowled at her as his mother riffled through blouses on an overstuffed sale rack outside May Company. Julie fingered the tiny gold ball she wore on a chain around her neck, the only piece of jewelry she hadn't given away when she'd moved out to the Farm. It was real gold, round and perfect under her dusty overalls and coarse workshirts. It was an emblem of the incorruptible life within her, which was hidden deep within the rough husk of blood and bones and sweat and dirt.

She touched the necklace again, felt the scared-rabbit pounding of her heart, but walked right up to the child anyway. Yes, that was right, just to walk on over and not think about it so much. She pulled a small leaflet from a bulging back pocket.

"Would you like this little book to color? It's something special just for kids." That was what she had decided to say for starters, and she had the rest of it pretty well memorized, too. Get the child talking about the pictures in the book, Jud had coached her this morning on the Farm bus—a heart black with sin on the first page, then the heart washed clean and white by Jesus—and often the mothers would start talking to you, too. But the child had shoved the book in his front overalls pocket, and the mother—not much older than Julie, probably married right out of high school—was wiggling two fingers impatiently at the child.

"Come *on*, Joshua, Mommy's going to try these on now." Then she spoke to Julie. "You know, I appreciate your efforts and all, but we're Catholic. We've got our own church." The mother gave her a tiny crooked smile and walked away toward the blue-and-mauve walls of the junior department. The child trailed after her, still staring.

Julie sank onto a bench outside the May Company. There was an old man at the far end of the bench, skinny and pale as a picked chicken inside his polo shirt and golf pants. He cleared his throat several times, whinnying. The ribbed nylon socks had slid all the way down into the backs of his shoes. Julie wanted to pull them back up, and to smooth the nubby stretch fabric of the shirt over the man's bony shoulders. She looked sideways at him, trying to catch his eye. But he was scraping at his teeth with a horny yellowed thumbnail.

Jud would know what to say. He could march right up to strangers and ask if they knew what would happen to them if they were to die right this second, where they would go to spend eternity. He had a real burden for reaching unbelievers—he actually *saw* people, he had told her once, as though they were standing at the edge of a cliff, about to plunge over into eternal sorrow, and it was up to him to put out a hand and warn them.

Melinda, too, would have said something about the Lord by now, something in that easy California drawl of hers. It was a voice smooth and rich as butter, and it soothed and stroked and patted away at people's defenses.

Julie remembered the mink-coat lady, who, just last week in this same exact mall, sat next to Melinda and five-month-old Elijah. Melinda had gotten the lady talking about when you were supposed to introduce solid foods to your baby and what brand of iron-fortified cereal was the best to use, Gerber's or Beech-

Nut. The woman dandled the baby on her fur-covered knee, singing trot-trot to Boston, trot trot to Lynn, while Elijah girgled over the softness of the coat beneath him, raking his plump fingers over the brown furrows.

Julie'd noticed the purplish lipstick that had way overshot its mark, and the swollen feet in little sparkly shoes. But Melinda looked past all that and told the woman that it was surely a lovely coat.

"Thank you, dear," the woman answered, sighing. "It was a gift from my late husband. He passed, oh, ten, 'leven years ago now."

Then Melin sort of petted the fur on the woman's arm; she could do that without it looking strange because the woman was still holding Elijah with that arm, and so Melin was touching Elijah at the same time.

"This coat of yours," she'd said. "When I see it I can't help thinking about Jesus. I mean, think of all the little animals that *gave up their lives* to make it. Sort of like Jesus, pouring out His life for us."

Julie turned pink around the ears, remembering. She just might rather die than say something like that. But that was okay, to feel shame and pain now and then. It was a sign that the old self was dying off, bit by scabby bit. She would share Jesus with this old man here, no matter what it cost her. The bigger fool she was the better.

And then the joy of the Spirit, which came and went as it pleased, descended upon her. It was, as always, like warm water poured down her back, surging toward her toes and fingertips, and making her head pound. Things looked different when the joy came; something barely perceptible about light and shade maybe, as if the glory spread itself around like a fine sprinkling of fairy dust. Once she'd had ear wax suctioned out at the doctor's, and afterwards sounds were bright and clean, as though they'd been scoured of a thick gray residue. It was like that now, the dull film stripped away to reveal glory everywhere. Behind her the glass exit doors were opaque with it, shot through with sunlight.

And the old man. Julie could see in him the face of the child he had once been and perhaps still was in God's eyes, since God wasn't bound by time. It was the opposite of those artist's renderings of what famous people would look like in thirty years' time—Jackie O. or Twiggy or Robert Redford with eyebags and throats gone to turkey-wattles. She was going back in time instead, fleshing out the man's gaunt hands, extracting from the sunken jaw a rounded child's mouth, turning the withered ears to little peach halves.

She smiled encouragingly at the old man, who turned toward her, childlike and doddering all at the same time, all in the same face. He smiled back. They held the smile between them, like folding a blanked together, and then the man said something, or maybe he was just clearing his throat. He said it again.

"Yaw a heffah!" That was what it sounded like.

"Exuse me?"

"Heffah!" He began to laugh, making little sawing noises in his throat; but it was kind laughter, really, as if the two of them were old friends sharing some enormously funny joke. Only she didn't know what the joke was.

She looked down at the zipper of her rucksack. It was jammed with a corner of her red kerchief. She began to ease the cloth from between the metal teeth; but he was saying that thing again, whatever it was. She looked up and tried to smile even though she couldn't understand him, to show concern and interest, but the corners of her mouth had turned to starch.

"HEF-fah." He spit a little, saying it. When she didn't answer, he looked away, defeated. She had hurt his feelings.

"Oh, *Arthur*." It was a voice from behind, belonging to a pair of shoes that came tapping quickly across the floor. Arthur looked over his shoulder, guileless, and the woman, wispy-haired, and smelling slightly of face powder, spoke to Julie in a stage whisper.

"He used to be a cattle man, so he always called girls heifers. You know, a young cow. One that hasn't had a calf yet," the woman added, as if that made everything clear. She glanced sidelong at Julie's dusty feet and ratty thongs, then eased Arthur off his bench, asking if he might like to go get a nice sandwich somewhere—McDonald's? Denny's? Carrow's?

And with that, the glory departed altogether, like the last slight circling of bath water down the drain.

Stiff-faced, she got up from her bench, walked down the mall toward a strobe-lit shop whose mannequins stood glowering in odd positions—shoulders hunched up and hips thrust forward, fingers distended like bird claws. The desire to be alone was swelling in her.

She turned into the shop. She would pretend to be trying something on, anything at all. She pulled three of the same kind of blouse off a swaying overhead rack, then realized her mistake. You had to take different kinds of things, of course; she'd forgotten what it was like to go shopping. She put two of the blouses back and took another, plus a pair of pants.

A bored clerk handed her a plastic number three, pointing at an empty cubicle.

It was pale blue inside, with two mirrors slanted at angles to each other, so you could see yourself front, back and sides. Above were acoustical tiles, the kind with irregularly-spaced holes. They would drive you crazy looking for a pattern to them.

She sat with her knees drawn up to her chest, her back to the mirrors, eyes shut tight so that she saw a warm orange-brown instead of that dead flourescent blue. She held one hand up in a gesture of surrender, and her lips moved soundlessly.

—Lamb of God, who takes away the sins of the world. Have mercy on me, a sinner.

That was what Jud prayed over her the day she was saved, his big hands pressing down on her head, telling her to repeat it after him, and to keep on repeating it, and repenting of all her sins, until the Spirit descended.

"Be patient, little one," he'd told her then. "This isn't a magic trick, something you conjure up like saying a spell. I've waited on the Lord all night before, on my knees, sometimes longer than that. You just turn yourself inside out, now; give everything to Him. His Holy Spirit can't fill you unless you're all clean and swept-out."

They were down at the creek then, down under the big ragged eucalyptus tree. Even now, almost a year later, she could recall that menthol smell from the tree, and the slight breeze ruffling her hair as she said the words over and over until she really meant them, nearly swooned with wanting that mercy. Melin had stood next to her, a hand on Julie's shoulder, making soft sounds that wove like tendrils around the thick vine of Jud's voice.

It had grown to be all light inside her head, brilliant white-hot light. The others were so close she could feel them breathing on her face and neck and shoulders, and they were singing about the Lord on his throne, high and lifted up, and the angels crying holy, holy, holy is the Lord. She saw something of the glory and the mercy, then; clutched at the lambent hem of it, anyway. It was colors and wheels and fiery jewels, and a face—she caught the eyes of that face and then, in what seemed the next instant, she was wondering why the bed was so hard, and why people were trying to prod her awake.

"You were singing in the Spirit. And then you went down, just like a bowling pin," Melin said, helping her up and then brushing the dirt and grass from Julie's hair with gentle fingertips.

"One of the sweetest songs I've ever heard," Jud added. "And we likely won't hear it again—not exactly the same one, anyway—until we're all in glory together. Sing it for us then, will you? At the wedding feast of the Lord."

Yes, oh yes. She would count it all joy to do whatever he asked, then and now. And right now she ought to be out there in front of Sears, passing out tracts and letting her light shine, instead of in here hiding it under a bushel basket.

She got up, seeing amoeba-like spots on the cubicle wall. "Just be a channel for Jesus," Jud had told her on the way down this morning, spacing his words carefully between the bangings and rattlings of the old school bus. "Just let Him come on through. If there's too much Julie clogging things up, people won't be able to see Him. You see how that works."

She left the cubicle behind, handing a tract to the dressing-room attendant along with the clothes and the plastic number. The girl was cat-eyed and sullen, her blue dress pulled tight under the arms. Julie felt her chest swell with love and grief both.

"I won't bother you while you're working; I just wanted to leave this with you. It tells about the spiritual laws that govern our lives, just like gravity governs our physical lives. Maybe you could read it sometime."

But the girl turned to adjust the clothes hung on the rack behind her, her slim little backside to Julie.

Lord, she was tired.

Her old self was dying off, for sure. She could feel it going, like tattered sunburnt skin getting peeled away. At the edges, though, were tender patches not ready to come off. Being here, doing what she was doing, was like having that live skin pulled right off her back.

But when Jesus came again, all of that would matter precisely not at all.

He would come like the morning sun, and would call out to His own, to the ones the Father had given Him from before the beginning of time.

This calling-out and gathering-up could happen a minute from now, a second, even.

Just the thought of it made her catch her breath, and go weak-kneed and aching with desire.

Patricia C. Hanlon owns and runs a small handmade-furniture and art gallery business in Gloucester, Massachusetts. She has a linguistics and rhetoric degree from Northeastern University and has taught writing there and at Gordon College.

"Passing out 'Four Spiritual Laws' tracts to strangers is something that would be excruciatingly difficult for me to do, so it was intriguing to get inside Julie's mind and find out how she was feeling. Also, friends of mine lived at communities like Glory Farm back in the mid-seventies."

Patricia plans to keep writing, raise her three children, and build up the family business. Her latest writing project is a novel

BLACK ICE

His father stole the puck and now Jimmy gripped his stick as his father broke clear of the pack and bore down on Johnny Ryan's father in goal. Mr. Ryan moved out from the net to meet him, trying to cut down his angle, but he was too slow, his father was on him now and Jimmy held his breath. His father's left shoulder dipped, Mr. Ryan bit. A graceful sweep right, then the backhand flip into a wide open net. Piece of cake, Jimmy imagined him saying. He relaxed the grip on his stick, let out a long, deep breath and started to smile.

Out on the pond his father did a tight pirouette from the goal and glided over to the keg of beer he'd provided. He was a beer salesman and got it at discount, and wouldn't think of letting anyone else chip in. Jimmy watched him fish a plastic cup out of the sweaters strewn around the keg, saw the heads of the other men thrown back at something he'd said. His father's own laughter, faint yet jarring, broke the silence in the cove and suddenly it all came back to Jimmy, the night before, what his father had said, and he stopped smiling. He looked away now, as if by averting his eyes he could close his ears to the sound.

The ground was cold under his father's faded green Marine Corps duffel bag, serving as a seat cushion, and he shivered slightly. He looked down at his new skates dangling over the bank, their untested silvery blades safely removed from the surrounding mix of dirt and snow. Beyond them the black ice stretched the length of the cove like a new-washed pane of glass, so clear he imagined being able to reach down to touch the dead leaves littering the pond bottom. Their clarity unnerved him, for some reason, and he shivered again. He'd grown up skating on black ice; it was the best ice there was if your skates were sharp, and he knew it was thick and hard because he could see the proof in the thin white cuts his father's skates had made. Still . . . he wondered where the ice turned to water, down there. He couldn't tell really. It was so dark, that icy water; its darkness seemed to fill the cove, as if to darken it from below.

He let his stick fall gently onto his lap and hugged his arms tight to his stomach. Past the thick spires of pines keeping the cove in perpetual shade the rest of the pond shimmered in the winter sun and the glare off the bluish-white surface hurt his eyes. He could see where the black ice left off and the other began and to him it might as well have been the distant line of the horizon on some flat, arctic ocean. His father had the puck again. He could have been a million miles away.

They usually approached the pond from the main beachfront down the way, but for some reason his father had driven to this end today. Jimmy heard the cries of the kids down there, but couldn't see them for all the trees penning the cove. Johnny Ryan would be down there, and Frankie Russo and Eddie Joyce. Briefly he considered cutting through the woods to join them, but no. He couldn't tromp through the woods in his new skates. Besides, he always played with the men on Saturday. His friends were still at the ankle-bending stage, it was easy for him to dominate their games. But Jimmy had started young. Already he could keep up with most of the men.

Saturday was their day, his and his father's. The day they forgot about tests at school, hassles with customers. On Saturdays they even skipped their daily ritual of attending Mass, so they could catch the good ice. Later it got soft from the sun and the sharp blades digging at it, chewing it up. But the early morning ice was hard, like glass. They were always the first ones on it, and seeing the lone cuts of their skates Jimmy sometimes imagined God's eyes watching, approving that it was them christening the virgin ice. When it was just the two of them like that his father would make him leave his stick behind and just skate.

"Stay low! From the hips!" he'd bark, his long shadow in front of Jimmy like a third skater as they whirled side by side from one end of the pond to the other. Jimmy's eyes never left his shadow as he matched it stride for stride, mirroring it down to the swing of its arms. Eventually the others would show up and the game began. But nothing beat their early morning skate, when they had the pond to themselves. Then the wind in his hair, the sound of his father's hard breathing next to him seemed to lift him right off the ice, until he imagined himself skating on air.

A thin, beckoning finger of light from the slow-rising sun beamed through a crack in the wall of pines, reflecting off one of his skates. Jimmy followed the current of light back into the trees. It reminded him of the way the light left Father Martin's gold chalice when he raised it during the consecration, a single, flashing, sharp-edged light. The sun was getting up there; the regular Mass would have ended and Father would be at the side altar by now. Jimmy pictured him alone at the altar and felt a flick of guilt. Poor Father: no one there to pour out his water and wine, to answer his prayers. He stared into the trees but, mysteriously, the

crack had closed, the light had disappeared. The cove was dark
again.

Father Martin set the altar boy schedules and lately had been
assigning more and more daily Masses to Jimmy. Or "Mr. Doyle,"
as Father called him sometimes. He liked that, "Mr. Doyle," and
since becoming an altar boy he did feel older, different somehow. He no longer worried so much about school, wasn't so
easily goaded into fights by his older sister Katie. He'd even taken
to padding around the house the way Father moved on the altar:
softly, quietly. It drove Katie wild.

"He's doing it again, Mommy," she'd complain bitterly. "He's
sneaking up on me again."

He knew he was becoming a great favorite of Father Martin,
and hadn't Father complimented him just last week on the way
he rang the bells during the consecration?

"Beautiful job with the bells today, Mr. Doyle," he'd said.

"Thank you, Father."

"You know, I might have you give a little clinic at my next altar
boy class. The awful noises some of those guys make," Father
clucked. "Why, it's a wonder old Haggerty hasn't had a heart
attack, the racket Joyce makes sometimes. Imagine the poor
man's shock, Jimmy. One minute he's traipsing o'er the green
fields of home, the next there's a three-alarm fire going off in his
head."

"My grandfather's from the same place in Ireland as Mr. Haggerty," Jimmy blurted.

"I know Jimmy, I know. And it wasn't easy for them when they
came here, believe me." Father's face grew thoughtful. "No, not
easy at all." He looked down at Jimmy, then brightened again.

"But that was a long time ago. Nothing for my favorite little
bell ringer to worry about," and he ruffled Jimmy's hair.

Blushing, Jimmy almost said, "It's all in the wrist, Father," but
caught himself. He didn't want to seem swell-headed. After all, at

ten he was the youngest altar boy in the parish. Besides, if there was anything his father hated it was a show-off. "Stop shapin'!" he growled whenever he thought Jimmy was getting too full of himself. Like the time a couple of weeks ago when he'd raced his friends across the pond and started skating backwards, teasing them as they tried to catch him. He'd sensed his father's watchful eyes, turned to see his shaking head and slipped on a dead leaf frozen into the ice. His crowing friends whizzed past and he lay still, waiting for his father to lift him off the ice, the way he used to when Jimmy would fall. But his friends' shouts were dim whispers on the winter air when he realized his father had skated away. Slowly he'd picked himself up, dusting the snow from his legs.

"Kid's a born defenseman. You should see him skate backwards," he heard his father tell his mother that night, when he thought Jimmy wasn't around to overhear.

He'd found out about the side altar Mass a couple of months ago. He'd just walked off the altar one day after serving Mass for Father Chioffaro when he was mystified to see Father Martin setting out his vestments. Outside of a funeral there was only one Mass scheduled on weekdays. He didn't say anything, but after hanging up his cassock and surplice he lingered in the back of the church, and when Father came out to the side altar with the chalice and the cruets filled with water and wine it dawned on him: a priest has to say Mass every day, he remembered. Without a word he'd walked over to the side altar and taken up his post, behind Father and to his right. It was a close call to make it to school on time that day. But he ran all the way and just made it.

Now every weekday the chapel emptied after Mass and he waited alone in the pews off to the side. He loved the peace of those early mornings: the sleepy light filtering soft through the stained-glass windows, muted by the dark brown pews and confessional closets lining the wall. The candles in rows between the side and main altars, short red ones in front, behind and above them taller, blue ones, casting vague shadows on the crucifix nailed into the dark wall above. Sometimes in the flickering shadows Jimmy imagined His sad eyes looking down on him and he strained in the dim light, searching them out, forgetting all about Father until the sweep of Father's cassock on the floor broke his trance. Then he moved to the small altar set into the sacristy wall and here, against the white altar cloth and white-washed walls, the shadows deepened and took shape. Father in a simple white cowl spoke his Latin softly, so softly the words might have come from his shadow on the altar. But Jimmy didn't have to hear to know when to whisper back the right response. At Mass's end Father simply nodded his thanks and Jimmy stole out the side door, then ran for school.

Of course, Sunday was the big day for everyone else. Jimmy sat benignly through the sermon, bemused at mothers and daughters in pretty dresses, fathers and sons in suitcoats and ties and fresh-shined shoes. From the altar he looked out on Miss Leary his teacher, prim in a dark dress; old Mr. Haggerty, drowsy already in the back of the church; his friends in a whispery huddle, Ryan and Russo and Eddie Joyce. They were such kids!

There'd be his family all in a row. Mom in her favorite blue dress and black felt hat with its thin-meshed veil, Katie scowly beside her, then the three little ones fidgety, buffed and polished like prized red apples on display in a supermarket. His father impassive as Father Martin spoke from the pulpit: "For all men He suffered . . ." The shifting of feet, scattered coughs. Sunday pretenders! The racket of his father honking into his handkerchief would ring out. Incredible, the volume of that honk, like a wounded goose.

He heard the honk now and looked up to see him glide into the cove. He set his teeth to stop their chattering. His father pulled up, stuffing his handkerchief back into his pocket, then leaning casually on his stick. He reminded Jimmy of a Confederate soldier leaning on his long musket, broken-nosed, gaunt and hungry-eyed, like the one pictured in his history book.

"Hey kid, we could use some fresh legs out there."

Jimmy shrugged and looked down at the black ice. Below the surface a bright orange carp swam slowly, aimlessly back and forth, as if trying to stay warm. The sound of ice meeting ice boomed like a thunderclap somewhere out on the pond.

"Must be awful cold just sittin' there, huh? Ya cold?"

"No."

"Feel sick?"

"No."

His father looked down, idly tapping his stick against the snow caught in his skates.

"Hmm. He's not cold, he's not sick." He looked up. "What're ya, a sissy?"

Jimmy stiffened. There it was again, that same flat, hard voice from the night before and now it all came back to him, the feeling from the night before that the voice came from someone else, from some impostor pretending to be his father. He stared at his father now and tears started in his eyes. *Don't cry,* he told himself, *whatever you do, don't let him see you cry.*

He looked down at his new skates, gleaming again from another patch of light breaking through the trees. He'd been so excited the night before when his father brought them home. New Bauers, just like the pros wore! He could still smell the sharp leather, could see his father's smile when, trembling, he'd taken them out of the box. In his rush to try them on he'd cut his thumb on the edge of a blade. "Easy, kid," his father had laughed, applying a band aid to the wound. Idly now Jimmy picked at the bandage until it came loose. He rubbed a fingernail around the frozen cut, feeling the dry, wrinkled skin.

"C'mon kid, you're missin' all the good ice," his father said, softening. "You wanta try out those new skates, don't ya?"

Jimmy started picking out patterns on the dead leaves under the ice. Softly, he said: "I should be at Mass."

"What?"

"I should be at Mass. Father will be all alone today."

"Christ, can't you take one lousy day off from those priests? Huh?"

It was his father who'd started him going to daily Mass, before he was old enough for school even. Jimmy remembered how he used to trail after him, struggling to keep pace as they left the house; two silent, shadowy figures in the pre-dawn darkness, the crunch of their boots on the dry snow echoing in the still morning air. Then arriving at the church and always that fresh feeling of rediscovery, as if he were entering an old familiar world. Sometimes they were the only ones there and Jimmy couldn't help feeling it was a world made specially for them; a mysterious, dark-lit, timeless world, far removed from the slow-wakening world outside. Kneeling together in the soft light and warmth of the chapel, Jimmy would mimic his father's every move, down to the modest bow of his head, the clasp of his hands.

But now by the time his father's honking sinuses woke the house Jimmy was out the door, alone in the snowy street, arriving at the sacristy early to tend to his duties. Filling the cruets with water and wine, lighting the candles, setting out the Book. Then leading Father to the altar, to another even more private world where nothing beyond the altar rail mattered. Afterwards he had his side altar Mass to serve, by which time his father would be gone.

He felt his father's gaze and raised his to see him shaking his head.

"Sit there all day, makes no difference to me." He turned, did a little hop to accelerate and headed back out to where his friends were circled around Mr. Ryan, who'd just stopped a hard shot with his head. Jimmy watched him leave the cove. The shivering he'd stifled broke with a pent-up energy, like an imploding crystal of glass. He looked out at the fresh cuts of his father's skates on the black ice and with a final, convulsed shudder closed his eyes and forced himself still.

"He, he didn't dent my puck, did he?" His father's shout, like clanging metal in an empty room, echoed through the still cove.

The night before, when Mr. Ryan came over to watch the hockey game with his father, Jimmy had joined them in the basement. They liked having him around to fetch their beer for them, and he felt privileged in this role, in a way. No one else in the family was allowed down there when his father had company. Although Mr. Ryan could be a pain. He drank faster than Jimmy's father and always seemed out of synch, so Jimmy would no sooner make a run than Mr. Ryan sent him up to the kitchen again.

"Kid." The game had just started and his father pointed to his empty beer can.

Jimmy automatically looked to Mr. Ryan, but there was no signal there and he ran upstairs. Returning, he caught his father in mid-sentence.

". . . so I says to the guy, whattaya mean you only ordered ten cases? I got it written down right here, twenty cases of bar bottles. What's it, my fault you had a slow week? I gotta pay for your problems?

"So he says 'Well, I don't remember order no twenty cases.' He no speaka the Inglaise too good, know what I mean? At this point I go into my act."

His father stood up and slowly lifted his hands, palms upward, to the ceiling. Rolling his head onto his neck, he said in a loud voice, "God, why me? What did I do, that you put me here in the South End with these people, me with five kids and guys half my age cleanin' up out in Brighton and Newton? Tell me, what did I do to deserve this shit? Willya tell me please?"

He shook with laughter. "I'm tellin' ya, I did everything but strike my breast three times. That poor spic didn't know what to do. Finally he says, 'Okay, okay, I take the twenty.' "

"Did he really order twenty cases?" Mr. Ryan asked.

"No you dummy, that's the whole point. I padded my order, see? Christ, I've been cheatin' those Puerto Ricans down there for years. How d'ya think I feed these kids? By charity work?" He sat down, picked up his beer and turned back to the game, still chuckling. Jimmy couldn't tell what his father thought funnier, his own performance or Mr. Ryan's dimwittedness.

"Only you, Doyle, only you," Mr. Ryan said, laughing himself now.

When the game ended and Jimmy went to bed he lay still, trying to go to sleep. From the den downstairs he heard the rustle of his mother's newspaper, the crack of a beer opening. There was a plopping sound as his father settled into his chair.

"So how was your day?"

"Not bad," he heard from his mother. There was a pause, as if she were considering something. "Jimmy's teacher called today. He was late for school again."

"That kid." Jimmy pictured his father's shaking head. "At the church?"

His mother must have simply nodded.

"Christ, don't those priests know he's got school?"

"They don't ask him to do it; he volunteers. Father Martin says he's the only kid who's ever done it, in his memory."

"Well, it's time we put an end to it."

"I suppose." There was another pause, then his mother laughed. "Father calls him his shadow. Says he's never seen such a serious little kid."

"Too serious for his own good, if you ask me. He spends too much time with those goddamn priests."

"Oh, come on Jim . . . "

His father cut her off, his voice a weary growl. "It's a hard world out there and it's about time he realized it. He's gettin' older now."

Suddenly alert, Jimmy rose halfway from his bed, straining for his mother's response. The house was still. He lay back then turned onto his side, arms wrapped tight over his stomach. He closed his eyes, but soon his father's snores began to drift up from the den, deep snores that filled the quiet house. In between, his low whistling breaths were like spent waves.

Jimmy exhaled noisily, as if trying to blow the pressure in his stomach right out of him. It was not good, though, he saw it still too clearly: the dull flush of his father's broken-veined face when he'd stood, the crooked smile. The too loud voice when he'd said, "God, why me?" Did his father really have to cheat, to feed him and Katie and the others? He wondered if the Puerto Ricans cheated, to get food. And if so, whom.

There was a loud snort from the den. The air whooshed out of his father's chair, there was a lurching step, a muttered "good night." His father tripped on the stairs and cursed. Through hooded eyes, Jimmy watched his shadow pass his door.

He pulled his blanket tight around him. His mother always turned down the heat after putting them to bed. Already the house seemed cold. Shivering slightly, he curled around the lump in his stomach and stared into the darkness. "For all men He suffered . . . " Father had said. Jimmy closed his eyes again, and now he could hear Father's soft voice, could see him at the altar, his face furrowed in prayer. Suddenly drowsy, he began his own whispery prayer. Our Father . . . father . . . Father . . . father . . .

Now he shook uncontrollably. The thin cuts his father's blades had made on the black ice stared up at him like an accusation. He lifted his head in time to see someone's stick catch in his father's skates, sending him crashing to the ice. The spill made him wince and he held his breath. *Get up, Dad, get up* he urged silently, but his father lay in a heap where he'd fallen.

Jimmy stood up. Throat tight, he took a tentative step onto the ice and his legs, cramped and weak, buckled and nearly collapsed. Like a newborn foal, he righted himself and pushed off with his skates. He glided slowly out about ten yards into the cove, holding his breath, as if to make himself lighter. The ice was hard and sure. Exhaling deeply, he pivoted and glided back to the bank, where he stopped and turned. His father lay still on the ice.

Jimmy stared out at the fallen figure of his father and gripped his stick. Head down, he dug the inside edges of his blades into the black ice and began to skate. Halfway across the cove he sensed his speed pick up and churned ahead with fury, pushing hard from side to side. From the hips, just like Dad taught me, he spurred himself on. Leaving the dark cove, he felt the pressure explode out of him, mingling with the light and the wind and the cold air and seeming to lift him right off the ice, propelling him forward.

"Dad!" he cried. "Dad!"

His father turned and jumped to his feet just in time to catch Jimmy in his arms. Grinning, he lifted him and held him close.

"All right, here he is. We'll see some moves now."

"Dad, are you okay?"

His father smiled. "Sure, I'm okay, kid. I was just takin' a little rest."

"I thought you were hurt."

"Naw, who could hurt an old Marine like me?" He laughed.

Jimmy was panting. His frozen nostrils, loosened by his sprint across the ice, ran freely and he gulped in the cold air.

"You had me worried," he gasped.

"Ah, you're like your mother. You worry too much."

A flooding warmth broke inside Jimmy, melting out to his hands and feet. The cut on his finger throbbed. He stared into his father's eyes and blurted: "Dad?"

"Yeah, kid?"

"You won't cheat the Puerto Ricans anymore?"

His father met Jimmy's stare with silence. Gently, he dropped him to the ice.

"Dad?"

"Yeah, sure kid. No more cheating," he said quietly, so quietly the wind rushing over the pond seemed to steal the words right off his lips. But Jimmy was sure he'd heard them.

He swallowed freely, warm in his father's shadow, and looked around him. Out in mid-ice his father's cronies battled for a loose puck. Down by the beachfront the kids played whip-the-whip. The cove and its black ice sat off in the distance.

"Hey kid, whattaya say we show these guys where we come from."

"Yeah, let's show 'em where we come from."

Jack McNamara works as mail clerk in Cambridge, Massachusetts and fills non-working hours with literature and music. "Black Ice" came from his own memories: " . . . sitting on the bank of a pond, staring at an expanse of black ice, and being filled with dread that I would fall through if I stepped out onto it. The story is a fictional attempt to explain how a young boy can overcome his fear, in this case by an overwhelming need to re-connect with his father." He has a "drawerful" of story ideas and intends to keep developing them.

THE BODY

*N*athan woke up one morning feeling odd.

It frightened him so he took one look at the rumpled sheets vacated an hour ago by Betty, listened to make sure she had left for work, then jumped up and went into the bathroom.

He faced his image in the mirror. Couldn't see the bald spot from in front, but it was there. He felt it with a soft hand; it was up there, certainly bigger today than yesterday, growing like a cancer, chomping at the rim of black hair, yawning wider and wider like the deep and indifferent mouth of age. That wasn't odd. Awful, but not odd.

The soft stomach wasn't the odd thing either. What do you expect of the stomach of a forty-five-year-old man?

"What's so odd about *me?*" he asked himself while sitting at the table eating his figs and sipping his warm milk. Morning sunlight streamed through the windows and the yellow curtains.

"I'm a normal guy. Let's not have any more of this oddness nonsense. It'll go away." He went to work.

But it didn't go away. There was no work to be done downstairs at the firm this morning so he sat in his office drumming his fingers for a few minutes. He felt funny. He opened his deep drawer and took out this month's magazines. He leaned back in his large swivel chair, cradling the half-dozen magazines on his lap, deciding which one to look at first. None was particularly good this month.

"Let's not make a big deal out of this," he said aloud, though in a careful undertone (which you got used to employing in the building). "Let's just take the top one."

The top one had a layout of girls on convertible sports cars. The smirky brunette was his favorite one—the only one where it didn't look as if the girl were lying on a slab. He leafed through the rest. Threw the magazine back into the drawer.

The next magazine liked to have its girls tan and oiled up. It didn't look like real flesh. Looked preserved.

He leafed through the back pages of the next one, which had personal ads. He wasn't interested in any of them.

Bodies. Bodies. He threw them all into the drawer and checked his watch for the date. Next month's magazines wouldn't be out for fourteen days.

He swivelled around and looked out the window. Then he called Jill, his girlfriend.

An hour later they sat in Harvey's Ice Cream Boutique pretending not to be special friends. He *always* felt odd with Jill, but not this kind of oddness. It was such a small town. She was dressed vanilla—white ruffled skirt that was very short when she crossed her legs under the glass table. Nathan felt that she sat back farther from him than usual. A pretty little blonde, he thought as he watched her talking; she should have gone to college last year. Ah well, she needed money for that, and Nathan knew he was a good prospect for money. Isn't anybody genuine anymore; is everybody after something? It occurred to him that she seemed to edge farther away from him every minute—and she always did that when he met her during working hours. Up until this very moment he had thought she did that so as not to look like a Special Friend; now he realized that he probably had a smell. It was in his building. He couldn't smell it anymore, but others could.

All these years my wife put up with the smell? he thought as Jill talked. Then he looked closely at Jill. She smelled his odor. Jill must tell her friends: "I'm dating a married mortician. You can smell it on him; he has this sick, dead body smell and all those chemicals . . . "

He carefully put his thin stainless steel spoon into the stiff white milkshake, feeling a sick, revulsive thing in his stomach.

"Say, Jill, I just remembered I have an appointment. I'm sorry. I've got to run."

He stood and she said, "I'll pay for the milkshakes."

"Oh!" Nathan exclaimed. "I forgot! No, no! I'll pay for this." He reached into his pocket and rushed to the cash register, his head reeling a little bit. The world seemed to be going a little faster than he was, and he was trying to catch up at the edge of his balance, trying not to look inebriated or throw up or fall down. He stood thinking of nothing as he got his change.

Nathan walked up the street to the mortuary, thinking that suddenly the leverage had slipped and the world was out of hand for him, and it was time to stop this nonsense. Just a little sitting quietly in his office. Maybe read something out of one of the devotional brochures.

He entered his office thinking he should have a headache. But he didn't. The office was odd. Heavy, thick walnut. His desk looked substantial, solid. The panelling on the walls was smooth and rich, shiny. Actually it was only veneer-thin stuff, but it looked solid.

The phone rang. The interoffice button was lit. He and Elvin, the President of Elvin Roberts Funeral Home, were the only ones in the building. Nathan felt his hand buzz a little—or thought he did—as he picked up the phone.

"Yes?"

"Nathan?" Elvin's voice sounded odd too! It was tentative. Elvin was never tentative with his employees, especially not with Nathan, and he usually called him Lydell. "Nathan, did you make the arrangements for this client we have down here?"

"Uh, I . . . No, I haven't made any arrangements today."

"*Nathan,* would you come down here please?"

Oh, no. Nathan put the receiver down and absently felt his stomach. There was something wrong. It's what you're always afraid of, Something Wrong. The whole profession is a veneer over Something Wrong. *Why does Elvin have to sound so urgent and so funny?*

"Unprofessional," Nathan said aloud as he went down the stairs. He pulled on the light, turning up the brightness all the way, then walked through the casket room. He ran his hand along the walnut model. At the other end he turned off the light, then pulled it on again, and went across the tile hallway to the embalming room.

On the table was the naked body of a brutalized man, a cloth over his face. Nathan felt perfectly normal now, professional. Elvin was a little watery around the eyes and his bald head trembled as usual as he talked, but both men being there together reassured each other and they got on with it. Elvin pointed out the brutal marks all over the body.

"He's been whipped, all over."

"Everything happens these days, even in small towns in Ohio, unfortunately," Nathan stated.

"Nathan," Elvin said evenly and somewhat angrily, "I want you to look carefully at the wrists and the feet."

Each wrist had a hole through it, as did the feet.

"This is sick, very sick," Nathan said. "I imagine you've called Don."

"Don is the sheriff."

"I *know* that," Nathan said. He didn't know why he was so annoyed at Elvin. "If this man is the victim of some kind—"

"Didn't you *look?*" Elvin said fiercely, his fat face sweating. He clenched his teeth. "What the hell is this, Nathan? *Nathan?* Look at the marks. Look, look! All over the body. The back is *shredded.* Below the middle the strokes are upward, above the middle the strokes are downward. Bruises. See? Here. Here. Nathan, I want you to see the face."

"I don't want to look at the face."

"All right. For now we won't look at the face. I want to tell you what is on the face."

"Blood. Bruises."

"Yes. Blood and bruises. And a line of puncture marks across the forehead and all around the head, Nathan. Do you *understand me?*"

"Just a minute," Nathan said. "We need to back off from this body. Let's go outside for a few minutes and discuss this. O.K.? Let's do that."

Nathan took Elvin by the arm and they walked out of the room and across the hallway and through the casket room, and then Nathan let go of Elvin's arm and they walked up the stairs. Nathan opened the door and they went out onto the veranda and sat on a wrought-iron bench.

You could see that Elvin wanted to cry. He wanted to put his hands to his face and cry. Nathan squared his shoulders. But his voice was not steady.

"What is it you think we have, Elvin?"

"Nathan, Nathan! What we have here is the body of Christ!" He looked at Nathan threateningly. "It's the *body* of *Christ.*"

"In the Elvin Roberts Funeral Home."

"Nathan, you saw it. You *saw* it. There is nothing wrong with me. There never has been anything wrong with me."

"I know."

"And there's nothing wrong with me now. What do we have here, Nathan? I want *you* to tell *me*."

"We have a victim of a murder. We have had murder victims several times. They duplicated the wounds of, of Christ on this man—"

"I want you to see the *face*, Nathan." Elvin gripped Nathan's arm; Elvin was a weak man and the grip was mush. "I want you to see the face!"

"I'm not going to *look* at the face." Nathan stood. "Listen, I'm not going to look at the face. I'm not. All right? I'm not."

"Sit down." Nathan sat, and Elvin Roberts dragged his shirt-sleeve across his forehead. Elvin was graying. He owned two small apartment buildings and a grocery store, and drove a Cadillac, and Nathan saw that Elvin Roberts was a boy, a fat boy who knew nothing and never had, and everybody always went along with him. He was nothing but a little boy.

"The Presbyterian Church doesn't train a guy well for such things, does it?" Nathan said calmly. "Nor does mortuary school. I think we'd better call Don. Everything will be all right."

The little boy Elvin Roberts looked Nathan in the eye. "You've always been strange. I've put up with you all these years."

"Strange!"

"And now I'm giving you an order."

"You can't—"

"Who else is going to employ you? You get fired here, are you going to take one of your girlfriends and start a business of your own here? Listen to me, Nathan, if it's the one and only and last time you ever do."

"This is unnecessary."

"Listen. Today is Friday. Nobody is going to touch that body, nobody is going to *know* about the body, until Monday morning. Do you understand?"

"I certainly don't understand. We have to embalm the body, we have to notify—"

"Nobody!" Elvin grunted viciously, his teeth clenched. "We notify *nobody* until Monday morning. I'll fire you, Nathan Lydell, if you let word of this out to *anybody.*" Elvin's face and his fists were shaking.

"We have to embalm the body!" Nathan shouted, standing.

"No!" Elvin stood.

"It's the *law.* If you want me to keep quiet and I don't know *why,* I'm not going to—at least I'm not going to stand by and have the law broken. We are professionals. Look, what's the matter here?"

Elvin took a deep breath. "If you want to embalm the body, go ahead. But no word." He moved his index finger slowly back and forth in the air. "No word."

"I don't understand this, Elvin."

Elvin calmed himself carefully. "You think we have an ordinary body down there, a body somebody brought in without our knowledge. And I think it's the body of Christ."

"Oh, Elvin."

"And I won't have a thing done, nothing said, until Monday morning."

"Then what?"

"Then we'll see whether you're right or I'm right. And I know I'm right."

"Of course you're not right. Of *course* you're not right! My gosh, Elvin, what's going on here?"

"You just look at his face."

"No Elvin. I said I wouldn't."

"You're going to embalm the body, aren't you?"

Nathan did not want to look at the face because he already believed.

Elvin understood that now. "Listen, it's all right. You go down and look at his face. There's nothing wrong with that."

"Holy," Nathan said. "If you're right," he added.

Elvin looked at Nathan very closely. "I don't know why you believe it, or why it happened here, or why I'm in charge. Please look at his face and tell me what you see."

Walking downstairs and going into the embalming room and lifting the linen cloth took more courage than Nathan had ever exercised, but he lifted the cloth and he saw that it was Christ, and he carefully put the cloth aside and he walked back upstairs and outside.

"He is to be embalmed," Nathan said. "It is a physical, human body, and it must be embalmed."

"I won't do it," Elvin said. "I couldn't."

"It has to be done. I'm going to do it. Will you help me?"

"No."

"*Please* help me."

"I . . . I'm sorry. No. No, I won't."

"All right. I'll do it myself. I want to tell someone else, Elvin."

"No."

"We have to tell Father Gerton."

"No. And not my minister either."

"They should know. It's insane not to tell the Church!"

"He came to us. He came to somebody who refuses to tell."

"Why do you refuse to tell?"

"Same reason you want to embalm Him. This isn't a world for Him to come to. There'd be people and cameras and tourists and shysters all over the body. Just *think* a minute!"

Nathan kept staring at Elvin's face. "Do you know what I am?" he asked calmly.

"What do you mean?"

"I'm an adulterer. And do you know I've been stealing from you every way I could for the past fifteen years?"

"Yes. Everybody knows."

"And you're afraid of *other* people desecrating the body? What are *you?* How holy are *you?*"

"You know."

Nathan sat on the bench. All at once he was completely exhausted. He was thinking rationally.

"If we are right, and we both believe we are right, there is no reason to wait. There is no embarrassment to fear."

"It isn't embarrassment—"

Nathan held up a hand. "Maybe this is the sign the whole world has been waiting for. Maybe this is the Second Coming. It's our job to get the publicity out."

Elvin walked to the corner of the veranda, rubbed his sweaty neck with his hands, sat back against the white wood railing. He blew a breath of air to release tension. "I feel this is private."

"How—"

"Nathan, I feel this is private. If it's the human image of God we have no responsibility, there's nothing we can do, unless we're told to do something."

"Great Scott, Elvin, what's coming *here* but telling us!"

"Telling us what?"

Nathan did not know.

"Then until we know, we do what we feel."

Nathan did what he felt by washing and embalming the body. He went home and told Betty all about it, and she believed.

———

The embalmed body was their secret over the weekend. It was an odd feeling for all of them; unprecedented, hence odd.

Nathan threw out all sorts of things in his office.

Several women in and around town received phone calls from Nathan canceling things and calling whole things off; though Nathan no longer felt odd he was certainly acting oddly.

From Friday evening onward the Funeral Home was closed and all business was to be referred to their competitor, except nobody died; Elvin and Nathan and Betty and Elvin's wife took turns sitting out on the veranda, two at a time, including Friday, Saturday, and Sunday nights, all night.

———

The first night, Friday, had been a strange night. It seemed to Nathan as if the body were swelling and swelling, down there in the embalming room, filling up the whole room, mysteriously filling the whole funeral home, cracking timbers and plaster and somehow making them disappear, making the plush carpeting dissolve, crushing the caskets and even the vault corner samples into figments of memory. It is a great responsibility to have a body, Nathan thought.

You don't realize it until the body is dead.

He looked at Betty, asleep beside him, curled under an afghan with her head on a cushion from one of the other chairs on the veranda. Would he ever have to embalm her? He wouldn't. He would have the other funeral home do it. No, he wouldn't. He would do it himself; he wouldn't let anybody else do it.

———

You can't find what's alive among the dead.

So why do I do this?

Nathan questioned his occupation once in awhile.

But Saturday night it was as if the body lay right behind him. It was more real than anything else. It seemed as though Nathan must give an account: What are you doing with the body?

Nothing much, Nathan said to himself. Watching it age. Using it to distract myself. Forty-five years old and just waiting.

How odd I am, Nathan thought. Here is the actual physical image of God. Not a photograph, but like a photograph, except made into human muscle and bone and skin and everything. He knew it was God's image, a body of God's earthly visitation; he had known it as soon as he saw the face; he just had known. Can't explain it; don't need to.

And what was Nathan doing? SITTING on this veranda! What else to do? It wasn't as though he was ignoring the body of Christ there, right there. IT'S FILLING ALL MY THINKING! Yet what am I doing? I'm doing all I can to forget, to distract myself; doing things just as if everything were normal, the same way that people who've had someone close die go on and carry on and do the little things in a normal way so as to forget and be normal. Nothing odd; nothing odd. Isn't that how we are! God presses in on us, and we go about life every day as if the whole purpose of life were to forget about it. Nuts—everybody's nuts! It's a mad world! Of course the body of Christ is dead; we spend all our waking hours killing it. Here I have the Body of Christ, right there thirty or forty feet from me, and I'm trying to act normal! That is real oddness. Insanity.

I will think about the Body of Christ, then. I will not try to be normal.

Nathan thought. The blood had seemed too precious to pour into the drain, but he had done just that. Being normal. Insane! It should be drunk. What? Are we beasts? It was actual human blood, actual human blood. Christ's body or not Christ's body, it was actual human blood, and you don't drink that.

Think about it some other way. Think about the Body of Christ. Meditate, contemplate.

There is nothing odd about it.

Everything else is odd. I'm odd.

Then Nathan's odd body went to sleep.

———

Sunday night about 2 A.M. Nathan began to wonder whether he should have embalmed the body. Elvin was asleep beside him, his bald head supported by a couple of little satin pillows, his mouth open. Nathan was terrified by guilt; he felt twisted-out all over. It would have worked if he had left things naturally; but he had drained the blood and now the body was full of embalming fluid—chemicals.

"Oh God," he prayed. "Oh God!"

He sat alone with his consuming agony. Elvin had been right. You don't violate authority; you don't violate authority; you don't violate authority.

A little after 4 A.M., just as a little light began to suggest itself in the east, Elvin woke up, rubbed his hand all over his face, un- zipped his jacket, and nodded toward the sidewalk. "This is going to be embarrassing," he said.

"Uh," Nathan responded, seeing a man coming along the sidewalk carrying a fishing rod. "We've been lucky so far. Just smile and nod. It's probably too dark for him to see us," he whispered.

"Hi," Elvin said quietly, raising a hand for a little wave. Nathan was exasperated.

"Good morning. What're you fellows doing out here so early?" The man came up the walk. "Didn't think I'd see anybody until I got to the brook."

"We're just sitting here," Nathan said.

The man set his lunch bag on the railing and leaned the two sections of his flyrod just next to it. Nathan tried like everything to remember the fellow's name but couldn't because he was so embarrassed. He recognized the face; he wasn't one of the Hoggedorn men, though he had the short grizzled beard and prematurely gray hair. One of them had had a heart attack last fall and all the brothers had shown up.

"Didn't even get a bump yesterday," the guy was saying. Elvin knew him.

In fact, Elvin began to tell him all about the body.

Gad, it's Elvin's brother-in-law. How many are we going to let in on this?

Yet Nathan, now that Elvin had set an example, felt like talking about it. There are those guys who look pretty much like bums that sometimes you feel instinctively you can tell all about yourself. When a man was out of his shirt and tie and dressed in fishing clothes . . . As it became a little lighter Nathan realized he more or less knew the man and wasn't talking to a stranger. Later today the whole thing would be out, all over town.

"Would you mind not telling anybody what we've told you about this? We try to help people with grief and if they thought we were a couple of crazy men . . ."

"That's no problem." The man smiled. "I figure to be out all day and trout fishermen don't gab much. Just let me know what happened when I come back."

Nathan fought the rational idea that the man would tell everybody he found, and in fact wouldn't even go out fishing. He'd hang around the funeral home with a few of his friends. But Nathan dismissed the idea because the man seemed perfect and he wanted to know his opinion.

"What do you think we should do if the body is gone this morning?"

The guy scratched his lined, tan face. He needed a shave. "I'd just tell your friends or the newspaper or whoever you felt like. Why not?"

"Ha!" Elvin exclaimed. He seemed to feel jovial. Nathan felt mildly insulted that Elvin needed a relative to make him feel comfortable about this whole thing. Nathan's company hadn't done anything for Elvin, evidently.

"Well," the guy said, "I don't see how it matters whether people believe you. You just tell 'em what you want, and let it go at that."

"Do you believe us?"

The man didn't answer. He fiddled with his lunch bag.

"Do you believe that downstairs right behind us in this house the body of Christ is lying on an embalming table?"

"Well." The stranger cleared his throat. "I can't honestly say that I do. No. But that doesn't mean I wouldn't go fishing with you fellas. Everybody makes a mistake now and then."

"You think we've made a mistake?" Nathan asked. He didn't know whether he was angry or disappointed or just tired.

"Yeah, I s'pose you have."

"Elvin, I think he should go downstairs and look."

The fisherman held up a hand. "No thanks."

"Nathan, can you think of any ordinary person who'd want to go into the basement of a funeral home in the middle of the night and look at a body? But say," he turned to the man; "why don't you have a look? I think it would be worthwhile."

"One of you come down with me?"

Nathan and Elvin shook their heads.

"Then I think I'll pass," he said, smiling, almost laughing. "You two guys have been sitting out here too long. You're tired and hungry and—thirsty?" He reached into his creel and took out a can of beer. Nathan knew the type. "I got a couple of peanut butter sandwiches in this bag. I won't eat 'em both."

"The idea of a peanut butter sandwich and a can of beer at four in the morning is absolutely nauseating," Elvin said. "But I sure am dry."

"I didn't say a whole sandwich; I'm saving one." The man cracked the can open and handed it to Elvin, who took it and gulped and grimaced and gasped gratefully. The fellow put the sandwich back into the bag and took out a big cellophane pouch of peanuts. He tore it open, grabbed a handful and reached it toward Nathan.

Nathan saw that the hand was strong and dirty; not the hand of a businessman, or a loafer. Suddenly he felt an impulse to grab all the peanuts and look closely at the whole hand. He took a few peanuts. Elvin handed him the beer.

They ate peanuts and drank beer for a few minutes. It was getting almost light enough to see individual branches on the elms along the street. Nathan felt awakened. He knew there was no body of Christ in the basement; an ordinary working man had made him see things the way they were. He wondered whether he had ever seen things the way they were. Was it too late to get a manual job, maybe spend some time fishing?

"So what do we do with the body down there?" Nathan asked cither of the two. The man stuffed the lunch bag into the creel. He had the nearly empty can in his other hand.

"Nobody's called to claim it?"

"We put our phones on the answering machine," Elvin said. "Maybe we better go get those calls."

Nathan wanted to say one more thing to the man. "We're nothing, you know? We wanted to think we had the sign, the scoop, that would change the world."

Nathan could see the man's good smile in the half light. "Bible says a wicked and adulterous generation seeketh after a sign; and there shall no sign be given unto it but the sign of the prophet

Jonas." He picked up his flyrod and nodded to them and went down the steps.

Nathan and Elvin watched him walk down the sidewalk and away down the blocks. "I thought he was your brother-in-law," Nathan remarked quietly.

"Never met him before." They sat still, and after a while Elvin looked at Nathan with a long, firm stare, his child's face very intent, and Nathan looked back very carefully and steadily. Did not our hearts burn within us?

Kent Gramm is an English professor whose articles have been widely published in journals such as *The Christian Century*, *Theology Today*, and *Christianity & Crisis*. In 1988, he won the Hart Crane Memorial Poetry Prize, and in 1991 published his first literary novel, *Clare*. He enjoys fishing and sailing and lives with his wife, Lynelle, and three children in Lake Geneva, Wisconsin.

PENELOPE J. STOKES

MANSFIELD FISHER AND THE REVELATION BARN

For the foolishness of God is wiser than man's wisdom . . .
1 Corinthians 1:25

When word came down from On High that Mansfield Fisher had bought the widow Randolph's place out on the highway, everybody in Turner's Crossroads raised cane. The rumor was reliable, all right: Sylvia Munson, who worked in the County Office of Records and Assessments over in Marshall Forks, knew most of what was bought and sold in Angstrom County, and she broadcast more than she knew.

"Ol' Angstrom would turn over in his grave, he would," spat Eddie Bjerke. He set his coffee cup down with a clatter and looked at the familiar weathered faces of the farmers around the center table at the Four Korners Kafe. He knew his sentiment was upheld by most of the citizens in Turner's Crossroads.

"He would," echoed Marvin Angstrom, great-grandson of the revered First Settler in the county. "My gran'pa, and his pa before him, worked hard to make this into a town, a respectable town. He wouldn'ta wanted the likes of Fisher to come in bringin' his trashy ways."

"Ain't there somethin' we can do?"

"Syl Munson, she says the papers are all signed and the place is paid for—all legal and done. Guess we're stuck with Manny junking up the place for the next twenty years."

"Less we convince him to move on." Johnny Leland, the youngest of the group and one of the few whose family had not settled Angstrom County three generations ago, shifted a toothpick back and forth in the space between his front teeth. He sucked on the chewed-up wood thoughtfully, then pointed it at Marvin. "You remember, we got rid of that welfare thief a few years back—"

"Johnson? Sure, but we had reason to show him the door. He really robbed us all blind before that spineless jellyfish of a Sheriff got close enough to put the cuffs on him. Fisher's honest enough—and not a bad guy, really."

"He's just odd, that's all. Won't come to church. Hermits himself up. Don't talk to nobody."

"And—" Bjerke concluded, putting on his cap and jacket and heading for the door, "he'll have that nice place at the corner of 18 and 32, the first thing anybody sees of the Crossroads, made into a junkyard in three months' time."

———

But Mansfield Fisher surprised them all.

Off and on for two weeks, Eddie Bjerke had led a slow-moving caravan of pickup trucks snaking by the intersection of County roads 18 and 32, just to see what was going on at the Fisher place.

"Can you believe it?" Bjerke said when they had returned to the cafe. "Manny's actually fixing up the place!" He jerked his hands with the force of his words, sloshing his coffee onto the stained green formica of the table top.

Johnny Leland laughed and poked Bjerke across the table. "Ah, Eddie, you're just sore becuse he's proving you wrong—you said he'd trash the place."

"Something's happened to Manny," Bjerke said seriously. "I dunno what it is, but it's something."

———

It was something, all right. On Sunday, to the shock and disbelief of the entire congregation of St. Thomas' Lutheran Church, Mansfield Fisher, scrubbed pink, in clean overalls and a new white shirt, marched up the aisle and sat down in the second row.

The word went forth, whispered, from one row to the next: "Manny Fisher's here . . . what do you suppose . . . well, if that isn't something!"

Manny paid no attention. Nobody heard a word of Pastor Carlson's sermon except Manny, who smiled broadly and nodded in agreement at various points. He stood straight and tall in the second row, head thrown back, singing the hymns at the top of his off-key voice.

Near the end of the service, the pastor came down the steps and stood facing the congregation at the head of the center aisle. "I have a blessed duty to perform this morning," he said quietly. "One of our number has returned to the fold and wishes to be baptized." He paused. Mansfield Fisher stood up and walked to the front of the church.

Everyone drew in a collective breath as Fisher humbly bent his massive girth and leaned his head down over the baptismal font. In total silence the church waited, hearing the murmured words and the splash of water. At last Manny lifted his balding head and turned to face the congregation, his radiant smile met by looks of incredulity, even hostility.

After the service, Manny stood at the sanctuary entrance with the pastor. Eddie Bjerke tried to escape out the side door, but Pastor Carlson's exuberance wouldn't let him get away. "Isn't it wonderful!" the pastor said, shaking Bjerke's hand and passing him on to Manny, who stood waiting.

"Wonderful," Bjerke muttered, trying to extricate himself from Manny's enthusiastic pumping. At last Bjerke looked up into the shining, moon-shaped face. Fisher was smiling, but his eyes probed into Bjerke's with a look of compassion and knowledge that shook Eddie to his roots. Flustered, Bjerke broke free and ran for it.

"It was like—I don't know—like he *knew* something . . ." Marv Angstrom, like everybody else in the Four Korners on Monday morning, was talking about the strange effect of Mansfield Fisher's baptismal coming-out.

Eddie Bjerke, relieved that he wasn't the only one who felt it, agreed. "Yeah, he just looked me in the eye and, well, it was like he was looking right through me."

"I think you guys have been out in the sun too long," said Mavis Kitchens, the morning waitress. "He seemed harmless enough to me." She set down a plate of donuts and walked back behind the counter.

"Harmless, maybe," Johnny Leland said. "But we'd better keep an eye on him anyway."

Marv stared hard at Leland. "Who died and made you king?" he snapped.

"Ah, c'mon, Marv," Johnny protested. "Just because your great-grandpa settled here first don't give you the right—"

Marvin shut him up with a look that said, *Remember your place, sonny; your folks have only been around for fifty years.*

As it turned out, everybody was keeping an eye on Mansfield Fisher. Four or five cars a day cruised by on Manny's farm road—in Angstrom Country, a regular rush hour.

Then one day, during afternoon coffee at the cafe, Syl Munson walked in and slumped into a booth at the back. "He's done it," she muttered to nobody in particular.

"Who's done what?" Eddie Bjerke said.

A crowd had gathered where Sylvia had flopped into the back booth. She shook her head and waved her hands distractedly. "Manny Fisher's painted his barn."

Marv Angstrom shook his head and mouthed the word *Women!* "Well, now, Syl," he said, "that doesn't seem to be anything to get so depressed about. I mean, after all, we didn't want to see the place junked up—"

Sylvia's head shot up and she glared at Marv venomously. "Go out and see for yourself."

They did. In four pickup trucks, the leaders of Turner's Crossroads made their way down the rutted gravel roads to the intersection of County Roads 18 and 32.

Manny was nowhere in sight. The house, glistening with a fresh coat of white paint, shone like a pearl against the green velvet of the recently-mowed lawn. Two of the outbuildings had been painted barn red, and the grove stood like a well-groomed park, completely free of the usual farm litter of old gas engines and worn-out tillers.

Nobody could believe how good the place looked. In silence the men gaped at the transformation, then their eyes focused on the massive barn. Whitewashed, it looked twice its normal size, and across the side in red, clearly visible from the road, the neatly painted words read: REPENT, FOR THE KINGDOM IS AT HAND.

"What does he mean, *repent?*" Marv said through gritted teeth.

"Repent means to ask forgiveness, to—" Eddie began. Marv silenced him with a look. He knew very well what the word meant, of course; he and Eddie Bjerke had gone through confirmation class together at St. Thomas' Luthern under old Pastor Tollefson, back in 1949. But repentance was something you talked about in church, and rarely enough even there. It wasn't something you splattered across the side of your barn for the whole world to see. Religion was a private matter, especially in Southern Minnesota. Mansfield Fisher may have "come back to the fold," as Pastor Carlson had put it, but if this was his idea of becoming a good Lutheran, he had gone too far.

Nobody said a word on the ride back into town. When they pulled up in front of the Four Korners Kafe, Marv shut off the engine and sat in the truck, still as a statue. Johnny Leland parked next to Marv, got out of his pickup, and came over to Marv's side to lean in the window.

"What're we gonna do about him?" Johnny said.

Marv shook his head. "I don't know. I gotta think about it."

———

In the next few days, Marv Angstrom thought of little else besides the message written on the side of Mansfield Fisher's barn. The verse worked on him like an incantation, dredging up memories he thought he had buried long ago: the time he had painted over the rust on a used car and sold it to Leif Hanson for full book price; the lies he had told his wife Addie the time he had gone to Minneapolis alone for a week.

For the first time in six years, Marv had dreamed of the woman he had met in Minneapolis that week. He was sure, when he turned over the next morning and looked into Addie's eyes, that she knew. She knew, all right; the pain was there, a vacant emptiness he had never seen before. How could he have missed it?

All along, Marv had made excuses when the little twist in his gut told him he was wrong to go out with the woman, wrong to sell a defective car to poor ignorant Leif, wrong to take a tax deduction three years running on the tractor he had traded back to John Deere after the axle got bent.

On those rare occasions when Pastor Carlson had preached about repentance and forgiveness and Marv had listened, he always assumed that the message was for someone else—for Hans Midthun, who drank himself senseless every weekend and went home to beat his wife and kids; for Tennie Hovland, the buxom waitress at the truckstop on the highway, who flaunted her wares and auctioned herself off to the highest bidder. Now *that* was sin.

But the pastor's sermons didn't apply to Marv. He was a good man, a hard worker. He loved his kids, took care of his wife, lived as decent a life as anybody else. He'd had a few slip-ups in his life; who hadn't? Nobody was perfect. Yet now, because of a few words on the side of a barn, he was being turned inside out with memories he didn't ask for. His sense of well-being was gone, vanished. And it was all Mansfield Fisher's fault.

———

When Marv Angstrom showed up at the Four Korners Kafe on Thursday, everybody was talking about Mansfield Fisher's barn. Marv didn't want to hear it, but he had to listen anyway. Most of the people in Turner's Crossroads were upset about it, but nobody seemed to be having the kind of trouble Marv was experiencing. Nobody said a word about having old memories surface, about seeing the past come back to haunt them.

When the crowd had thinned and most of the folks had gone back to work, Eddie Bjerke faced Marv across the cafe table and clenched his coffee cup in his hands. He looked directly into Marv's face, his eyes narrowed with intensity.

"Marv," he said, glancing over his shoulder nervously, "we've been friends a long time."

Marv nodded, waiting.

"Well—" Eddie hesitated. "Aw, it's probably just my imagination."

Marv perked up. "Is this about Fisher's barn?"

Eddie stared at him. "How did you know?"

"Never mind. Go on."

"Well," Eddie said, "ever since we saw that message on Manny's barn, things have been going on in my mind—strange things." He paused. "I know this sounds really stupid," he said at last, "and it doesn't sound like me at all, but I've been remembering things, wondering about things that I haven't thought about in years."

Marv nodded. So it wasn't just him!

"I tried to ignore it," Eddie said. "I mean, I'm just as good as the next guy, right? But—" He shook his head. "I just couldn't get it out of my mind: *Repent, for the Kingdom is at hand.*"

"So what did you do?" Marv prodded. He felt sorry for Eddie's misery, but he was glad Eddie was saying this to him, and not the other way around.

"I kept going back out there, every day," Eddie said. "You been out there since Monday?"

Marv shook his head. "No."

"Well, there's more. Tuesday, in addition to the first message, it said: *The wages of sin is death.*"

Marv winced. "And Wednesday?"

"Wednesday he had added, *The pure in heart shall see God.*" Eddie slammed his hand down on the table. "Who does Fisher think he is, anyway—accusing us like that?"

Marv shook his head. "I don't know, but . . ."

Eddie stared hard at his friend, a light of understanding dawning in his eyes. "Ah," he said. "So you've felt it, too."

Marv was caught, and he knew it. "Yeah," he muttered. "Ever since the first message, I've been remembering a lot of stuff I've done wrong over the years."

"Me, too." Eddie heaved a sigh of relief, glad that the truth was out.

Silence hung between them for a moment. "You know what, Eddie?" Marv said at last

"What?"

"For the last couple of days I've been mad, real mad, at Manny for putting that stuff up on his barn for everybody to see. It was like he had written all my secrets in plain view. I coulda killed him. But now with what you're telling me about the rest of it, about the pure in heart seeing God, I wonder if maybe the messages are coming not from Manny, but from—well, from somewhere else."

"From God?" Eddie couldn't keep the sneer out of his voice.

"Maybe." Marv averted his eyes. He played with the spoon until it clattered noisily to the table.

"Eddie," Marv said finally, "Do you suppose other people are feeling the same way?"

"I don't know," Eddie said. "People around here don't talk much about religion."

"Yeah, yeah," Marv said. "I know. It's a private matter. But Manny's sure making it public. He's forcing people to think about their lives, and nobody's very happy about it, far as I can see."

The following Sunday, you could have heard a pin drop in St. Thomas' Lutheran Church. Even the children were quiet, riveted to their seats as if waiting for something to happen.

Mansfield Fisher took his seat on the second row, and a hundred pairs of eyes bored into the back of his skull. He didn't seem to notice. He smiled and nodded and sang the hymns at the top of his off-key voice.

Pastor Carlson stood up to give his sermon. "My text for this morning comes from Matthew chapter five, verse eight: 'Blessed are the pure in heart, for they shall see God.' "

Eddie Bjerke's head snapped around and his eyes fixed on Marv Angstrom, three rows back. Marv was staring straight at Pastor Carlson, his face blizzard-white, a sheen of sweat across his brow. The pastor spoke in quiet tones for a few moments about the necessity of forgiveness. Then he came down and stood in the center of the aisle, where a week before Mansfield Fisher had been baptized.

"We're going to do something this morning that we rarely do in the Lutheran church—and maybe we should do it more often. Before we come to communion, we always have a time of silence and reflection, a time for repentance of sin. This morning I'm going to ask any of you who wish to make that repentance public to come up to the altar to pray. None of us is perfect; we all have need of forgiveness. But if we want to be pure in heart, and be able to see God at work in our lives, we need to begin by being honest with him."

The pastor returned to his seat, and Lavonne Amundson began to play hymns softly on the organ. Nobody moved; nobody even breathed. Then, after three full minutes of total stillness, a shifting of hymnbooks and purses and papers began to ripple through the sanctuary. Pastor Carlson got up from his seat and went to kneel at the communion rail. Everybody watched, amazed, as his shoulders slumped and then gently began to shake. He was crying!

Eddie Bjerke shot another look back at the Angstroms. Marv didn't see him; he had hold of Addie's hand and was leaning toward her, whispering. The two of them got up and went slowly forward to the rail.

Eddie closed his eyes and breathed deeply, trying to steady himself. For a fleeting moment he considered joining them; something inside of him prodded him to get up, but he fought against it. Whatever he might have felt when he saw the messages on Mansfield Fisher's barn, he had to get a grip on himself. Religion, after all, was a private matter.

When he looked up again, the altar rail was nearly full, and people were milling up and down the aisle. On the back row, a few stony-faced women glared at the spectacle, then got up and stalked out the back door. Eddie shook his head. He felt embarrassed, ashamed for Marv Angstrom and all these other fools who were letting their emotions run away with them.

Eddie watched. Marv and Addie Angstrom came back down the aisle past him, smiling, and resumed their seats. In a few minutes it was all over. When the communion liturgy began and Lavonne hit the opening chords for "This is the Feast of Victory for our God," Mansfield Fisher's off-key voice was drowned out by the volume of a hundred other voices.

———

That afternoon, after Sunday dinner and the newspaper, Marv Angstrom took his wife for a drive in the country. They happened to pass by the Fisher place and stopped to read the barn. All the previous verses had been painted over, and across the side of the whitewashed wall one message stood out: THOUGH YOUR SINS BE AS SCARLET, THEY SHALL BE WHITE AS SNOW.

Manny stood in the driveway, still dressed in his Sunday overalls and white shirt. He waved, then turned and went back in the house.

Word got around quickly about the odd goings-on at the church in Turner's Crossroads. The Four Korners Kafe was crowded to capacity at nine o'clock Monday morning, and the conversation, as expected, centered around Mansfield Fisher's barn.

A lot of the people in outlying areas hadn't seen the barn for themselves; they had only heard the rumors. At ten, a line of cars that looked like a funeral procession for the governor rounded the curve at the intersection of County Roads 18 and 32.

The house, glistening with a fresh coat of white paint, shone like a pearl against the green velvet of the recently mowed lawn. The grove resembled a well-groomed park. Everyone was impressed with how beautifully kept up the place was.

And there, across the driveway from the house, stood the barn. Whitewashed, it looked twice its normal size. A dozen newcomers got out of their cars and hung on the open doors, staring.

The reports that filtered back in to the Four Korners Kafe on Monday afternoon varied. Some said there were no messages at all on the barn; others described elaborate paintings of the Four Horsemen of St. John's Revelation. One man claimed to see the face of Jesus on the barn door.

Eddie Bjerke drove out one last time to see for himself. The barn was whitewashed; all the messages were gone. He parked his pickup on the side of County Road 32 and sat for an hour, a sense of loss and loneliness overwhelming him. By the time he started his truck and headed back toward Turner's Crossroads, he had convinced himself that it had all been a figment of his imagination.

It was dangerous, this religious fervor. It made people imagine things about themselves, doubt what they knew was true. He wasn't such a bad guy, after all. He wasn't perfect, of course; but who was? Right then and there, on the road back into Turner's Crossroads, Eddie made his decision. Next Sunday he would go out to North Creek Church, where people believed that religion was a private matter.

Penelope J. Stokes is a freelance writer/editor in Blue Earth, Minnesota. When not writing she spends her time reading, watching old movies, and restoring her 100-year-old Victorian house. Her story is based on a real "gentleman who filled his yard with huge billboards, quoting Apocalyptic scriptures and proclaiming the imminence of the End Times. It struck me as an odd kind of evangelism; 'Mansfield Fisher' was based on the premise that God can use all manner of strange methods to communicate truth to the human heart."

Penelope has six books on the market with another due to be published in 1993, a collection of stories about the characters who inhabit Turner's Crossroads.